SUMMER NIGHTS

SUMMER NIGHTS

Susan Mallery

CHIVERS

British Library Cataloguing in Publication Data available

This Large Print edition published by AudioGO Ltd, Bath, 2013.
Published by arrangement with Harlequin Enterprises II B.V./S à r.l.

U.K. Hardcover   ISBN   978 1 4713 2682 0
U.K. Softcover   ISBN   978 1 4713 2683 7

Printed and bound in Great Britain by TJ International Limited

My thanks to all the librarians
who have supported me, loved my
books and talked about them endlessly.
So many of you have shared that just
once you'd like to read about a
librarian who is fun, smart and
sexy — without the buttoned-up
cardigan and unflattering hair.
Annabelle is my gift to you.
I hope you adore her as much as I do.

CHAPTER ONE

Shane Stryker was determined enough to never walk away from a fight and smart enough to know when he'd been beat. The beautiful redhead dancing on the bar might be everything he wanted, but pursuing her would be the worst decision he could make.

Her eyes were closed, her long, wavy hair swayed in rhythm with her body. The sensual beat of the music hit Shane square in the gut. He shook his head. Okay, it hit him lower than that, but he ignored it and the draw he felt. Women who danced on bars were trouble. Exciting, tempting, but not for him. Not anymore.

He might not know her, but he knew the type. Attention-seeking. Deadly — at least for a guy who assumed marriage meant commitment and monogamy. Women like the one on the bar needed to be wanted by every man in the room.

Slowly, regretfully, he turned away from

the woman and headed for the exit. He'd come into town for a beer and a burger. He'd thought he could catch the game, maybe hang with the guys. What he'd found instead was a barefoot goddess who made a man want to forget all his hopes and dreams in exchange for a single smile. His dreams were worth more, he reminded himself, glancing over his shoulder one last time before stepping out into the warm summer night.

Annabelle Weiss opened her eyes. "It's easy."

"Uh-huh." Her friend Charlie Dixon put down her beer and shook her head. "No."

Annabelle climbed off the bar and put her hands on her hips. It was her attempt to look intimidating. Kind of a feeble gesture when she considered the fact that Charlie was a good eight or ten inches taller and had muscles Annabelle didn't want to know existed.

She was about to make her case, maybe even throw in a line that it was for the children, when the mostly female crowd broke into spontaneous applause.

"Great dance," someone called.

Annabelle spun in a circle. "Thank you," she called. "I'll be here all week." She looked back at her friend. "You have to."

"I'm pretty sure I don't."

Annabelle turned to Heidi Simpson. "You talk to her."

Heidi, a pretty blonde who had recently gotten engaged, glanced up from studying her diamond ring. "What? Oh, sorry. I was busy."

"Thinking about Rafe," Charlie grumbled. "We know. He's wonderful, you're happy. It's getting annoying."

Heidi laughed. "Now who's cynical?"

"It's not news. I've always been cynical." Charlie grabbed her beer and led the way back to their table. The one they'd abandoned when Annabelle had offered to show them both the dance of the happy virgin.

When they were seated, Annabelle turned to Charlie. "Look, I need to raise money for my bookmobile. Being in the town festival is the best way for that to happen. It's a ride on a horse. You know how to ride. You even own a horse."

Charlie's blue eyes narrowed. "I'm not dancing on a horse."

"You don't have to. The horse dances. That's why it's called the Dance of the Horse."

"Mason is not a horse who dances."

Heidi leaned forward. "Annabelle, this is your bookmobile project. You're the one who has the passion. Why don't you do the dance?"

"I don't know how to ride."

"You could learn. Shane could teach you. I've seen him working with the rodeo cowboys. He's very patient."

"I don't think there's enough time. The festival is ten weeks away. Could I really learn to ride a horse well enough for it to do the dance by then?" She turned to Charlie. "More than a thousand years ago the Máa-zib women left everything they knew and migrated up to where we are today. They were powerful women who wanted to make a home for themselves. They settled here and their strength and determination flows through all of us."

Charlie sipped her beer. "Good speech and no, I'm not doing the horse dance."

Annabelle slumped over the table. "Then I've got nothing."

Heidi poked her in the arm. "Like I said, do the dance yourself. You're the one always going on and on about the Máa-zib women protecting their daughters from sacrifice by leaving. They were tired of their daughters being killed before they'd ever had a chance to live so they came here where they could be free. Embrace that spirit."

Annabelle straightened. She was hardly

the type to lead a parade, she thought. She was quiet, more of a behind-the-scenes person.

She opened her mouth to say "I can't" but the words got stuck. Because she could if she wanted. She could do a lot of things. But all her life, she'd been conventional in an attempt to fit in. From trying to please her parents to making herself over to suit every guy she'd ever dated. She considered herself accommodating, not strong.

Charlie stared at her. "You okay? You look funny."

"I'm a pushover," Annabelle said. "A doormat, in the most honest, unflattering terms."

Heidi and Charlie exchanged looks of concern. "Okay," Charlie said slowly. "You're not having a seizure, are you?"

"No, I'm having a revelation. I've always been the one to bend, to sacrifice what I wanted for another person's needs and desires."

"You were just dancing on a bar," Heidi said with a shrug. "It doesn't get more independent than that."

"I wasn't drunk. I was showing Charlie the dance of the happy virgin in an effort to convince her —" She shook her head, then stood. "You know what? I'm going to do it.

11

I'm going to learn the dance myself. Or learn to ride. Whatever. It's my bookmobile. My fundraiser. I'm taking charge. I'm putting myself out there. The spirit of the Máazib women lives on in me."

"You go, girl," Charlie told her.

"You were home early last night."

Shane turned off the water in the barn and glanced up to see his mother walking toward him. It was barely dawn, but she was up and dressed. More important, she carried a mug of coffee in each hand.

He took the caffeine she offered and swallowed gratefully. Visions of a fiery redhead had haunted the little sleep he'd managed.

"Jo's Bar turned out to be more interesting than I'd thought."

May, his still-attractive, fifty-something mother, grinned. "You went to Jo's Bar? Oh, honey, no. That's where the women in town hang out. There's shopping and fashion playing on the TV, not sports. You should have talked to your brother about where to catch the game. No wonder you didn't stay out late." She reached out her free hand to stroke the nose of the mare hanging her head over her stall door. "Hello, sweetie. Are you adjusting? Don't you love Fool's Gold?"

The mare nodded, as if agreeing that all was well.

Shane had to admit his horses had settled in more quickly than he'd anticipated. The drive from Tennessee had been long but the end results worth the journey. He'd bought two hundred prime acres in the foothills outside of town. He'd already drawn up plans for a house and, more important, stables. Construction would start on the latter within the week. Until then he was boarding his horses in his mother's stable and he was staying up at the house with her seventy-four-year-old boyfriend, Glen, Shane's brother Rafe, and Rafe's fiancée, Heidi. Talk about a crowd.

Shane reminded himself he was doing exactly what he'd always wanted to do in a place he planned to settle down. He had the horses, the land, family close by enough to make it feel like home but, once his house was built, not so close that they would get in the way. If only he could get the image of that woman out of his head.

"Mom, do you know —"

He bit back the rest of the question. His mother was the kind of woman who would know everyone in town. Give her a name and within fifteen minutes she would get back to him with four generations' worth of details.

He wasn't looking for trouble. He'd already done that, had married and then divorced the kind of woman who haunted a man. He'd had enough excitement to last him until he was ninety. Now was the time to settle down. To find someone sensible, someone who would be satisfied knowing that one man loved her.

His mother looked at him, her dark eyes so much like his own. Her mouth curved in a slow, knowing smile.

"Please, please say you're going to ask me if I know any nice girls."

What the hell, he thought, then shrugged. "Do you? Someone, you know, regular." No one like the bar-dancing goddess.

His mother practically quivered. "Yes and she's perfect. A librarian. Her name is Annabelle Weiss. She's lovely. Heidi was telling me Annabelle wants to learn to ride a horse. You could teach her."

A librarian, huh? He pictured a plain brunette in glasses, cardigan buttoned up to her neck and practical shoes. Not exactly exciting, but that was okay. He'd reached the place in his life where he wanted to have a family. He wasn't looking for someone to rock his world.

"What do you think?" his mother asked anxiously.

"She sounds perfect."

"Returning to the scene of the crime?"

Annabelle grinned at her friend. "There was no crime."

"You know that and I know that, but rumors are flying, missy."

Annabelle held open the door to Jo's Bar, then waited while Charlie preceded her into the brightly lit business. It was lunchtime in Fool's Gold and women already filled nearly a dozen tables. Jo catered to the female population, decorating with girl-friendly colors like mauve and cream. During the day the big TVs were either off or turned to shopping and reality shows. The menu had plenty of salads and sandwiches, with discreet calorie counts listed to the side.

Annabelle followed Charlie to a table and took a seat.

"Everyone is talking about you dancing on the bar."

Annabelle laughed. "I don't care. It was for a good cause. Even if it didn't convince you to be in my festival. But that's okay. I'm going to do it myself." She frowned. "You are telling people I wasn't drunk, right?"

In fact she hadn't bothered to finish her single glass of wine. Getting on the bar last night had been more about feeling unsettled than wanting to show off and had nothing to do with any alcohol in her system.

Charlie grinned. "I swear, I'm sticking to the one-glass-of-wine story. The archaeologists were intrigued, though. I think the dance of the happy virgin is giving you street cred with them."

"Yes, because they're so wild."

Last fall, construction workers on a building site had blown away a bit of the mountain, exposing Máa-zib gold. Archaeologists had stormed in to take charge of the discovery. After the pieces were researched and catalogued, they would be returned to the town.

"Are you helping them?" Charlie asked.

"I'm more unofficial liaison," Annabelle told her. "My minor in Máa-zib studies gives me enough information to be annoying to the professionals."

"Most professionals need a little annoying."

Annabelle appreciated the loyalty. "Then my work here is done."

The door opened and Heidi walked in. She saw them and waved.

Heidi hurried over. "Shane said yes. He's

16

going to teach you to do the horse dance. Well, ride a horse. I don't think his mom mentioned the dancing."

"Probably better to sneak up on him with that one," Charlie said.

"You're right." Heidi grinned. "He's a successful horse guy. He's not going to be into the dancing thing. You'll need to introduce the idea gradually."

This was what she loved, Annabelle thought happily. Her friends and, for the most part, her life. She had a great job in a town she adored. She belonged. If she got a twinge of envy when the light caught Heidi's gleaming diamond engagement ring, well, that was okay, too.

In truth, she didn't care about the rock — it was what the rock represented that gave her a couple of pangs. Love. Real love. Rafe wasn't trying to change Heidi. He didn't accept only parts of her. He was all-in. Annabelle had never had that. Her revelation from last night had stayed with her. She wanted more than conditional love. She wanted it all — or nothing. Messy, inconvenient love, where both parties gave with their whole hearts.

Not that she had a bunch of guys lining up, begging her to take a chance.

She pulled a folder out of her large tote.

17

"I have the information I promised." She withdrew the pictures she'd taken at the two florists in town, along with pricing sheets.

Heidi sighed. "You're amazing and wonderful and I really appreciate the help."

Charlie bristled. "Hey, I tasted cake. I wouldn't do that for just anyone."

Heidi looked at her. "Are you sure?"

"Okay, I *would* taste cake for just about anyone but I did it for you because you're my friend."

"You two are the best," Heidi said, her eyes getting bright. "Seriously. I don't know how to thank you."

Charlie held up a hand. "I swear, if you start crying, I'm outta here. You're emotional. Are you sure you're not pregnant?"

"Yes. I'm sure. It's just everyone is being so wonderful about the wedding."

Heidi had been engaged all of two weeks, which wouldn't be notable except the wedding had been scheduled for the middle of August, giving everyone barely two months to get it all arranged. Heidi's only family was her grandfather, so Annabelle and Charlie had stepped in to help with the details.

They looked over the flowers. Heidi studied arrangements and prices. They paused when Jo stopped by their table to find out what they wanted for lunch.

"By the way," Jo said, handing them each a small card with a price list, "the party room is going to be opening in about a month. You were asking about it for the bridal shower."

Heidi leaned forward. "You're making it like you said?"

Jo grinned. "Yup, just as girly as the rest of the bar, with very flattering lighting. Lots of tables, a private bar, big-screen TV and a small stage. I'm working on the menu right now. We can do appetizers and finger sandwiches or regular meals. Whichever you want."

"Champagne?" Heidi asked.

"Lots."

"I love it," Annabelle said. "Want to have your shower here?"

"The room can hold up to sixty," Jo told them.

"You wouldn't have to limit your guest list," Charlie told her.

"Sounds like a plan," Heidi said happily.

Annabelle nodded. "We'll get back to you on dates."

"Great." Jo took their lunch orders. Salads for Annabelle and Heidi and a cheeseburger for Charlie.

"Fries for the table," the firefighter added,

then glared at her friends. "I know you two. You'll steal mine otherwise."

"I would never do that," Annabelle lied cheerfully.

"Hi. I'm Annabelle Weiss."

Shane looked up from the saddle he'd been cleaning and immediately came to his feet. Instead of a mousy, stern-faced woman wearing glasses, with an oversize cardigan and stockings bagging around her ankles, he stared into the slightly amused green eyes of the petite, redheaded bar dancer.

She had on one of those tight, strappy dresses women liked to wear and men liked to look at. Which was usually the woman's plan all along. It was white, with flowers scattered all over. Skinny strips of fabric had been braided together to hold the whole thing up. The dress was fitted, following her impressive curves to just above her knee.

Technically she was covered, with not a hint of anything risqué showing. But the outline of her body was enough to bring the strongest of men to his knees. Shane would know — he was a breath or two away from going down in a heap.

His first instinct was for self-preservation. Moving forward wasn't an option — that would put him too close to her. So he took a step back and nearly tripped over the stool he'd been sitting on. The stool started to go over. He grabbed for it, as did the woman. His fingers somehow got tangled in hers and damn it all to hell, there it was. The to-the-groin jolt of awareness, of hunger.

"You're Shane, right?"

He inched away from her and managed a quick nod as he twisted the rag he held in his fingers.

"Heidi said you were willing to teach me how to ride." Her expression shifted from entertained to confused, as if she was wondering why no one had mentioned he was a can or two shy of a six-pack.

"A horse," he clarified, then wanted to kick himself. What else but a horse? Did he think she was here to learn to ride his mother's elephant?

One corner of Annabelle's perfect, full mouth twitched. "A horse would be good. You seem to have several."

He wanted to remind himself that he was usually fine around women. Smooth even. He was intelligent, funny and could, on occasion, be charming. Just not now, with his blood pumping and his brain doing nothing more than shouting "It's her, it's her" over and over again.

Chemistry, he thought grimly. It could

21

turn the smartest man into a drooling idiot. Here he was, proving the theory true.

Aware he was still holding a rag in one hand and leather cleaner in the other, he set both on the battered counter.

"You're interested in pleasure riding?" he asked, careful to keep his voice even.

Annabelle sighed. The action caused her chest to rise and fall. It took every ounce of willpower he possessed to rip his gaze away.

"Actually, it's kind of complicated," she admitted.

Complicated? He didn't think so. She was a beautiful woman. He was a man who had to have her or the world would come to an end. What could be simpler?

Only she wasn't talking about what he was thinking and if she knew what was on his mind, she would run him through with a pitchfork, tear screaming into the afternoon, then back her car over him for good measure. Not that he would blame her.

But he knew better. He was a regular guy looking for a regular kind of life. He knew women like her. Make that, he'd known one woman like her. He'd married her and then had been tormented all through his marriage. Women like her wanted men — all men. They weren't happy unless the world was drooling over them. No way he was go-

22

ing to make the same mistake again. No falling for wild women who could turn him on with a single breath. Right now, boring sounded excellent.

"I'm a librarian in town," she began.

"You sure about that?"

The words popped out before he could stop them.

Annabelle raised her eyebrows. "Fairly. It's my job and so far no one has told me to go away when I show up for work."

Smooth, Stryker, he thought. *Very smooth.*

"I was expecting someone wearing glasses. You know. Because librarians read a lot."

The raised eyebrows turned into a frown. "You need to get out of the barn more."

"Probably true."

She hesitated, as if not sure he was being funny or just incredibly slow. "Okay."

Telling her the truth wasn't an option. Admitting she was the sexiest creature he'd ever seen and that the reason he sounded so much like a mindless idiot was because all his blood was pooling in his groin would most likely cause her to bring him up on charges. Starting over seemed the only option.

"Tell me what you had in mind," he said, staring into her eyes, determined not to even think about the steady rise and fall of

23

her chest, or the way her painted toes on her tiny feet were just so darned cute. "Let me guess. You've wanted to ride since you were a kid?"

Annabelle laughed. "Have you seen me? Horses are big animals. Why would someone as small as me want to risk my life on the back of something that could crush me with a thought?"

As she spoke, she shifted, holding out one gorgeous leg to show him the four-inch heel on her sandal.

He supposed she'd done it to make a point about her height. All he could think was that she was small enough and light enough that supporting her weight would be easy. The image of them up against a wall, her legs around his waist as they . . .

He closed his fists against the visual, reminded himself that his mother knew he was meeting with Annabelle and thought about horse racing stats. When that didn't help, he worked a couple of fractions in his head.

"Size has nothing to do with it," he said, then wanted to hit his head against the wall. "Jockeys are small and they control fast, powerful horses."

Amusement danced in her green eyes. "Sure. Logic. The last male refuge."

He managed a smile. "I work with what I've got. So we've established riding wasn't a childhood dream."

"Hardly. Although I would have loved to be a ballerina. Anyway, I need to ride because I'm raising money for a bookmobile. We just finished up the new media center the first part of this year. It's wonderful."

"Isn't a bookmobile old-school?"

"As in anyone can get anything off the internet, including a book?"

He nodded.

"I wish. We have a lot of shut-ins who can't get to the library and don't own computers. Older couples up in the mountains who don't come down in the winter. A few folks in wheelchairs. That sort of thing. Right now we have a sad little van that makes trips, but it can't hold much in the way of material. Plus, I was hoping to raise enough to have a few laptops and portable Wi-Fi, so we could introduce the shut-ins to the magic of computers. Open up their worlds."

He hadn't thought of anyone still being computer illiterate, but realized there was probably a fair percentage of the population either unable or unwilling to step into the electronic age.

"I've already picked out my dream vehicle," she said, her voice crackling with excitement. "It's huge and has four-wheel drive. That means it can go up into the mountains in winter."

"How much do you need to raise?"

"A hundred and thirty-five thousand dollars."

He opened his mouth, then closed it. "That's a lot of vehicle."

"Some of the money will go for stocking it with books and computers."

"And the Wi-Fi."

"Right."

So much for simply handing her a check. "So how does learning to ride fit into all this?"

She smiled. "This is where we test how much you learned in history class. I'm going to ride in a ceremony celebrating the Máa-zib tribe."

Shane grimaced. "That class was a long time ago." He paused, then nodded as something he'd learned in fourth or fifth grade drifted into his brain. "They settled the area eight hundred years ago. Maybe more. They're Mayan women who founded their own civilization here. And maybe there was something in the news about gold recently?"

"You were a good student."

"Not really. I would rather have been outside."

"Not me. I always had my nose in a book. Anyway, yes, those are the basics. At the end of summer, there will be a festival that will include authentic Máa-zib crafts and lectures, and me on a horse performing the traditional ride of the female warrior. It's more of a dance, really. Technically it's called the Dance of the Horse."

"You're going to dance on a horse?"

"No. The horse is going to dance while I ride it."

This time Shane remembered about the stool when he took a step back. "Do you have a dancing horse?"

"Um, no. I thought maybe we could work on that, too."

He took another step back. "You want me to teach you to ride and teach a horse to dance?"

"Isn't that possible?"

Her gaze settled on his, rendering him immobile, so when she moved closer, he was unable to ease away. She smiled up at him and put her hand on his arm.

"Heidi said you're gifted when it comes to horses. It's just a little dance. A few steps. For a good cause."

27

He doubted she was doing anything extraordinary. In most parts of the country, a beautiful woman touching a man's arm was considered a perk, not the least bit dangerous. But she wasn't just any woman. This was the one he'd seen dancing on top of a bar. The one he, for reasons of chemistry and Fate having a hell of a good time at his expense, found irresistible.

Why couldn't she have been the cardigan-wearing boring stereotypical librarian he'd been expecting? Or maybe librarians weren't like that at all. Maybe they were all wild, like Annabelle, and the cardigan thing was a giant joke they played on a world too self-involved to see the truth. Either way, he was lost. Lost in a pair of green eyes and a sexy smile that hit him like a fist to the gut. Only it wasn't a fist and the parts of him responding weren't exactly his gut.

He wanted to say no, but he couldn't. Not only because the bookmobile was a good cause but because his mother would give him a look that told him how he'd disappointed her. Despite crossing thirty a few years ago, he couldn't stand that look.

"I'm a tough, macho guy," he growled, then held in a groan as he realized he'd spoken out loud.

Annabelle raised her eyebrows, then

stepped back. "I'm, ah, sure that's true. Big horse man."

He swore under his breath.

Before he could figure out how to extricate himself from the conversation and somehow recover what was left of his dignity, he heard a loud neigh from one of the corrals. He turned and saw the white stallion standing by the gate, his dark gaze fixed on Annabelle.

She turned in the direction of the sound. "Oh, wow. That horse is beautiful. What's her name?"

"His. Khatar. He's a stallion. Arabian."

And a sonofabitch, Shane thought. The kind of horse who wanted to make sure everyone knew he was in charge. Khatar's previous owner had been too aggressive, trying to break the horse's spirit. Now Shane had to fix the mistake, which was turning out to be a challenge. But he would do it — he had to. He had way too much money riding on the physically perfect animal.

He turned back to Annabelle. Even in her four-inch heels, she barely came past his shoulder. He figured he could get her on one of his calmer geldings and have her riding in a week or two. As to the dancing, he would deal with that later. When he could speak in full sentences.

"When do you want to start?" he asked, impressed he was able to string the words together.

She turned back to him and smiled. "How about tomorrow?"

"Sure." The sooner they started, the sooner they would be finished. Better for both of them to get her out of his life. She could go on tormenting other men and he could stop acting like an idiot. It was close enough for him to call it a win.

Chapter Two

Annabelle didn't completely understand the science of growing fruit. Not only had she been raised in a city, her ability to grow anything was hampered by having what she cheerfully referred to as the black thumb of death. If she got too close to a plant, it visibly recoiled. If she dared to take one home with her, the poor thing withered and died within a couple of weeks. She'd tried watering, feeding, sunlight and playing classical music. She'd read books on the subject. Nothing worked. It had gotten to the point where the Plants for the Planet, a small local nursery in town, refused to sell her anything except cut flowers. Something she tried not to take personally. So the agricultural cycle of life eluded her.

What she did know was that fruit that grew on trees matured later than fruit that grew on vines, or bushes. That strawberries arrived first and that cherries, which grew on trees and therefore should have been later in the summer, were available by mid-June. She also knew that several families spent their summers living in small trailers by the vineyards and orchards. They worked the various crops and after the grapes were picked in late September and early October, they moved on.

Annabelle drove up to the circle of trailers and parked. Before she'd even opened her door, children spilled out of the trailers, jumped off swings and raced from the grove of trees shading the area. They circled her car, laughing, pulling open her door and urging her out.

"Did you bring them? Did you bring them?"

Annabelle stood and put her hands on her hips. "Bring what? Did you ask me for something?"

The children, ranging in ages from maybe four to eleven or twelve, smiled eagerly at her. One little boy darted behind her and pulled the latch that opened her trunk. Immediately the children hurried over and began searching through the bins of books she'd brought.

"It's here."

"That one's mine."

"The second *and* third book in the series? Sweet!"

By the time the kids had found their requested books and disappeared to begin the magic of getting lost in a story, the mothers had appeared, most carrying infants or toddlers in their arms.

Annabelle greeted the women she knew and was introduced to a few she hadn't met yet. Maria, a slight woman in her early forties, leaned heavily on her cane as she gave Annabelle a welcoming hug.

"The children were watching the clock all morning," she said, leading the way to a small outdoor table by the largest trailer. Maria's husband managed the group of workers and spoke for them when dealing with the local farmers. Maria acted as unofficial "den mother" for the younger women.

"I'm glad," Annabelle said, settling in one of the folding chairs. "When I was their age, summer was all about reading."

"It is for them, too. Since last year, when you first found us, the little ones want books."

After moving to Fool's Gold the previous year, Annabelle had started driving around to explore the area. She'd discovered the enclave of trailers, had met several of the women and made friends with the children. Maria had been the first to welcome her and had been enthusiastic about her idea of bringing books to community.

This year, Annabelle had created several reading lists, based on the ages of the children. She was working on getting donations so that when the families left, they would take plenty of books with them. Enough to last until they returned next year.

Maria had already set out iced tea and cookies. Annabelle poured them each a glass.

"Leticia is going to have her baby this week," Maria said. "Her husband is frantic. Men have no patience with nature when it comes to their children. He asks every day, 'Is it now?' As if the baby is going to tell him."

"He sounds excited."

"He is. And frightened." She called out something in Spanish.

"*Sí*, Mama," came the response.

Maria smiled. "They're writing down the titles of the books they took, and what they want for next time."

"I'll be back next week." Annabelle lowered her voice. "I have several of those romances you like, as well."

Maria grinned. "Good. We all like them."

Annabelle wanted to offer more, which was why she was focused on getting the money for the bookmobile. With luck, this time next year she would be bringing a lot more than three or four bins of books in the trunk of her car. She would be able to offer free internet access. Maria and her friends could email with family members in different countries and use various web resources to supplement their children's education.

"Blanca's engaged," Maria said with a sigh.

"Congratulations."

"I told you, good men are out there."

"Yes, in Bakersfield. You told me." Maria's eldest daughter had studied nursing, then moved to central California.

"He's a doctor."

Annabelle laughed. "Every mother's dream."

"She's happy and that matters most, but yes, I like saying my daughter is marrying a doctor. Have you been to the hospital lately?"

"That was subtle."

"You need a man."

Just then a little boy ran up to her, a small jar in his hands. He stopped in front of Annabelle and grinned. "We found 'em and saved 'em. Because you bring us books."

She took the jar full of pennies. "Thank you, Emilio. This is going to help a lot."

He darted off and she carefully held the precious gift. Technically it was only a couple of dollars, but for the children who had collected the pennies, it represented a fortune.

"You've made a wonderful home for your children," she said. "All of you. You should be very proud of them."

"We are. But don't think I've forgotten what we were talking about. Finding you a good man."

"I'm ready for a good man," she admitted. She thought about her post-bar-dancing revelation. "One who wants me for me. Not someone who wants to change me. I haven't been lucky enough to find him yet."

"Luck can change."

"I hope so."

She thought briefly about Shane who brought the cowboy fantasy to 3-D life. The man looked great in jeans, but he was a little strange. She was trying to figure out a polite way to ask if he'd maybe been dropped on his head as a baby.

Besides, cute didn't equate with good and she was done making bad choices when it came to her love life. The next man she allowed in her world and her bed was going to adore her for exactly who she was.

"Wait," Shane yelled, watching the teenager on the horse. "Wait."

Elias, nineteen and sure he knew better, jerked back on the reins. The gelding dug in hard and came to a stop. Elias's rope fell about three feet shy of the calf who darted away.

Elias swore. "Damn calf is laughing at me."

"He's not the only one," Shane grumbled. "Why are you here if you're not going to listen?"

"I'm listening."

"No. You're doing what you want to do and look where it's getting you."

Elias muttered something under his breath and reached for his rope. "If I wait too long, I'm gonna miss."

"Waiting too long isn't your problem."

"Now you sound like my girlfriend."

Shane chuckled. "You'll get better with practice on both counts. Now let's try this again."

"See, you need to be working with me, Shane. What have you got going on here that's better than the rodeo?"

"A life."

"Not much of one. You're stuck in this

small town. I swore, once I got out of mine, I was never going back. I can't believe you could live anywhere and you're here."

Shane thought about the couple hundred acres he'd bought and the stables and house he would have built. "I've got everything I need."

Elias grimaced. "Well, help me win and I'll take care of everything I owe."

"Kid, you got heart, but you're going to need a lot more practice. And I'm out of the game."

Elias nodded toward the far corral, where Khatar watched everything going on. "How much did you waste on him? Coulda bought a whole ranch with what you paid for that one."

"He's worth it."

"In your dreams."

"He's perfect," Shane said, not bothering to glance at the stallion.

"If he doesn't kill you first."

"He has a reputation, I'll grant you that. But I'm not convinced he's as mean as everyone says. You interested in practicing or are you here to flap your gums at me? I've got better things to do than stand around listening to you tell me what you don't know."

Elias grinned. "I'm here to learn."

"That's what I thought."

"Until three. Then I have to head to Wyoming." Elias opened his mouth to say something else, then closed it and gave a low whistle. "I sure wouldn't mind getting me a piece of that first, though."

As the teen spoke, Shane felt a prickling on the back of his neck. He didn't even have to turn around to know who had arrived, didn't have to see to understand that his afternoon had just taken a jog toward the impossible.

Elias slid off his horse. He dropped the reins and pulled off his hat, then walked to the fence.

"Afternoon," he called, his eyes wide, his lips curving in a stupid grin.

Shane gave in to the inevitable and shifted so he could watch Annabelle approach.

She'd replaced her fitted summer dress with jeans and a T-shirt, which shouldn't have been sexy, but were. The jeans hugged impressive curves, and while her legs weren't all that long, they were well-shaped. She'd pulled her wavy red hair back into a braid. Her green gaze met him and damned if he didn't want to go down on his knees and beg. He wasn't sure what for, but at this point he would gladly take anything she offered. Although if it was hot, took a long time and was illegal in several states, he could like it even more.

"Yours?" Elias asked, speaking under his breath.

"No, but stay away."

"But I —"

"No."

Elias huffed in annoyance and spun his hat in his hands.

"Hello, Shane," Annabelle said as she stopped in front of him. "I'm here for my lesson." She smiled and held up a tiny foot. "I bought cowboy boots. I want to tell you that you should be impressed, but honestly any excuse to buy new shoes is welcome." The smile blossomed. "It's a girl thing."

"They're real nice," Elias said.

"Thank you."

Shane gave in to the inevitable. "Annabelle, this is Elias."

"Nice to meet you," she said easily.

"My pleasure." Elias looked her over thoroughly. "I was supposed to be heading to Wyoming. It's my grandma's birthday in a couple of days. But I could stay put for a while."

"No, you couldn't," Shane told him, watching Annabelle to see if she was going to start flirting with the younger man.

"We should let the lady decide."

Annabelle watched them both, then frowned. "I'm sorry. Do you mean me?"

"Elias wants to know if he should stick around," Shane said. "For you."

A delicate frown pulled her eyebrows together. "I don't understand."

"We could go out to dinner," Elias offered. "Or back to my place."

"You don't have a place," Shane reminded him. "You stayed with me last night."

"I could get a place."

"You have a girlfriend."

Elias turned back to Annabelle. "It's not serious."

"You're nineteen."

Elias glared at him. "Don't make me hurt you, old man."

Annabelle shook her head. "I'm still confused. I'm, ah, here to learn how to ride."

Shane winked at Elias. "That was a no."

"Like you're going to do any better."

Shane knew that was probably true. More important, for reasons of self-preservation, he needed to stay clear of Annabelle Weiss. Even if she was a temptation.

"About the riding lesson," she began.

Elias sighed. "Is it an age thing? Everyone thinks I'm real mature."

Shane slapped him on the back. "Is that

what they're saying?"

"You stay out of this, old man. This is between me and the lady."

Old man?

Annabelle's green eyes widened. "Are you trying to ask me out?"

"If you have to ask, then I'm doing it wrong," Elias muttered.

"Something else the girlfriend says?" Shane asked quietly.

Elias glared at him. "Shut up."

Shane patted him on the back. "Give it time, kid. You'll get the hang of it."

"I do just fine."

"Uh-huh."

Shane turned his attention back to Annabelle. As he'd suspected, she created trouble wherever she went. He was torn between regretting his offer to help and wondering how he would survive if he didn't get to see her. She was the kind of woman who —

He was interrupted midthought by a whole different kind of trouble approaching from the direction of the barn.

Annabelle was willing to admit she had a sucky track record when it came to men, but she'd never found them quite so perplexing. The young cowboy was hitting on her, which was flattering, but made no sense. She was too old for him. Sure, her new boots were cute, but she'd yet to meet a guy who was that into shoes.

It was the height thing, she thought with a sigh. Because she was small, people often assumed she was younger than she was. Or incompetent. Or both.

As for Shane, who was even better looking in person than in her memory, he seemed more amused than attracted to her. Probably for the best. At least he was acting more normally today. Maybe he hadn't been feeling well the last time they'd met.

"Don't move," Shane said in a low voice.

She blinked at him. "Excuse me?"

"Don't move. Stay exactly where you are. Elias?"

"On it, boss." The teen slipped between the rails of the corral and started walking in a wide circle.

"It's going to be all right," Shane said, never taking his eyes from her.

Annabelle realized this wasn't some strange game, that there really was a problem. Her body went cold as she imagined a large snake approaching. One with big fangs and poisonous venom designed to kill in six painful seconds. Or maybe she was being stalked by something worse, although right now she couldn't imagine what could fit

43

that description.

"A bear?" she asked hopefully. Being mauled seemed better than anything to do with a snake. "Is it a bear?"

"A horse."

"What?"

She turned and saw the large white stallion they'd talked about the day before. Apparently he'd let himself out of his enclosure and was now trotting toward her.

He was beautiful — like something out of the movies. His mane and tail shimmered, muscles rippled and his hooves were a shiny black. Dark eyes locked with hers as he headed directly for her.

He had the most gentle expression, she thought, her nervousness fading away. Almost as if he were trying to reassure her.

She put her hand on her chest, just below her throat. "You scared me. I thought it was a snake. While I hate to be one of the crowd, I share the typical female fear of snakes." She turned toward the horse. "Hey, big guy. You're beautiful. I assumed I would be afraid of horses because you're so big, but you're sweet, aren't you?"

"Annabelle, stay calm." Shane's voice was insistent, almost fearful.

"Okay," she said. "I can do that."

"Move back slowly."

From the corner of her eye she saw Elias approaching with a rope. The teen was bent over at the waist, practically running. Over-react much, she thought, as Khatar reached her.

"Hey, baby," she murmured, reaching up and stroking the huge animal's face. "Who's a handsome boy?"

Khatar shuffled closer and placed his face near to hers. She smiled at him and breathed in the scent of horse. It wasn't as over-whelming as she would have thought. She patted his neck.

"You're very strong," she told him. "Do all the girls say that? I'll bet you're very popular with the lady horses."

He put his head on her shoulder and leaned into her. The action nearly sent her to her knees, but she managed to stay stand-ing. She wrapped both arms around him and would have sworn he sighed.

"What's the matter?" she asked, stepping back and rubbing his cheek again. "Are you lonely? Does mean old Shane ignore you?"

She glanced over her shoulder and saw both men staring at her. Elias's eyes were wide, his mouth hanging open. Shane looked surprised, but slightly less comical.

"What?" she asked.

"Stay calm," Elias told her, sounding

oddly desperate.

"I am calm. What is with you two?" She glanced around, half expecting to see a marauding snake or twelve.

Shane and the teen exchanged a whispered few words, then Elias began to circle the stallion. Khatar, still nuzzling her, casually kicked out a back hoof. Elias jumped back.

"Annabelle, please step back."

Shane sounded stern. She did as he asked. Khatar followed. She rubbed his shoulder.

"Will I be riding him?" she asked.

"No!" The two men spoke as one.

"Okay, okay." She returned her attention to Khatar. "Are you valuable? Is that the problem? You're pretty enough to be worth a ton. Although I suppose *handsome* is a better word, right? Who's a handsome boy?"

Elias and Shane had another whispered conversation.

"Annabelle, we're going to put a halter on Khatar," Shane said in that slightly annoying, reasonable voice.

"Want me to do it?" she asked. "He seems to like me."

"No. I want you to slowly step away, while I get between you and him."

She took the horse's big head in both her hands and lightly kissed the hair above his nose. "You be good for Shane, you hear me?"

His eyes flickered and his gaze shifted to the cowboy. Then his ears went back.

She didn't know much about horses, but that didn't seem like a good sign.

"Why don't I stay close," she offered. "That way he'll be calm."

"She's not crazy, boss," Elias said. "Look at him."

She's not crazy. Wow — maybe she could get that made into a bumper sticker for her car. Talk about a way to step up her game in the romance department. Men would be flocking.

Shane hesitated for a second, then nodded. "Be careful," he told her. "Watch out for his hooves. He's likely to kick."

"How do you know that? Has he kicked you?"

"No, but —"

She folded her arms across her chest. "Has this horse done even one mean thing since you got him?"

"No, but —"

Annabelle exhaled. "Why do you think he's a problem?"

"I don't. He's a great horse. Okay? Happy now?"

Shane moved in. Khatar stiffened slightly.

Annabelle rubbed his neck.

"It's okay, big guy. He's not going to hurt you and I'm right here."

Khatar relaxed and Shane slipped on the halter. She grabbed the rope hanging down.

"Now I have you in my power," she joked. Khatar took a step toward her. She glanced at Shane. "I guess I can take him wherever you want him."

The two men both looked stunned. Again. Shane pointed to the corral where Khatar had been kept before. She led the way, stroking his neck as they walked, his head right beside hers. When they reached the enclosure, she walked him in, closed the gate and then unfastened the rope.

"Home again," she said with a smile.

Khatar sighed. Or maybe snorted. She couldn't tell.

Shane secured the latch on the gate. "Annabelle, slowly move to the railings."

She glanced at him. "Seriously, you don't need to talk in that 'let's keep the crazy horse calm' voice. He's fine. Too bad I can't ride him."

"You can't," Shane told her. "Now please come out of the corral."

She did as asked. Khatar followed her to the fence, then stared at her, looking lost and a little stricken.

"I think he's lonely," she said. "Can't you pay attention to him more?"

Elias walked up. "Ma'am, that horse is a killer."

"He's not a killer," Shane said quickly. "He's difficult. Or has a reputation for being difficult."

"You didn't find out for yourself?" she asked. "You just assumed?" Annabelle looked at the forlorn expression on Khatar's sad face. "Maybe you should do a little more checking."

"I'll get right on that," Shane told her.

The world looked different from the back of a horse, Annabelle thought thirty minutes later. She was perched on Mason, her friend Charlie's large horse, hanging on to the saddle with both hands. Although she'd read a couple of books on riding, none of that information had prepared her for how far away she was from the ground.

"I don't think I can do this," she said desperately.

The horse stood perfectly still, which was a good thing. If he took even a single step, she was pretty sure she was going to start screaming.

"Just relax," Shane told her. He held on to Mason's bridle and patted the horse's shoulder. "Get used to how it feels."

It felt too high and way too scary, she thought frantically. A hundred or so yards away, Khatar ran back and forth, keeping close to the fence line as he called out to her.

"If you're telling me to be careful, I'm so listening," she murmured, knowing the horse couldn't hear her. Riding while a horse danced? What had she been thinking? "Maybe I'll try a car wash instead. That would raise money, right? I can wash cars."

Shane flashed her a grin. "Come on, Annabelle. I was riding a horse before I could ride a bike. It's not that bad."

"I'm too small." Her short legs were sticking out so much they were practically parallel to the ground. "Does he even know I'm on his back? What if he thinks I'm a bug and decides to shake me off?"

"Mason's a good horse. You'll be fine. Now take the reins."

She shook her head. That would mean letting go, which was so not going to happen.

"Use your left hand," he instructed. "You can still hang on with your right."

"I don't want to," she whined, but then slowly, carefully, picked up the reins. The thick leather was worn and softer than she would have thought. She still kept a firm hold on the massive saddle, but felt slightly more horsewoman-like, perched there and actually holding reins.

"Now think about him moving forward and gently kick him."

"What?"

"You want him to move, right?"

"Not really."

She was up to sitting on a horse while the horse stood still. Everything else seemed a little too risky. She reminded herself this was for a good cause. But kicking?

"I don't want to hurt him." Or piss him off. At this point, as far as she was concerned, the horse was seriously in control of the situation.

"Then don't," Shane told her. "Like I said. Be gentle."

She sucked in a breath and lightly touched her heels to his side.

Nothing happened.

She did it again. This time Mason turned and stared at her, as if asking if that was her or just a leaf.

"It was me," she informed the horse. She wiggled in her seat, urging him forward. "Walk."

He took a lurching step.

Actually it probably wasn't lurching, it just felt lurching to her. The entire world seemed to jerk slightly as he walked. She screamed, dropped the reins and grabbed onto the saddle with both hands.

She heard something that sounded suspiciously like a laugh but was hanging on too hard to look in Shane's direction.

"You're not helping," she yelled.

"You're doing fine."

"This is not fine. This is flirting with death."

"Relax. Move with him instead of against him. You're fighting movement you can't control."

Not information designed to make her feel better. She sucked in a breath and tried to relax. As her muscles unclenched, she realized the movement wasn't as lurching as she'd first thought. She was staying in the saddle and didn't feel that she was in danger of slipping off. While she kept a tight grip on the saddle with her right hand, she once again picked up the reins with her left.

"Good," Shane said, his mouth twitching suspiciously. "Just like that."

"Are you mocking me?"

"Only a little."

Thirty minutes later, Annabelle had figured out the walking thing and had even been slapped around during a very bone-crunching trot. She'd managed to let go of the saddle and hang on to the reins like a real rider.

"Not bad," Shane said as she drew Mason to a stop.

"Thanks," she said, bending over and patting the horse's neck.

"I was talking to him."

She wrinkled her nose. "Very funny. So how do I get down?"

She'd used wooden steps to get up to horse level, but wasn't sure she was comfortable dropping onto them. If Mason wasn't in exactly the right position, she could easily fall off the stairs and snap a bone or something.

"Swing your leg over and drop to the ground," Shane said, moving in to hold on to the horse's bridle. "I'll keep him still."

She looked all the way down to the ground, then shook her head. "I don't think so."

"You can't stay up there forever," he pointed out. "You'll be fine."

"Do you know how short I am? It's farther for me than most people."

"By a couple of inches."

Inches could be significant. As a man, he should know that. Still, his point about not staying up in the saddle for the rest of her life was a good one. So she followed his instructions on how to position her hands and then swung her right leg over Mason's wide and very high back. Holding on to the saddle, she reached down and down and finally felt the solid earth with her toe. She released and sank back. Only to find herself unable to stand.

Annabelle's arms went up and out as she staggered, her legs too wobbly to support her. It was as if the muscles had suddenly become al dente pasta.

Just before she hit the ground, strong arms came around her and saved her.

She found herself pressed up against Shane, staring into dark eyes that were bright with humor. This close, he looked even better. She liked the firmness of his jaw and the shape of his mouth. She was aware of his hands — one on her waist and one resting at the small of her back. Her body nestled against his and there was heat everywhere.

"Your muscles take a minute to recover after riding," he murmured. "I probably should have warned you."

She felt the first serious zing of attraction ricochet through her. It left her weaker than being on horseback riding ever could and alerted her to fifty kinds of danger.

Apparently Shane should have warned her about a lot more than riding.

CHAPTER THREE

"I found it," the little girl said proudly, holding up the latest edition in the Lonely Bunny series. This one — *Lonely Bunny Goes to the Beach* — showed the now-famous rabbit in a sun hat, on a towel with the ocean in the background.

"You're going to love the story," Annabelle told the girl. "It's one of my favorites."

"I can't wait!"

The girl ran off to show her mother.

Summer mornings were crazy busy in the library. The summer reading program coordinated between the schools and the library brought in plenty of kids and many of their parents.

For the librarians, the hours were shorter, but the time spent at work was more frantic. Getting the usual amount of work done in less hours with more people milling around. Annabelle loved when the library was crammed, most of the seats taken and the computers hummed with activity.

Normally she didn't work in the children's section, but the regular librarian was on vacation and Annabelle was happy to fill in. The unfamiliar work gave her less time to think — a good thing considering the man on her mind.

She hadn't been able to stop thinking about Shane since "the incident on the horse." Although technically it was the incident getting off the horse, but she didn't feel the need to be that picky.

She'd been able to deal with Shane's good looks with no problem. He was a handsome, if slightly strange, man who was going to teach her to ride. Then she'd seen him joking with Elias and she'd found herself intrigued by his sense of humor. Which would have been fine if she hadn't ended up pressed against his body yesterday. Seriously pressed, with heat and tingles. A dangerous combination.

She knew that when it came to men, she had the word *disaster* tattooed on her forehead. She was always trying to be whatever the man in question wanted. She had to learn to be herself. Could she do that? Could she let Shane see who she was and take things from there?

If only he weren't so appealing, she

thought ruefully. Because honestly, thinking about the very yummy Shane and his powerful chest, long legs and surprisingly large hands made her want to figure out exactly what he found most appealing and be all that. Which would only get her into trouble.

"I want the real thing," she reminded herself in a soft voice. That meant breaking old patterns, being strong and, mostly, being herself. So if Shane was into short, plant-killing women who like to read and hang out with their friends, then they had a chance. If not, she was going to have to ignore the tingles he generated and move on.

Not that he was actually asking her to do anything at the moment.

The good news was tomorrow was the Fourth of July. Which meant no library and no riding lessons. She would lose herself in the fun that was a holiday in Fool's Gold and forget all about the rugged cowboy with the tempting smile.

A small squeal alerted her to the arrival she'd been waiting for. Annabelle walked toward the children gathered around a very worried-looking dog and the pregnant woman holding his leash.

Montana Hendrix Bradley smiled. "We're here."

Annabelle's automatic "Thanks for coming" got lost as she stared at Montana's huge belly. "Are you okay?" she asked instead. "You look . . ."

"Huge?" Montana rubbed the small of her back. "I'm counting the days, let me tell you. I can't get comfortable anytime. I don't sleep." She lowered her voice. "I pee every fifteen seconds. Let's just say I'm not one of those women who glow during pregnancy."

Annabelle felt a little swish of envy. "But you'll have a baby."

Montana smiled. "That's the best part. Just a couple of weeks to go and then we'll have our precious little girl."

"How's Simon dealing with the waiting?"

At the mention of her husband, Montana's expression softened. "He's making me insane, hovering all the time. He phones me every other minute and treats me like I'm breakable."

"You love it."

"I do and him. We're both excited to start the whole kid thing." She glanced around at the children swarming Buddy. "Okay, let's get this started."

It only took a couple of minutes to get the first reader settled with Buddy. Montana had started the reading program the previous year. Buddy, a trained service dog, was the perfect choice. He had a perpetually worried expression and children instinctively wanted to make him feel better. When they read, he relaxed.

During the school year, Buddy traveled to various schools in the district. In the summer, he was a regular tutor at the library. Annabelle had seen the difference he made to the children who had trouble reading. While a child might be uncomfortable reading to an adult, a dog never judged or criticized.

Once Buddy and the first reader had flopped down on the beanbag chairs provided, Montana rejoined Annabelle and carefully lowered her pregnant self into a chair.

"You look as worried as Buddy," Montana said, tucking a strand of blond hair behind her ear. She still wore it long, with bangs. One of three identical triplets, Montana was as beautiful as her sisters. All three of them had been married the previous New Year's Eve in a memorable wedding at The Gold Rush Ski Lodge and Resort.

"While I have plenty of research material on giving birth, what with this being a library and all, I'm not ready to put it into practice," Annabelle admitted.

Montana laughed. "Don't worry. The hospital is close and trust me, Simon would make sure I got there. My poor gynecologist is used to dealing with anxious husbands, but with Simon being a doctor, he's starting to ask her technical questions. I suspect she'll be threatening to sedate him when I go into labor. How are Heidi's wedding plans coming?"

"We're still in the early stage," Annabelle said. "Heidi's getting organized and Charlie and I are doing as much as we can to help. Between the remodels on the house, her goats, the growth in her cheese business and being engaged, she's juggling."

Montana's eyes brightened with amusement. "Charlie isn't exactly the wedding planner type."

"Not girly?" Annabelle asked with a giggle. Charlie was a wonderful friend, but more the type you'd take car shopping than ask to help you pick out linens for a wedding.

"Not exactly."

"She's trying because she's a good friend. And it's kind of fun to watch her get out of her comfort zone."

"Tell Heidi I appreciate her holding the wedding nearly a month after my due date. It gives me time to squeeze back into a regular kind of dress, rather than one of the attractive tents I've been wearing."

"You look wonderful. And you do have the glow, no matter what you say."

Montana grinned. "Don't tell anyone, but it's not a glow. It's panic."

"You'll be a great mother."

"I hope so. Anyway, my mom is thrilled. She went from having only one grandson for eleven years to discovering Ethan had a son he hadn't known about to Dakota adopting Hannah last year to Dakota having Jordan Taylor and me having a girl this year." She drew in a breath. "That's a really long sentence."

Annabelle laughed. "No baby name for you yet?"

"We're still negotiating." Montana's gaze turned speculative. "I heard Rafe's hunky brother has moved to Fool's Gold permanently. Have you met him? Is he all they claim?"

"Shane? He's attractive." Annabelle hesitated, not sure what else to say. She wasn't ready to admit the tingles to anyone.

"I do love a cowboy," Montana said with a sigh. "Not for anything serious, of course. Simon is about the best man on the planet. I'm so lucky to have him." She grinned. "But a girl can always enjoy a floor show, right? Have you seen the third Stryker brother? Clay?"

"I've seen his butt." Clay was a professional model and butt double in the movies. His, um, assets had been featured in more than one film.

"Impressive," Montana said with a grin. "He's one confident guy."

Too pretty for her tastes, Annabelle thought. Shane was handsome in a rugged way. Clay would always be the best-looking guy in the room. That was more pressure than she would be comfortable with.

"So what about your love life?" Montana asked. "Just to give you fair warning, weddings tend to come in threes lately. You're friends with Heidi, so that means you're at risk. Or lucky, depending on how you look at it."

"No, thanks," Annabelle said easily. "I'm not interested."

"Not a big believer in the big L?"

"I do believe in love. It's just . . ." She shrugged. "I thought I had bad luck with men, but maybe I'm as much to blame. When I finally found who I thought was the one, I ended up with a controlling, egotistical husband who expected me to play the part of the fawning wife."

"Ouch."

"It wasn't pleasant. But lately I've been

wondering if it was all him, as I would like to say, or if some of it was me? I think I shelved a big part of myself in order to please him and it was only when things got really bad that I realized he had no idea who I really was. I haven't been strong enough. You know, like the Máa-zib women. I want the real thing, but only if the guy in question also wants the real me. I want love that's honest and messy. I'm done with safe and polite."

With her past, she'd been so determined to make the right choice. To be part of one of those couples who stayed together for sixty or seventy years, then died holding hands. Lewis had made her believe he was exactly who she'd been looking for and she had done the same for him. But the truth was, they had never been right for one another.

"Sorry," Montana said, touching her arm. "I didn't mean to bring up bad memories."

"It's fine. I wish things had been different. Honestly, I've practically given up on finding the one."

"How about dating?"

"Not successful so far."

"Don't forget to have a little faith," Montana told her. "Love shows up when you least expect it. Look at me. The first time I met Simon, I thought he was some stick-up-the-butt jerk with the sense of humor of a rock." She laughed. "He thought I was a twit, but a very sexy twit. Now we're together and having our first baby. Sometimes I wake up and wonder what I did to get so lucky."

Her friend made falling in love sound wonderful. Annabelle wanted to believe, but she'd been wrong before. It was time for a new strategy — one that involved staying true to herself.

Fool's Gold knew how to put on a party, Shane thought as he made his way through town on the Fourth of July. There were carnival rides, food vendors, kid-friendly games in the park and plenty of people. Although it was still early in the afternoon, the sidewalks were crowded and he found himself getting separated from his brother and Heidi.

Not a bad thing, he reminded himself, pausing to let more distance come between them. When Rafe had suggested Shane come along to see how the town celebrated, he'd agreed without thinking the details through. Like the fact that Rafe and Heidi were crazy in love and watching them make goo-goo eyes at each other reminded a guy how alone he was. And how that was unlikely to change.

He was glad his work-only, work-always brother had loosened up enough to find someone as great as Heidi and hoped they would be happy together. But Shane didn't need the 3-D illustration of what he would never have. Not while he was obsessed with Annabelle.

If he could forget about her, maybe he would have a shot with someone more . . . regular. A sensible kind of woman who had a great smile. A woman he could grow to love in a rational way. That's what he wanted. A safe relationship. Not heat and fire and desperate longing. In that kind of situation, he was going to end up little more than a pile of ash on the sidewalk.

Up ahead, Heidi started looking around. When she spotted him, she walked back and linked arms with him.

"What do you think?" she asked. "Is this a great town or what?"

"I remember the Fourth being a big deal when I was a kid, but this celebration is more impressive than I remember."

"I'm glad." She leaned against him. "You never had Rafe's issues with the town?"

"No. I liked it here."

Rafe, the oldest of the Stryker children,

had been the one to try to step into the role of caretaker after their father died. He'd still been a kid himself, but he'd worried about his siblings and their mother, had worked too hard and often gone hungry so everyone else had enough to eat.

It had taken Shane years to figure out what his brother had given up. By the time he had, Rafe had already been in college — Harvard, on a scholarship — and on the road to success. For Shane, Clay and Evangeline, Fool's Gold had been the best place in the world. For Rafe, it was where he'd been poor and scared and hungry.

"I'm sorry I haven't been more help with your house," Heidi said. "Between the goats and the wedding, I'm swamped. But I'll make time."

He was having a house built, or he would as soon as he approved the plans. He knew exactly what he wanted with the stables, but the decisions for the house baffled him. There were hundreds of different kinds of door handles. He couldn't understand why his contractor was uncomfortable making those decisions.

"It's not your problem," he told her. "I'll figure it out."

"You could ask your mom when she gets back."

"No, thanks." Not only was she traveling with Glen, Shane didn't want to live in a house his mother had built. He was sure she had great taste, but that was too strange for him. "It's a few fixtures. I'll be fine."

"I hope so." Heidi patted his arm. "Want to ride a pony?" she asked with a grin, pointing to the line of small children waiting their turn. "My treat."

He shuddered. "No."

"Not a pony fan?"

"They're mean."

"Not every single one on the planet."

He groaned. "Now you sound like my mother."

He was going to say more, but before he could speak, he felt a heat flare in his body. Were he out in the wild, he would assume he was being stalked by an animal. Here, in this crowd, there was only one danger. And it, or she, was getting closer.

He turned and spotted Annabelle talking to a firefighter. It took him a second to tear his gaze away from the stunning redhead long enough to recognize Charlie Dixon, the woman who owned Mason and boarded him at the ranch.

Annabelle looked up and saw him and Heidi. She waved, said something to Charlie and the two women approached. He braced himself for impact.

Today Annabelle had dressed to cause mayhem wherever she went. The swingy little sundress was pale green, with skinny straps. Her hair was a mass of wavy curls and tumbled down her back. Shane had to hang on to every fiber of self-control to keep from pulling her under the nearest bush and taking advantage of her in every way possible.

"Hi," Annabelle said as she approached. "Shane, do you know Charlie?"

The firefighter, tall and muscular with big blue eyes and an appealingly sarcastic eye roll, sighed. "I keep my horse on his family's ranch. Of course I know Shane."

"Right." Annabelle grinned. "She's crabby. Charlie hates the Fourth of July."

"I don't hate the holiday," Charlie muttered. "I hate people being stupid and today is one day they're experts at it. Do you know how many calls we're going to get because idiots who can't read simple instructions will catch somebody's roof on fire with fireworks? It's pyrotechnics, people. Know what you're doing or leave it to the professionals."

Annabelle patted her arm. "Deep cleansing breaths."

"I'll be calm tomorrow." Charlie drew her

eyebrows together. "What about the animals at the Castle Ranch? Can they hear the fireworks?"

Heidi shook her head. "We're too far out of town. Don't worry, though. Shane's heading back early and will be taking care of them."

"Thanks. I'm concerned about Mason," Charlie admitted.

"You're a good horse mom," Annabelle told her. "And Mason is really nice. He was very calm with me. Although I think he's mocking me when I flop around on him."

"He is," Charlie told her cheerfully. "But he's a good guy. Imagine what a horse with attitude would be thinking."

"Like Khatar," Heidi murmured. "He scares me."

"Khatar?" Annabelle shook her head. "Why would he scare you? He's so sweet."

Shane had used the distraction of the women's conversation to talk himself off the sexual ledge. Now he managed to clear his throat and actually speak.

"Khatar got out while Annabelle was over a couple of days ago. He seems to like her."

"For lunch?" Charlie asked.

Annabelle grinned. "Even I know horses are vegetarians."

"If one was going to make an exception, it

would be him. You be careful."

"I'm fine. He was practically snuggling. He's not what you think."

Heidi looked as doubtful as Charlie. "Keep your distance, Annabelle. He's nothing like Mason or Shane's other horses."

"I'll keep her safe," Shane said.

One of Charlie's eyebrows rose, but she didn't say anything.

"At least Khatar won't be in the way much longer," Heidi said.

"Where's he going?" Annabelle asked Shane. "You didn't sell him, did you?"

"No. I bought about two hundred acres next to the Castle Ranch. I'm having stables built, along with a house."

Annabelle grinned. "What? You don't want to live with your mother and her boyfriend forever?"

He groaned. "Not to mention my brother and his fiancée? No."

"Speaking of your brother, I'd better go find him," Heidi said.

"I'll walk you," Charlie told her. "I have to get back to the station."

Shane expected Annabelle to go with them, but she stayed with him and seconds later, despite the hundreds of people milling around them, he found himself alone with her.

"Come on," she said. "I'll show you the town. You can tell me how it's different from when you were a kid here."

There was no polite way to tell her no and, in truth, he liked the idea of spending time with her. Assuming he could figure out a way to keep his hands to himself and think about something other than the way her mouth would feel against his.

His grand plan fizzled to dust when she linked arms with him and leaned close. "As you know," she began. "Fool's Gold is the festival capital of the country. Maybe the world." She glanced up at him and smiled.

Her mouth was moving, so he knew she was still talking, but he couldn't hear anything but a buzzing sound. Heat hit him with the subtlety of a bull rider slamming into the group. There was something about her face — the perfect shape, the dark green of her eyes, the thick lashes, the flash of white teeth when she smiled up at him.

Even in the middle of the crowd, with food stands all around, he could breathe in the soft scent of her perfume. Or maybe it was just her. A combination of vanilla and invitation.

"Shane?"

He promised himself when he got back to the ranch he would bang his head against the closest wall until he knocked some sense into himself.

"Sorry," he murmured.

"It's okay. Now, what do you remember about being a kid here?"

He focused on the question. It was a whole lot safer than focusing on her. "That I loved the ranch. There was always so much to do. I had my brothers, my friends. When Mom told us we had to move, I threatened to run away. We were all sad to leave — except for Rafe."

"Heidi mentioned he didn't want to come back." She laughed. "He's stuck now. Falling in love will do that to a guy." She turned her head and her long hair brushed against his forearm. "Was it always your plan to move back here?"

"No. I knew I wanted my own ranch, and I've been planning for that, but I hadn't settled on a location until Rafe and my mom told me that they'd bought the Castle Ranch. I came out to visit, saw the land next door and bought it."

"Impressive. And here I am excited that I just paid off my car." She frowned. "There's no house, right? You're having that built."

He drew in a breath. "Yes, but it's slow going. The stables are easy. I know what I want and don't want. But the house is a pain in the ass. Every time I turn around, the contractor has more questions. Lights, sinks, countertops, appliances."

"Not a big shopper?" she asked, her green eyes bright with amusement.

"No."

"If only there was a kit, right? Generic house surfaces and finishes. You pick one from column A, two from column B and, voilà, a house."

"You're mocking me."

"A little. But mostly because it's easy."

"Thanks," he grumbled. "Did you build your house?"

"No. I'm renting a charming rambler and it came with things like sinks and appliances. I would love to make some changes, but my landlord doesn't share my thrill for interior design. He has let me paint the walls a color other than white, which I appreciate." She grinned. "I confess I love all those decorating shows on TV and I'm the first one to read the home style magazines when they come into the library."

They paused by a row of food carts. He motioned to the offerings — everything from fresh-squeezed lemonade to cotton candy.

"What would you like?" he asked.

"I'm good."

He'd been hoping she would get a drink and maybe something to eat. Anything that would cause her to untangle herself from him. Not that he didn't enjoy her pressed up against him, but that was part of the problem. He enjoyed it too much.

Two boys ran past, nearly bumping into her. Annabelle shifted out of the way, which brought her breasts in direct contact with his chest. He clenched his jaw and did his best not to groan as the sensual burn seared through him.

"Sorry," she said, stepping away. "I do love the life in this town, but it can get a little crowded during holidays."

"How long have you lived here?" he asked, willing himself to think about granite and tile choices. Anything to keep the blood from pushing south and taking up residence.

"I moved here last year. I got lucky. I was looking to start over and found this job right away." She glanced at him. "I was married. After my divorce, I wanted to settle somewhere far, far away."

"Where did you move from?"

"North Carolina."

"That is far. You don't have a Southern accent."

"I grew up in Arizona."

"How do you like this coast?"

"I love it. There are seasons here. We have snow." She smiled. "I was a little nervous about learning to drive in the white stuff, but it wasn't too bad. I have great tires and nerves of steel. Or maybe just a really strong plastic. Either way, I survived. I took my first snowboarding lesson."

"How was it?"

She laughed. "Horrible. I swear my instructor was twelve and he couldn't stop laughing at me."

Shane doubted he was laughing *at* her. "You'll do better this year."

"I hope so." The humor faded. "I was nervous about starting over, but it's been good." She glanced at him from under her lashes. "I understand there's an ex–Mrs. Shane Stryker in your past."

"There is."

"Regrets?"

"About it being over? No. Rachel was a mistake from start to finish. I never should have married her."

Annabelle came to a stop in front of him. "Wow. Still putting energy into what went wrong?"

"No, but I'm grateful every day to be apart from her."

"What was she like?"

They were standing less than a foot apart.

Everything about her tempted him. If he closed his eyes, he would still be able to picture everything about her. Worse, would be able to hear her laugh — a sound that had become as appealing as the rest of her.

"A disaster."

Annabelle grinned. "You're not going to answer the question?"

He paused, then spoke the truth. "She was a lot like you."

"Mom's talking about getting you a wading pool," Shane said.

One of Priscilla's ears flickered with interest. "At least *you're* talking to me. That's something."

The elephant turned her large head toward him, her trunk lightly brushing against his arm, as if reminding him he had no one to blame but himself.

"I know," he muttered. "I'm the bad guy."

He hadn't meant to hurt Annabelle's feelings the previous day. When he'd said she reminded him of Rachel, her eyes had widened, she'd gone pale, then excused herself and walked away.

"Maybe I should have gone after her."

Priscilla's wise expression clearly asked, "You think?"

"But that would have meant catching her."

Stopping her, possibly by putting his hand on her shoulder. Then what? He had a bad feeling that a single touch was all it would take.

It was early, barely after dawn. Shane hadn't slept much the night before so he'd already been awake when it had been time to get up to take care of the animals. His horses and his mother's misfit collection of elderly llamas, sheep and Priscilla didn't much care about his state of mind. They wanted breakfast.

The back door slammed. Shane saw his brother stalking toward him and knew that word had spread.

Rafe came to a stop by the fence line and glared at him. "What the hell?"

"Morning to you, too," Shane grumbled.

"Heidi and Annabelle are friends."

"I don't want to hear it."

"I don't care. You're going to hear it. Annabelle's hurt, Heidi's pissed and I'm caught in the middle. What did you say to her?"

"We were talking about Rachel."

"Great first-date material."

"We're not dating."

"Good. Last I heard, even you weren't that stupid around women."

Shane let himself out of Priscilla's enclosure. He reminded himself he didn't want to fight with his brother, although at the moment, he couldn't figure out why not.

"She asked what Rachel was like and I said she reminded me of her."

Rafe stared at him in disbelief. "You ranted about Rachel," he began.

"I didn't rant."

"You always rant about her. You went on and on about how bad she was then told Annabelle she was just like her."

Shane thought longingly of the coffee he hadn't had yet. "Not just like her."

"Close enough." Rafe swore under his breath. "I don't like Heidi upset."

"I'll apologize."

"To Annabelle?"

Shane nodded. Maybe it wouldn't be an issue. Maybe Annabelle would avoid him now.

"She's nothing like Rachel," Rafe told him. "Rachel was a bitch. Annabelle's nice."

"Not in personality," Shane said quickly. "I didn't mean that. It's more . . ."

Rafe waited, but Shane just shook his head. No way he was going to confess that the need to possess was just as powerful as it had been with his ex-wife. The difference was, he enjoyed spending time with Annabelle.

"She's dangerous," he said at last.

"What? She's a librarian!"

"Have you seen her?"

"Sure. Short with red hair. So what?"

So what? She was temptation incarnate. "The librarian thing is a cover."

Rafe groaned. "You're in trouble. Just fix it. I don't want to have to hear about what a jerk you are from Heidi."

Shane nodded. "I'll take care of it."

If only he could figure out exactly how.

CHAPTER FOUR

Annabelle told herself she would be the bigger person. Possibly for the first time in her life, she thought, managing a smile. Maybe she was making too big a deal out of what Shane had said. It's just he'd obviously hated his ex and then to have him say she reminded him of the woman had been disconcerting. And okay, it had hurt a little.

"I need to learn to ride," she said aloud, then squared her shoulders and tightened her grip on the steering wheel. "For the bookmobile."

She needed to keep her eyes on the prize. The festival to raise the money would culminate with the dance. She was the one who had said she would learn to do it. Someone had anonymously donated the money for riding lessons. It's not like she was going begging.

Someone tapped on the driver's side window of her parked car. She yelped and jumped in her seat, then saw Shane standing there.

Her first instinct was to drive back home. But she was already here and they needed to come to terms.

She hit the button to lower her window. "Hi."

"Hi, yourself. I wasn't sure you'd show up."

She tried to tell if he was pleased or disappointed, only his dark eyes were impossible to read.

"I'm sorry," he said abruptly. "About what I said. I didn't mean it the way it came out."

"How did you mean it?"

He hesitated, then drew in a breath. "Can I pass on that one?" He reached through the open window and pulled up the lock, then opened her door and held out his hand. "I'd like very much to teach you to ride and teach one of the horses to do the dance. If you'll accept my apology."

If she'd been standing, she would have stomped her foot. Now he was being all nice and conciliatory. If she said no, she would look like she was pouting. Plus, she really did need the lessons.

"That would be great," she said, and placed her hand in his.

For a second, she thought she felt a little

tingle, but told herself she was imagining it. It had to be static electricity.

He helped her out of her car, then released her.

"I'll get Mason," he told her as he closed her car door. Shane suddenly stiffened and swore under his breath.

She turned and saw Khatar trotting toward them.

"I changed the lock on his gate," Shane said. "Stay back."

Annabelle ignored him and walked toward the beautiful white stallion. "He's smart and handsome. Aren't you, big guy? Who's a clever horse?" As she spoke, she reached up and stroked his face.

Khatar stepped closer, as if eager to be near. He angled his body between her and Shane, then lowered his head so he could press it against her chest.

"You're quite the kitten, aren't you?" She looked over his ears toward Shane. "You should let me ride him."

"I don't think so."

"Is it because he's expensive? I'll be careful. Doesn't he need exercise? Couldn't I do that? He's so sweet."

"He's not sweet."

If he hadn't looked so serious and worried, she would have laughed. "You must be confusing him with another horse," she said, and wrapped her arms around the horse's strong neck. "You wouldn't hurt me, would you?"

"You can't ride him."

There was something in Shane's tone. Something that made her want to stick out her tongue and remind him he wasn't the boss of her. Not exactly mature.

She told herself this was his horse and he had the right to say who could ride him and who couldn't. Still, Khatar was so friendly.

"Could I try?" she asked.

"No."

"For a minute?"

"He'll throw you then trample you."

"He won't. He adores me. I'll show you."

She was standing by the fence, with the horse between her and Shane. In one quick move, she climbed onto a lower rung and reached for the horse. Khatar moved toward her, turning to give her a better angle. Shane's entire body stiffened as his face went white.

"Annabelle, don't!"

His tone was frantic. She realized he wasn't kidding about his concern. She started to get down, only to slip on the wood and start to fall. She caught herself by grabbing onto Khatar. He stayed perfectly still, as if wanting to make sure she didn't get hurt.

Shane came around the front of him and stared. "Well, I'll be."

"Dangling here," she reminded him, her feet flailing as she started to slip.

Shane reached for her and grabbed her around her waist.

"Give me a leg up," she said.

For a second, he didn't move, as if he couldn't decide. Then he guided her foot to his thigh.

She pushed against him and found herself going up and over, then settling on Khatar's back. There was no saddle, nothing to hang on to.

"This might have been a bad idea," she whispered.

"That's what I said."

Khatar started walking. She hung on with her thighs and discovered she could easily adjust to his steady rhythm.

Shane watched them, then shook his head. "You win. I'll get the bridle and we'll see what he's willing to do."

He disappeared into the barn, then re-appeared with the bridle. Khatar walked over and stuck out his head toward the leather straps. Shane slid the bit into his mouth and then adjusted everything and handed her the reins.

"Go for it," he said.

They circled the barn a couple of times. When Shane held open a gate to a corral, she urged the horse in that direction and he did as she asked.

"He would look amazing painted," she said.

Shane winced. "I can trace his bloodlines back three hundred years."

"It's water-based paint. It would come right off."

"That's not much in the way of comfort."

"I have a costume," she offered. "If that helps."

"It doesn't."

"The ceremony also includes a male sacrifice. I'm supposed to cut out a guy's heart." She patted Khatar's shoulder. "Not for real, of course. Just pretend."

"Good to know."

"I haven't had any volunteers."

"Are you surprised?"

He talked her through a series of turns, then whistled the horse into a trot. The bouncing of her entire body on his bare back wasn't pleasant, but she survived.

"Had enough?" Shane asked a half hour later.

"I think my insides have turned into a

milkshake." Annabelle pressed her hand to her stomach. "But Khatar was great. I told you he was friendly."

"Just for you." He grabbed the reins and led the horse to the side of the corral. "You going to be able to stand when you touch ground?"

"I'll be fine," she said, hoping she wasn't lying, then eyed the horse's bare back. "What do I hold on to as I slide down?"

"I'll catch you."

She was less sure about that. Mason had been big, but at least there'd been a saddle to grab on to. With Khatar there was only his mane and she had a feeling that his good mood would disappear if she used that to lower herself to the ground.

Deciding she would be safer seeing what she was about to crash into, she swung her leg over his neck and sat facing Shane, then pushed off Khatar and slid down and down until her feet touched packed earth.

For a second she managed to keep her balance. Then her thighs gave way and she started to collapse.

"Didn't we already do this?" Shane asked, grabbing her around the waist and holding her up.

"I thought I would do better," she admitted, putting her hands on his shoulders and willing herself to stay upright.

The tingles she'd experienced earlier returned. Along with the zings and zips from the last time she'd been riding. Although it wasn't the riding that seemed to be a problem. It was being held by Shane. And maybe *problem* wasn't the right word. *Complication* seemed like a better fit.

Which was really interesting, because wasn't she the one looking for messy? And weren't complications really close to a mess?

He didn't wear a hat, she thought absently. Weren't cowboys supposed to wear hats? Not that she minded. His dark hair gleamed in the bright sun. He wore it short enough that the slight wave didn't turn into curls.

His eyes were made up of various shades of brown and there were crinkles in the corners from when he smiled. Only he wasn't smiling now. He was looking serious and sexy.

She told herself not to look at his mouth. Or think about what that mouth could do to her. So she kept her gaze on his eyes, which turned out to be equally dangerous, because it seemed to her a woman could get lost in his gaze. Get lost and never find her way back.

"I was an idiot," Annabelle said, poking at

her salad with her fork. "I stood there like a fifteen-year-old with a crush on the football captain."

"Did you babble?" Charlie asked before taking a bite of her burger.

"No. I ran. As soon as I could safely move without my legs giving way, I ran to my car and left."

Charlie chewed, then swallowed. "I would have paid money to see that."

"This is not you being supportive."

They were having a quick lunch at the Fox and Hound. Annabelle had felt the need to confess her reaction and knew she could trust Charlie to keep the information to herself. Normally she would have told Heidi, too, but with Heidi engaged to Shane's brother, it was feeling a little too incestuous as it was.

"So you wanted to have your way with Shane," Charlie said. "Big deal."

"I didn't," Annabelle protested, then dropped her fork. "Fine. I did. But I can't. He's teaching me to ride."

"So? He's a good-looking single guy. Last time I checked, you were single. What's the big deal? He's not a relative or your priest."

"No, but . . ." She picked up her fork again. "This was easier when I worried he'd been dropped on his head."

"Excuse me?"

"Never mind." She took a sip of her iced tea. "All I wanted was to learn to ride well enough to do the traditional dance of the female warrior. It's not a big dream, I know, but it was mine."

"You're still going to learn to ride. Shane will teach you. And if you're very good, he'll show you his manroot."

Annabelle burst out laughing. "His what?"

Charlie grinned. "Okay, better. I couldn't stand seeing you all depressed. You found a guy who probably thinks you're hot. You want him. That's good. Quit beating yourself up over that."

"Manroot?"

"I read it somewhere."

"I don't think I want to ask where." Her mood restored, she took a big bite of her salad.

Charlie was right. So she found Shane attractive. Lots of guys were. As to the tingles, she would think about them. Sure, he was a little too hung up on his ex, but that was all about passion, right? As long as he was totally over her. Because a man capable of that much feeling was the kind who put it all on the line.

"You're about to launch into a recap of your pathetic love life, aren't you?" Charlie picked up her burger. "Not every guy is your ex."

"I know. No recap, I promise. This despite the fact that I married Lewis. I dated him, I trusted him, I thought I fell in love with him and I agreed to spend the rest of my life with him."

"Are you sorry you left?"

"No. Of course not."

Lewis had been older, by twelve years, a somewhat successful, nearly famous author. He'd impressed her with his intelligence, his worldliness. He'd traveled everywhere, had lots of interesting stories. He was always the center of attention, so when he noticed her, she felt special. Wanted.

But she'd discovered that Lewis's stories were more fiction than truth and that while he seemed to know about many different topics, his information was superficial at best. He'd personified the concept of all flash and no substance.

"It took me a long time to figure out he wasn't what I thought," she admitted. "That he never really loved me, he loved what I represented."

"The trophy wife?" Charlie asked dryly.

"A little. Which is strange because he was always telling me that I was lucky he'd married me. That no one else would want me."

"Have you looked in the mirror?"

"Not lately."

"You should."

Annabelle smiled. "You're a good friend."

"I know. You should be sending me gifts and tweeting about my virtues on a daily basis." She picked up a French fry. "We all have secrets."

"What are yours?" Annabelle asked, not expecting an answer.

Charlie shrugged. "It was a long time ago."

Annabelle stared at her. "Want to elaborate?"

As a rule, Charlie didn't talk all that much about her past. Annabelle knew that her friend hadn't grown up in the area. That she was from somewhere back east. There had been hints of a difficult mother and a father who had died unexpectedly. But little else.

Charlie took a deep breath and seemed to steady herself before answering. "I was date-raped in college."

Annabelle's stomach clenched and the small amount of food she'd already eaten lurched threateningly. "No," she breathed. "I'm so sorry."

Charlie shrugged. "It happens."

"No, it doesn't. That's awful." She didn't have a lot of experience with the topic and wasn't sure what to say. "Do you want to talk about it?"

"No. Yes." Charlie rubbed her forehead. "This is why I don't usually mention it. It's done and over. Only I can't seem to move on."

She drew in a breath. "I went on a date in college with this really good-looking guy. He played football and was a senior. The whole cliché thing, right? But I didn't see it coming."

Annabelle winced. "You thought he really liked you."

"Exactly. Instead, he was using me for sex. Things went further than I wanted and when I tried to stop him, he raped me. I was a virgin and it was horrible."

"Did you report him?"

Charlie's mouth twisted. "Oh, yeah. I went to campus police and they brought him in. I was smart enough not to shower. There was DNA evidence."

"Then I don't understand. If you had proof . . ."

Charlie looked past her. "They didn't believe me," she said flatly. "I heard him talking to the cops. He actually laughed and said to look at me, then look at him. Was there even one person who wouldn't believe I'd have to be begging him before he would put out?"

She returned her gaze to Annabelle. "The police had called my mother. When she showed up and met him, she came and told me it was rude to lead a guy on. And that I shouldn't lie about something like being raped."

Charlie's expression never changed. Except for the tension in her mouth, there were no hints that something was wrong. Only Annabelle could guess the truth. That Charlie had been devastated, as anyone would be. But her pain had been worse because no one had taken her side and those she trusted most had thought it was a joke.

"I'm sorry," she whispered.

"Yeah? Me, too." Charlie picked up her burger, then put it down. "I keep telling myself it was a long time ago. That I'm over it. And I am. Sort of. But it's why I don't date."

"You're afraid to trust anyone."

"A guy," Charlie corrected. "I trust my female friends."

Annabelle raised her eyebrows. "And yet you don't want to date any of us."

Charlie grinned. "You offering?"

"No, but I could ask around."

"I'll pass."

"You haven't dated at all since the attack?"

"A little. But it never goes anywhere." Charlie's smile faded. "It's not like guys are lining up to ask or anything."

"That's because you make sure they know you're not interested." Annabelle turned the information over in her mind. "So you haven't, um, you know, done it since?"

Charlie shook her head. "Why would I want to? It was horrible. Everything about that night was terrifying. It's not like I miss it, right?"

Only her tone was slightly wistful.

Annabelle touched her hand. "You're the strongest person I know, Charlie. And the bravest. You can't let that jerk win."

"He's not."

"Yes, he is. You've shut off an important part of yourself because of him. Maybe you don't want to get married and have a family, but at least you owe it to yourself to find out. There are plenty of nice guys out there."

"Do you see me with a nice guy?"

"At this point, I think it would be a very good idea."

"He's not winning," Charlie repeated, but she sounded less sure. "I refuse to let him win."

"Better," Annabelle told her. "Have you thought about talking to a professional?"

Charlie rolled her eyes. "Therapy? Hardly. I'd rather take out my issues on a punching bag."

"Or the guy in question?"

"He's not worth it." Charlie sighed. "You're right. I've ignored what happened for years. I guess I need to work through it or something and move on."

"How can I help?"

"You're doing it just by listening. Thanks."

Annabelle nodded and returned to her salad. She no longer felt like eating, but knew that if she didn't, Charlie would get on her case.

Although she hated what had happened to her friend, she was glad she knew the truth. The situation explained a lot about Charlie's attitude on everything from trust to men. She had a long road back to find something close to normal. Still, Annabelle was confident she would get there and that her friends would want to make sure that happened.

"Thanks for meeting me," Shane said as Annabelle got out of her car and walked toward him.

"You were very cryptic," she said with a laugh. "How could I resist?"

Sunlight suited her, he thought, bracing

himself for the inevitable rush of wanting. It delivered right on cue, as he took in the soft wavy curls, the pale skin and temptation in her green eyes. Heat flared, desire exploded and he found himself wishing they were alone someplace quiet and dark. Like his bedroom. Or hers. He wasn't picky.

Instead they were in a parking lot outside his contractor's office. In the middle of the day. On the edge of downtown Fool's Gold. Not exactly the place for a rendezvous. Not that Annabelle was offering.

She approached on her ridiculously high-heeled sandals, her skirt flirting with her thighs. Her T-shirt was simple and shouldn't have been sexy, but was, hugging curves in a way that made his mouth water.

She stopped in front of him and waited, obviously expecting him to explain why he'd asked her to join him here.

"I need help," he said, hoping she didn't realize how true that statement was. "I told you before, I'm having a house built, along with stables and corrals. I can handle the horse-related decisions. I know how big I want the stalls, where the windows will be placed and all the hardware I need for their safety."

She smiled. "That's good because I

wouldn't have a clue. So what's the problem?"

"The house. Jocelyn keeps emailing lists of questions I have to answer and I don't have a clue. Do you know how many light fixtures there are in a kitchen alone? Overhead, pendant, under counter. There are switches and finishes and appliances. Paint colors, flooring." He didn't want to think about it all. "I don't have time."

"Or interest," Annabelle said with a grin. "Poor Shane. You're such a guy."

"Meaning?"

"You really do want a house kit. One that comes fully finished and all you have to do is pick the color of beige you want the walls before you move in."

"What's wrong with beige?"

She laughed.

He hadn't been kidding with the question, but okay.

"I take it Jocelyn is your contractor?" she asked.

"Yes. She's ready to break ground on the house, but I haven't approved the plans. I thought about asking my mom for help, but she and Glen are traveling and Heidi's busy with the wedding." There was more he wanted to say but he was having trouble remembering it. There was something about

98

the way she looked at him. It made him want to pull her close and . . .

He cleared his throat. "You'd mentioned you really like to decorate. If you help me with the house, I won't charge you for the riding lessons."

Her green eyes brightened. "Seriously? I have a donation to pay for them, but I could put the money into the bookmobile fund. That would be so great." She paused. "Are you sure? I feel like you wouldn't be getting your money's worth."

"It's a lot of house."

"Then sure. I'm happy to help." She moved close and linked arms with him. "Can we get a pink tub in the master? I've always wanted a pink tub."

Her breast pressed into his arm. He tried telling himself he wasn't sixteen anymore and that this wouldn't be the highlight of his day. But there were parts that didn't believe him.

"No pink."

"But it's pretty."

They headed for the office.

Once inside, he carefully stepped away, needing the distance. He couldn't think when she was close and if he wasn't careful, he *would* be agreeing to a pink tub.

Jocelyn, a no-nonsense woman in her early

99

fifties, was waiting for him in her small office. She looked capable, managed her crew with a fair but firm attitude and had agreed to a clause in the contract that basically gave him her firstborn if she didn't complete the stable on time. Just as good, she'd come highly recommended.

"This is Annabelle," he said by way of introduction.

"You didn't tell me you were married," Jocelyn said, holding out her callused hand. "I always need to meet the wife. I know who's the real power player in a relationship."

Annabelle laughed. "Not the wife. Just a friend who's going to help Shane with all the girly stuff."

They shook hands. Jocelyn grinned. "Got frightened by the list of finishes, right?"

"It was a longer list than I was expecting," he admitted.

"It always is." Jocelyn ran her hand through her short-cropped gray hair. "My advice is to give him maybe three choices in every category. No more. Men can't handle it."

Shane wanted to protest being talked about like that, but his bringing Annabelle along to help sort of proved Jocelyn's point.

She led them into a conference room

where the plans were laid out on a huge table.

"I need approval on the size of the house," she said, pointing to two chairs next to each other. "We can move walls around if need be, but I want to start pulling permits and reserving equipment. In a perfect world, we'd dig out the foundation in a couple of weeks, when we start on the stables."

"You can get started that fast?" Annabelle asked, taking a seat.

"If I get a little cooperation. This one knew everything he wanted in the stable, down to the paint color in the office. But I'd swear, he's never been in a house before."

"I've been in them," he grumbled, settling next to Annabelle, but being careful not to lean in too close. "I've never built one. There's a difference."

"Tell me about it." She handed Annabelle a printed list of questions. "Get me the answers to these and I'll be a fan forever. Before you leave, if possible." She started toward the door. "Try to keep the yelling down."

"We won't yell," Annabelle told her.

Jocelyn grinned. "Then you haven't done this before, either. Trust me, honey, there's always yelling."

101

She left, closing the door behind her.

Annabelle drew the plans toward them. "It's your house. We're not going to argue." She turned and smiled at him. "Because you're going to listen to everything I say, right?"

Her gaze captured him, holding him in place. Not that he wanted to go anywhere. "Not likely."

She chuckled, then turned her attention to the drawings. "Okay, the house. It's nice. I like all the windows. There'll be plenty of light in the winter. Big master. Good his and hers closets." She shifted slightly and her hair slipped off her shoulder to rest on the back of his hand.

The curls tickled and teased, making him want to weave his fingers through the strands. Even without trying he could breathe in the scent of her. He swore silently, reminding himself he had to maintain control.

"Hmm." She pointed to the kitchen. "This isn't going to work. Look at where the pantry is. Around behind the refrigerator? That's going to be a pain. And this wall here, closing everything off."

"You need the wall for cabinets."

"You need *a* wall for cabinets. There's a difference. The kitchen itself is great, but it's all catawampus."

He drew back and grinned. "It's what?"

"Catawampus? Askew. Turned around wrong."

"I know what the word means."

"I was trying to talk in cowboy terms. So we could relate to each other."

"You don't think we're relating now?"

Maybe it was wishful thinking on his part but he would swear she leaned a little closer. And that her lips parted as she drew in a breath.

"I do, but I wanted to make sure." She blinked a couple of times and turned her attention back to the plans. "All you'd have to do is shift everything ninety degrees. Then the kitchen would be open to the family room and the sink would still face a window. The pantry would be accessible, like this."

She picked up a pencil and drew a couple of quick lines.

He was more intrigued by her reaction than what she was doing. Was it possible that she felt it, too? The connection? Talk about a game changer. Not that he was looking to get involved, but there was a whole country of possibilities between interested and involved.

"I'll talk to Jocelyn," he told her, still

watching her as he spoke.

"You and I should probably schedule some time in the home improvement store so I can get an idea of what you like. For finishes and fixtures. That will help me narrow down the choices. I know everyone is crazy about granite, but I think there are a lot of manmade finishes you could consider. They're so easy to take care of."

More time with her? "Sounds like a plan."

"Good."

She turned toward him. Their faces were inches apart. Her mouth called to him in ways that left him hungry and determined. He wanted her and if she felt the same way —

"Shane?"

"Hmm?"

"What do you think of Charlie?"

It wasn't the question he'd been expecting.

"Charlie Dixon?"

"Yes. She owns Mason. You've met her. What do you think of her?"

Of course he knew Charlie. He took care of her horse. "In what context?"

Annabelle smiled. "Romantically. Would you like to go out with her?"

He'd been thrown from his share of broncs, but never had he landed on his ass like this. He stared at Annabelle, wondering what he'd done to deserve it. All he wanted was a regular kind of life with a normal woman. Someone nice and caring, someone he would be faithful to and take care of. Was it asking too much?

With that description, Charlie should be exactly who he wanted. She was a walking, breathing definition of sensible. Instead he was driven mad by the bar-dancing, horse-whispering redhead in front of him.

"Shane?"

He did the only thing he could think of. He grabbed her by her shoulders, pulled her a couple of inches closer and kissed the hell out of her.

Annabelle had been thinking Shane would either say he liked Charlie fine or that she wasn't his type. Honestly, she'd sort of been hoping for the latter, what with the tingles she'd started feeling when she was around him. But she hadn't expected this.

His mouth was warm on hers. Firm, a little demanding, but only enough to keep things interesting. He smelled good, tasted better and he held on like he would never let go. A quality she could appreciate in a man. He was —

Need shattered her. One second she was

enjoying how much she liked him kissing her and the next she was beyond frantic. Desperate, actually. She wanted to crawl into his lap and maybe inside of him. She wanted more kisses, along with some touching and even taking. Taking would be good. Very good.

She'd felt passion before, but nothing like this. Nothing had ever been so . . . desperate.

Moving as one, they stood, which was better. Now she could wrap her arms around his neck and lean into him. Now he could pull her even closer, then slide his hands up and down her back. She nestled against him, feeling the hard planes of his body against her curves. He wasn't the kind of man who yielded easily. A characteristic she could get used to.

She angled her head so she could deepen the kiss. He moved the opposite way, then stroked her bottom lip with his tongue. She parted for him, hanging on to his shoulders, knowing it was going to be a wild ride.

He didn't disappoint. At the first sweep of his tongue, fire danced through her. Her thighs heated, then went weak. The tingling returned, racing around her body before it settled in her breasts and between her thighs.

He kissed her deeply, teasing her tongue with his. She met him stroke for stroke, becoming more aroused by the second. His large hands settled at her waist. She wanted to pull them higher, to have him touch all of her. Tension made her surge against him, rocking her belly against his erection.

The proof of his need thrilled her. Although she'd managed to avoid being slutty for her entire life, right now the thought of doing it on the desk, right here, in the construction office, seemed feasible. Sensible even.

Shane broke the kiss and took a step back.

They stared at each other, their sharp breaths the only sound in the otherwise quiet room. A small measure of sanity returned, dulling the regret that he'd pulled away. Yes, it would have been amazing. Double yes, she would have had regrets.

But a girl could dream.

She cleared her throat, not completely sure she could speak in a normal voice.

"So, that would be a no on Charlie?" she asked.

"That's a no."

CHAPTER FIVE

"Annabelle! You're not listening."

Annabelle pulled herself out of the delicious daydream that had haunted her pretty much all day. The instant replay of Shane's kiss was nearly as powerful as the actual event had been. She wasn't sure if that spoke to chemistry or the empty tragedy that was her love life. Maybe both.

"Sorry," she said, smiling at the girl in front of her. "What is it, Mandy?"

"Is Shane a real cowboy? When we were at the Fourth of July festival last week, my mom said Shane was a cowboy and a half. I don't know what that means."

Annabelle held a smile, thinking it meant Mandy's mom had an appreciation for a good-looking man. Having a beautiful garden of one's own didn't mean a person couldn't admire someone else's garden.

She frowned, not sure why that metaphor sounded weird, then deciding to go with it.

"Shane is a real cowboy," Annabelle assured her. "Very much so. He has horses and knows how to ride. Oh, he was helping another cowboy with his rodeo skills, so I guess he teaches them, too."

"He's teaching you to ride, isn't he?"

"Uh-huh. For the Máa-zib festival at the end of summer."

"I want to learn to ride."

"Okay." Annabelle wasn't sure what to do with that information.

"My brother says only boys can be cowboys and that I can't learn to ride a horse." Mandy's blue eyes darkened with worry. "Is he right?"

"Of course not. You can ride as well as any boy. There's not much to do. Honestly, the horse does most of the work."

Mandy brushed her blond bangs off her forehead. She was maybe ten or eleven, a good reader who was always up for trying a new author. Even better, from Annabelle's perspective, the other girls listened to Mandy. If she liked a new book, they would try it as well.

"So I could try?"

"Yes. Of course. Riding is fun." Annabelle thought about her experiences on Khatar. "They're kind of big, so it's a little scary when you're first on them, but then it gets fun. You have to hold on with your legs and wow, was I sore afterward. But in a good way."

"Thank you," Mandy said with a grin. "I'm going to tell my brother he's wrong."

"Enjoy yourself."

Charlie put the dandy brush back in the box and grabbed Mason's body brush. His ears flicked in anticipation of what was his favorite part of being groomed. As she started at the top of his neck, prepared to work her way down and back, she was aware of Shane coming out of the barn. His gaze darted toward her, then as quickly shifted away.

Charlie had never studied any kind of criminal investigation but she knew enough about people to guess there was a problem. She and Shane hadn't known each other long, but they'd gotten along well enough. He took care of her horse when she was working and she let him use Mason for the guys who needed to practice their calf roping. Mason had been a rodeo horse before she'd bought him and he enjoyed the practice.

But ever since she'd arrived, earlier that afternoon, Shane had been hovering just out of conversational reach. They hadn't spoken beyond a brief "Hello" which wouldn't have bothered her except for the way he kept looking at her. As if he'd been spooked. She had a feeling she knew exactly what ghost had come calling.

"Shane," she yelled before he could scoot back into the barn. "Get over here."

He stiffened slightly, then seemed to brace himself. No doubt prepared for the inevitable, she thought grimly, continuing to use long stroking motions as she brushed Mason. His coat gleamed in the warm afternoon.

She'd tied him under one of the big trees to give them both shade. As the branches swayed in the gentle breeze, sunlight spilled onto his coat and the back of her hands.

Shane approached slowly but purposefully. If she were a different type of woman, she would torment him first. Just for sport. It was certainly in her nature, but men, at least in a romantic or sexual sense, weren't part of her comfort zone.

She waited until he was standing on the other side of Mason, then rested both her hands on the horse's back and stared at the man.

"Annabelle talked to you about me." She spoke flatly, not asking a question.

He pulled off his hat and ran his fingers

through his hair. After clearing his throat, he managed a strangled, "She might have said something."

Annabelle needed a good killing, Charlie thought, even as she told herself her friend had just been trying to help. Apparently with the subtlety of a bulldozer in a flower garden.

"You're not my type," Charlie told him, figuring bluntness was her strength and this was the time to go for it. "No offense."

He practically sagged with relief. "None taken. Not that you're not appealing," he added weakly.

"Of course. Practically keeping you up at night."

One corner of his mouth twitched. "Just like I do you."

"Right."

She returned her attention back to her horse and continued to brush him. "She's trying to help. Annabelle has a burr up her ass about me dating. God knows who else she's talking to."

"It's not just me?" Shane raised his eyebrows. "I'm devastated."

"I can tell." She glanced over Mason at him again. "Although I would say Annabelle was more to your liking."

Shane had been about to put his hat back

on his head. He paused, almost comically, his arms extended in the air, the hat frozen in time.

"I, ah, I'm not sure what . . ."

"Is that so?" Charlie relaxed, knowing they weren't talking about her anymore. Now she could afford to have a little fun. "Good to know. By the way, Annabelle is well-liked in town. Don't hurt her or you'll be sorry."

He managed to set his hat on his head. "We're not even dating and already you're imagining we've broken up and it's my fault?"

"She's my friend."

"I look after your horse."

"It's not the same." She looked past him to the fenced-in area across the property. Priscilla stood where she always did, watching what was going on, looking as solitary as it was possible for an elephant to look.

"Your girl there needs a friend. Don't elephants like companionship?"

He turned, following her gaze. "From what I've been reading, they do. I've tried the llamas, the donkey and a couple of the goats. She likes Athena, but they didn't really bond."

"What about one of your mares? Maybe the pregnant one. Priscilla might like to be a grandmother."

Shane hadn't been able to get an accurate read on how old the elephant was. Priscilla had come from a small circus that was disbanding. Her caretaker had guessed she was in her late twenties. Although elephants in the wild could live well past fifty, they didn't live as long in captivity.

His research had given him information on the best way to care for Priscilla. In the past month, a pond had been dug for her and he'd brought in trees and plants for her. But he hadn't been able to find her a friend.

"A pregnant mare is a good idea," he told Charlie. "I'm going to try that."

He walked toward Priscilla, wanting to check out the area next to her pen. As he approached, she shook her head and stomped her foot. Almost as if she were threatening him.

Shane paused. He had to admit he didn't have a lot of experience with elephants, but he and Priscilla had always gotten along.

"What's the matter, girl?" he asked, moving toward her more slowly. "You feeling okay?"

She raised her trunk and angled toward him. He stopped again. There was something familiar about what she was doing. A memory tickled in the back of his mind, but he couldn't quite . . .

She was protecting something, he realized, looking around for whatever had gotten into her area. A small dog, maybe? A raccoon?

He eased forward, holding his arms at his sides so she didn't think he was trying to make himself look bigger and more threatening. Not that she wasn't the bigger mammal.

At first he didn't see anything. Then he caught a flicker of movement. He eased forward, then crouched down.

"Damn," he murmured softly. "You're kidding, right?"

There, at the base of a tree, in a hollowed-out area in the trunk, was a cat and four kittens.

The mother was a calico, with tabby markings instead of black. Two of her kittens were tabby, one was a marmalade and the last was all black. They were tiny, maybe a week or so old.

Priscilla walked over to the tree, then bent down. Her trunk lightly stroked the cat. The cat closed her eyes and seemed to go to sleep.

He knew about the cats that came to visit when the goats were milked and this wasn't one of them. She looked more feral than the goats' daily visitors. He was also aware that while Priscilla would provide impressive protection and that there was plenty of water in the pen, the elephant was an herbivore. Whatever the mama cat was eating, she would have to catch it herself.

He stared at the elephant. "Because I needed one more thing?"

Her wise eyes seemed to crinkle with amusement.

He went back to the house, got some chicken out of the refrigerator, cut it up, then added cat food to the shopping list his mother kept. After taking the plate to the edge of the fencing, he slid it as close as he dared. Priscilla watched him warily, still standing guard over her new family.

He shook his head and walked away.

He'd gotten all of twenty feet when two SUVs drove onto the property and parked by the barn. What seemed like twenty, but was probably only five or six, girls spilled out and swarmed all around him.

"Are you really a cowboy?"

"Do horses bite?"

"Can I really learn to ride?"

"Can we braid the horses' tails?"

"Do any of the horses have blue eyes?"

"What's that smell?"

The drivers got out of the cars. They were both women he might or might not have recognized from his visits to town. Nothing about the situation should have been dangerous, but he couldn't help the feeling that his life had just taken a turn for the difficult.

"Ladies," he said, touching the brim of his hat. "How can I help you?"

"We're here for the horseback riding lessons."

Shane was waiting when Annabelle arrived at the ranch. He looked stern and rugged, in a sexy kind of way. Not that she was going to allow his killer smile to distract her. The man obviously needed his priorities set straight.

She got out of her car, but before she could start to complain, he said, "We have to talk."

"Good. I was thinking the same thing. I've been getting calls. Calls from mothers with daughters who are crushed that you won't teach them to ride. What's the big deal? You have horses, a ranch. I know you can do it. I saw you with that rodeo guy. He was learning and you were helping. These women are paying customers and this is your business. Why are you being so difficult?"

Shane pulled off his hat, set it on the roof of her car, then rubbed his face with his hands. "I need a drink."

"It's only three in the afternoon."

"It's been a hell of a day."

He moved closer and put his hands on her shoulders, then turned her so that she could see each of the corrals.

"Those are my horses," he said.

"I know that."

"What is it you think I do?"

She didn't understand the question. "Horse stuff," she said, stating the obvious. "You, um, raise horses and train them. And people. You're building a ranch where I guess you'll have more horses. Oh!" She turned to smile at him. "You have pregnant mares, so you breed horses, too."

"Two drinks," he muttered and released her shoulders.

She wanted to protest. The feel of his hands on her body was nice. Better than nice. His grip was warm, his fingers strong. He was a patient man and wasn't that the best quality in a potential lover?

"I started out in the rodeo. I took off when I was eighteen and got work where I could. Learned as I went. I did okay but I figured out early I would never be a champion. So I turned my attention to the horses. It turns out I have a knack for breeding. Thorough-breds."

She blinked at him.

118

"Horses that race. You know, like the Kentucky Derby."

She looked back at the horses grazing. At their powerful chests and long legs. "Racehorses?" She swallowed. "Aren't they expensive?"

"Yes."

"You've had horses in these races?"

"Came in second at the Belmont Stakes."

Another race she'd heard of.

She was starting to see that Shane wasn't exactly who and what she'd thought. She'd assumed he was a regular kind of guy who worked with horses. A man who kept a few around for, um, for . . . Well, she wasn't sure why people kept horses exactly. Charlie liked to ride Mason, but the world of racing and breeding was different.

Her gaze shifted to Khatar. "He's different from the others."

"Arabian."

She thought back to the conversations they'd had and her stomach lurched. "He was expensive?"

"Depends on your definition. He wasn't seven figures."

Seven? As in a million dollars?

"Well, sure. Why would you pay that much?" Her voice was faint. "But close, right?" Not that she wanted to know.

"Pretty damned close."

She was going to faint. Right there on the ground, she would collapse and possibly hit her head and then have to live with the resulting amnesia. The good news was she might then be able to forget this conversation.

"That's why you had me riding Mason," she said. "Because he's a regular horse and I couldn't hurt him."

"You can't hurt one of the other horses, either. It's that they're not riding stock. Certainly not for a beginner or a bunch of kids." He raised his hands, then let them drop to his side. "I'm not being a jerk about the kids, Annabelle. The truth is I don't have anything for them to ride."

"I see that now. I'll explain to the mothers. There has to be someone else nearby with appropriate horses. Because the girls were very excited by the opportunity. Maybe I could rent a horse for them or something."

He groaned. "Is that in your budget?"

"No. I work at a library. But I could figure something out."

"The walls are closing in," Shane muttered. "Have you talked to my mother about this?"

"No. Why?"

"Do me a favor. Don't. Tell you what. I'll

get some pleasure horses out here. Rent them for the summer or something."

"You don't have to. It's not your responsibility."

"You're right about that, but currently, it's my problem. If I don't rent them and my mother finds out, she'll buy some. Probably old horses. And I'll have to take care of them. This will be easier. I'll offer a few lessons and we'll take it from there."

While she appreciated the gesture, she still felt guilty and a little foolish. How could she have missed the truth about Shane?

Before she could figure out what to say, Khatar came strolling around the barn. She laughed as he headed directly toward her.

Shane turned. "What the hell? How did he get out?"

She reached for the horse as he approached and wrapped her arms around his neck. "Hey, big guy. How are you? Who's a handsome horse? Did you know you're expensive? You need to take care of yourself."

"He's insured," Shane said drily.

She leaned into the horse because it was easier than looking at Shane. "I can still help with your house. If you want me to. You know, to make up for all of this."

She expected him to say no, but he surprised her by agreeing.

"We never did decide on the kitchen," he said. "Maybe we can do that in the next day or so. Jocelyn is on me about wanting to pour the foundation."

"We can do it after our lesson, if you'd like."

"Sure. You have time?"

When it came to him, she was starting to think she had all the time in the world. She liked that even when he'd been annoyed, Shane's anger had been low-key. He'd never once yelled and he didn't say anything disparaging. Lewis, her ex, would have said she was stupid, would have gone on and on, blaming her. He would have done his best to make her feel small.

"I can stay," she told him.

Their gazes locked. She was aware of something hot pulsing between them. Something that would be very, very messy. Maybe he would want to . . .

A flicker of movement caught her attention. She saw one of the mares in the corral next to Priscilla's enclosure.

"Are you trying to see if Priscilla wants to be friends with one of the horses?"

Shane turned and nodded. "I found a cat with Priscilla yesterday. A mother cat with kittens. I went online and read about Asian elephants. The females need a group to belong to. I don't think a cat is going to be enough, so I'm trying the mares, one at a time, until we get a match."

"That's very sweet."

"Priscilla belongs to my mother. However, she has left the care of her menagerie to me, so I'll do what I can."

"Maybe she'll fall in love. Or at least start dating."

Shane swung his attention back to her. "Speaking of dating," he began.

Her heart fluttered. Was he going to ask her out? Did he feel the chemistry between them? Was he thinking that they should at least take their attraction for a test drive?

"I had an interesting talk with Charlie yesterday," he told her.

She winced. "Oh."

He raised his eyebrows. "Oh? That's it?"

"She needs to start seeing someone. I won't go into why, but she has to get back on the horse, so to speak, and you're a horse guy so I thought . . . But then you said you weren't interested and it probably wouldn't work." No way she was going to bring up their kiss. Even if she couldn't stop thinking about it.

"Anyway, that's what happened. You didn't hurt her feelings, did you?"

"Charlie firmly put me in my place. You would be proud."

"That's nice."

"Anyone else you want to set me up with?" he asked.

She shook her head.

"Other groups that will be showing up unannounced?"

"I can't think of any."

"Good. Ready for our lesson?"

She nodded. "Am I riding Khatar?"

Shane shook his head. "It's what you both want. Who am I to stand in the way?"

"But he's so expensive. I don't want to hurt him."

Shane sighed. "You won't."

Khatar stood next to her, his neck over her shoulder, his cheek against hers. "I'll be very careful."

"I'm sure you will."

Shane started toward the barn. She followed, Khatar trailing after her.

"You think I'm a pain in the butt, don't you?" she asked.

He turned. "I know you're not trying to be."

"I'm not. Usually I'm not the least bit difficult."

"Why don't I believe that?"

Before she could come up with a response,

he stepped toward her and grabbed her upper arms. He pressed his mouth against hers in one hard, hot kiss that seared her down to her toes. Before she could reach for him or even kiss him back, he released her.

"Khatar's never had on a Western saddle. You'll have to ride English."

Pleasure and need charged through her in time with her heartbeat. She drew in a shaky breath.

"Whatever you say, Shane."

He grunted. "If only that were true."

CHAPTER SIX

"Rafe and I have decided we'll hold the wedding here," Heidi said as she poured glasses of iced tea in the ranch's dining room. "It's more economical and we can have more people."

Charlie took the offered glass and raised her eyebrows. "Seriously? Rafe's worried about what it's going to cost?"

Heidi laughed. "No, but I've spent my life being frugal. That's not going to change anytime soon."

Annabelle figured her friend was in for a financial adjustment. Heidi and her grandfather had never had an excess of funds. Now Heidi was marrying a very successful businessman with millions to his name. She would bet that Rafe would pay for any kind of wedding Heidi wanted. But she also knew Heidi wouldn't see it that way.

"Besides," Heidi continued, "this is more about the room than the costs. I've made so many friends here in town. I want everyone to come and have a great time."

"More party than reception?" Charlie asked.

"That sounds perfect."

"I agree," Annabelle told her. "The weather will be warm but not hot and people will enjoy the more relaxed venue. You were leaning toward a less formal ceremony anyway."

May, Rafe and Shane's mother, walked into the dining room, several pads of paper tucked under one arm and a fistful of pens in her free hand.

"Am I late? Did you start without me?"

"You're right on time," Heidi assured her future mother-in-law.

"I saw you and Glen pulling into town about three this morning," Charlie told her.

"Our flight landed in San Francisco at midnight," May said, taking a seat at the table and passing out the pads of paper and pens. "We talked about grabbing a room by the airport but decided we would rather be home."

"How was Australia?" Annabelle asked.

"Wonderful. We're going back. The flight is long, but worth it. Do you know it's their winter now? We loved that. And the toilets really do flush the other way."

"As long as you spent your time on the important things," Charlie teased.

May laughed. "We saw the sights. I'll bore everyone with pictures later. But first we have a wedding to plan and I need to be caught up with everything that happened while we were gone."

"Just the usual," Heidi said. "There hasn't been any hot gossip."

May smiled, her dark eyes similar to her sons'. "You're not just saying that to make me feel better?"

Heidi touched her hand. "I promise I'm not."

Theirs was not a traditional household, Annabelle thought, watching the exchange. Most brides-to-be didn't live with future mothers-in-law. But last spring May and Rafe had moved in with Heidi and her grandfather. First Glen and May had fallen in love, then Rafe and Heidi. The older couple were having a small house built at the edge of the property and would be moving out as soon as it was finished.

Now Shane was living in the house, which made for crowded conditions. But Heidi seemed to be thriving with her new family. In truth, Annabelle felt a bit of envy. Her parents had split up when she'd been very young and they'd both made it clear neither of them wanted to be "stuck" with her. She'd been an only child and the house had been lonely. Having a lot of caring people around seemed pretty perfect to her. The sense of community that existed in Fool's Gold had been the main selling point for her.

"I hear Shane is teaching you to ride," May said.

Annabelle nodded. "It's going well."

"On Khatar?"

"He likes me."

"It's more than like," Charlie said with a grin. "She's his one true love. Shane can't figure out how to keep him contained when she's around."

May frowned. "He's a dangerous horse. Be careful."

"I will, but actually he's very sweet. So affectionate."

"It's true," Heidi told May. "You're going to have to trust us on that. Khatar wants to cuddle when he's around Annabelle."

"If you say so." May looked doubtful.

"There's more," Heidi said, her eyes twinkling with amusement. "Little girls have been showing up to learn how to ride. They want Shane to teach them because he's a real cowboy."

Annabelle sighed. "That's my fault. I

didn't realize all his horses were so valuable. I mentioned the lessons to a few of the girls who come to the library and it quickly got out of hand. Shane's being great about it," she added quickly. "He's talking about renting some horses."

"Renting? There's no need for that." May rose. "You girls go on with your planning. I'll be right back."

Heidi watched her go. "Uh-oh. I have a feeling a few more old animals are going to be showing up in the next day or so. Poor Shane. He's being thrown in the deep end of the ocean for sure. Talk about getting involved."

Annabelle winced, realizing that Shane's worry about his mother hadn't been in vain. Not that she was going to be the one to tell him. She reached for her iced tea and was about to take a sip when she realized Charlie was staring at her. "What?"

"Speaking of involvement," her friend said slowly. "Were you trying to set me up with Shane?"

Annabelle shrank back. "No. Yes. Maybe. I'm sorry."

"What did I miss?" Heidi asked. "Something fun?"

"Annabelle thinks I need to get out more," Charlie said, never taking her gaze from

Annabelle. "Start dating."

"Does she . . ." Heidi pressed her lips together.

Charlie finally looked away. "Yes, I told her about my past."

"I thought it would be a good idea to start with someone nice," Annabelle said weakly. "Shane's nice."

"Not my type and way too into you."

She sat up a little straighter. "Really? You think he likes me?"

Heidi looked at Charlie. "Looks like Khatar isn't the only one with a crush."

"I don't have a crush on Shane," Annabelle protested. "I said he was nice. There's a difference."

"Not when you're blushing," Heidi teased.

"You offered me to a guy you're interested in?" Charlie asked, sounding outraged.

Annabelle pressed her lips together. "I wasn't sure and you said you wanted to be fixed."

"Now you're making me sound like a stray dog. Look, I appreciate the effort, but I can handle this myself. I'll figure out a way to get over my mistrust of men or not. I don't need a man to have a family, right?"

"Well, you kind of do," Annabelle said gently.

"She's right." Heidi nodded her head as

she spoke. "But this is all good. You're facing the problem. I'm glad. I'm also a little surprised. I didn't think you liked kids."

"I grumble about them, but I like them okay. I always thought one day . . ." She shrugged. "Who am I kidding?"

"Don't," Annabelle told her. "You can't give up before you even start."

"I know. It's just you're both so normal and I have this horrible mother."

Annabelle knew her parents hadn't exactly been what anyone could call loving, but that wasn't the point. "She's still alive?"

"Last time I checked. She's famous. Or she used to be." She seemed to brace herself. "My mother was a ballet dancer. World-renowned. Dominique Guérin."

Annabelle frowned. "I think I've heard that name. Maybe seen a few of her DVDs. She's beautiful and very talented."

Charlie grunted. "She would be devastated to know your life doesn't revolve around her greatness. And I'm not saying that to be funny."

"Not the type to bake cookies?" Heidi asked.

"She has the maternal instincts of a rock."

Annabelle thought about the petite graceful dancer she'd watched as a kid and compared that image to the woman sitting in front of her. Charlie was tall — maybe five-nine or -ten, with broad shoulders and lots of muscle. She drove an engine for the Fool's Gold fire department, handled training of the volunteer force. She was competent, smart, loyal and a great friend. But she couldn't imagine a woman like Dominique having a daughter like Charlie. And based on the little Charlie had said, theirs hadn't been a loving relationship.

"Because of her, I never thought I should have kids," Charlie admitted. "I was afraid I wouldn't know what to do."

"Is that changing?" Annabelle asked.

"Sort of. Maybe. I don't know. Let's not talk about me anymore."

Heidi leaned toward her. "I was scared of love, too," Heidi said. "Of losing control, of being hurt. I wasn't even sure love was real. But now, with Rafe, I know it's worth it. What we have is so much stronger than the fear. I can give my heart and trust him completely. I never thought I would be able to say that about anyone."

Annabelle ignored the twinge of jealousy. Although she'd been married, she'd never experienced what Heidi described. With Lewis, she'd been flattered and grateful he'd even noticed her. Later, when he'd suggested they get married, she told herself what she felt was love, but she knew now her feelings had been nothing more than a desperate attempt to prove that someone, somewhere could love her. Only she'd been wrong. Lewis had only cared about himself.

She wanted the kind of passion she saw with Heidi and Rafe. Wanted to be with someone who loved her for her and whom she could love with all her heart. She wanted the dream.

Charlie's cell phone rang. She pulled it out of her pocket and glanced at the screen, before answering. "Now?" she asked, then paused to listen. "I'm at the ranch, with Heidi and Annabelle. Uh-huh. Yes, I have my list. I'll make the calls on the way. We'll be right there."

She hung up and looked at them. "Montana is having her baby. It's time to go to the hospital."

"Can you explain this?" Shane asked his brother in a low voice.

"No. One second I was at the ranch, minding my own business and now I'm here."

"Tell me about it. You know, it's gotta be something with the town."

Not anything mystical. Just a force more powerful than either of them were used to.

Nothing else explained why they were in the Fool's Gold hospital maternity waiting room. The most confusing part was neither of them knew the mother-to-be or her husband.

"We should go with it," Rafe said in a low voice. "It'll make Heidi happy."

"Something that matters more to you than me," Shane grumbled.

His brother grinned. "You got that right."

Shane shoved his hands in his jeans pockets and glanced around. The large waiting area was crowded with plenty of people he recognized and a few he didn't. From what he remembered, Montana was an identical triplet. Back when he'd been a kid, he'd known her brothers, but hadn't had much time for the younger Hendrix siblings. He spotted two other women who looked alike and figured they were the sisters.

From where he was standing, he overheard one saying to the other, "Sasha's pilot was picked up for a midseason replacement. It's a police ensemble with him playing the new rookie. He's going to be a national heart-throb about two days after it first airs."

"Finn will be so proud," the sister with short hair said, then laughed.

"Are you Shane?"

He turned and saw a tall brunette with

curly hair standing next to him. She held a child in her arms. A little girl maybe a year old.

"Hi. I'm Pia Moreno. I coordinate the festivals in town and I understand you're helping Annabelle with her horse dance."

"I'm teaching her to ride," he admitted. So far they hadn't gotten to the dancing.

"Good. Now there's a parade route of about a mile. The horse will just be walking for that. The actual performance comes at the end."

He felt that strong need to bang his head against a wall starting up at the base of his neck and spreading. "Parade route?"

"Didn't Annabelle mention that?"

"No, she didn't."

As Khatar had appointed himself Annabelle's love puppy, Shane had figured he might as well use him in the ceremony. But a mile-long parade route meant getting him used to riding around people.

"I'll get you a copy of the route," Pia told him. "It's very straightforward. A couple of streets and you're there. We're going to have a raised platform so everyone can see the sacrifice."

"Sure. You wouldn't want anyone to miss some poor guy getting his heart cut out."

Pia laughed. "It's going to be the highlight

of my day." She fished a business card out of her jeans back pocket and handed it over. "Call me if you have any questions. I'll get you the parade route in the next week or so. Don't worry about permits. We're very parade friendly in this town and we're folding in the ceremony with an existing festival."

"Lucky us," he murmured.

He watched her walk away, then felt his gaze slide just a little to the left. From where he was standing, he had a perfect view of Annabelle. Not that he wanted to watch her. He just couldn't seem to help himself. Like his stallion, he'd found himself in the unfortunate position of desperately wanting the feisty librarian.

He turned away before anyone caught him ogling and nearly ran into an older woman with white hair and a tailored suit. Something about her was familiar. Before he could figure it out, she stopped in front of him and supplied the answer.

"Mayor Marsha Tilson," the woman said. "You're Shane Stryker."

"Yes, ma'am." Had he been wearing a hat, he would have removed it immediately.

"I've been wanting to get over to the ranch to meet you, but town business is especially distracting these days. Please excuse my tardiness, Shane. I hope you're settling into life here in Fool's Gold."

"I am."

"Good. I understand you've closed escrow on the land you bought and will be building a stable and a house. Excellent." She smiled. "The town thanks you for your future tax contributions. And the employment of our local contractors. Jocelyn is one of the best. She's been in the Sacramento area for the past couple of years, working on a large subdivision. Thankfully she's returned home and plans to stay. You'll be pleased with her work."

Shane wasn't sure if the mayor was making conversation or giving him instructions.

The mayor pulled a small piece of paper out of her jacket pocket and handed it to him. "This is the name and number of a friend of mine. Your mother mentioned you were looking for some horses suitable for riding."

Shane didn't even glance at the paper. "I'm not buying any horses right now."

Mayor Marsha's blue gaze remained steady. "I understand you have your breeding program, Shane. These horses are for the children. You're giving riding lessons, aren't you?"

Even though the room was at a comfortable temperature, he felt the first itchy sensation of sweat on the back of his neck.

No. The word was easy enough to say. Riding lessons for kids? He was a busy guy with a small empire he was growing into a medium-size empire. Except he'd already agreed and backing out wasn't an option.

He swallowed.

"The horses come with all the necessary equipment. Saddles, bridles." She smiled. "I'm not familiar with the details." She continued to hold out the paper. "He's expecting your call."

It was as if a force he couldn't see or explain propelled his arm forward. His fingers closed around the paper and drew it back.

"Yes, ma'am."

Her smile widened. "Trust me. This is a good thing."

He was less sure.

"Oh, there's also the matter of Wilbur."

"He's the guy who owns the horses?"

"No. Wilbur is a pig. An unfortunate name, but there we are. Wilbur is available. For Priscilla."

Shane remembered getting a good night's sleep and having a couple of cups of coffee. His brain should be working just fine. But he couldn't seem to make the connections.

"You're offering me a pig?"

"For your elephant. I heard she was lonely. I don't think a cat is going to be enough of a companion. You have a couple of mares who will be part of the herd, but they won't match her intelligence. Pigs are very smart. Or so I've heard. He'll be arriving next week. If it doesn't work out, let me know and I'll have him returned."

She glanced toward the door. "It's nearly time for me to welcome the newest citizen to Fool's Gold."

With that, she turned and left the waiting area.

Shane stood in the center of the room, trying to grasp what had just happened.

"You okay?" Annabelle asked as she came up to him. "You look like . . ." She frowned. "I can't describe it."

"Me, either. Who is she?"

"Mayor Marsha? What's not clear from her title?"

"Is she a witch or something?"

Annabelle laughed. "Don't be silly. She's a lovely woman who has taken care of the town for years."

"No mystical powers?"

"Not that I know of. She's very connected. Everyone tells her everything. It's impossible to keep a secret around her."

"I figured that out for myself." He showed her the paper.

"You're getting horses?" She sounded delighted. "For the riding lessons?"

"Why not?" He hadn't felt he had much of a choice. "And a pig for Priscilla. His name is Wilbur. That seemed to bother the mayor."

"Wilbur? From *Charlotte's Web?* It's a children's book. Charlotte is a spider who . . ." She shook her head. "Never mind. I'll check out a copy for you at the library. Then you'll get the joke."

"It was a joke?" It seemed to him that Mayor Marsha was more like a tornado. She blew into people's lives and rearranged things, then disappeared. All that was left was the fall-out and a dazed sensation.

"I think a pig is a really interesting idea. They're supposed to be really intelligent."

"I'll make sure I leave out the daily crossword for them both."

She leaned against him, the scent of her body drifting to him. "This is what Fool's Gold is like. People care. They get involved. It's nice."

"It's extortion and entrapment."

"You're exaggerating."

"Maybe a little," he admitted, liking the feel of her against him. He dropped his gaze

141

to her mouth and he wondered if there was somewhere more private where he could take advantage of her.

She turned toward the waiting crowd. "Do you know everyone here?"

"Not even close. Rafe and I are trying to figure out what we're doing here, waiting for a woman we don't know to give birth."

"You're being supportive."

"Don't you think she would find that a little strange?"

Annabelle grinned. "You're so picky. Besides, you know her brothers. You have to. Rafe knows Ethan, so you should know Kent or the other one. I can't think of his name."

"Ford," Shane said absently, searching the room again. He spotted Ethan right away, talking to Rafe. Kent was with a boy who was maybe ten or eleven.

Kent looked up and saw him. He raised his eyebrows in surprise and headed over.

"I'd heard you were in town," Kent said, shaking hands with him. "It's good to have you back."

"It's good to be back. Do you know Annabelle Weiss?"

Kent nodded at her. "We've met at the library."

"Your son is an excellent reader," Annabelle said.

"Not in the summer. He's more an out-door kid when it's nice." Kent slapped Shane on the shoulder. "Just like you. I remember when you taught me how to ride a horse." He turned to Annabelle. "Shane here loved the ranch. He never wanted to come play with his friends after school. We had to go to see him. Man, remember when you dared Ford to jump over the fence?"

Shane winced. "I didn't think he would say yes. It was too high. The horse stopped and Ford didn't. He broke his arm. Your mom was so mad."

"Can you blame her?" Annabelle asked. "Typical boys." She looked at Kent. "I don't think I've met Ford. Does he live in town?"

"He's in the military. He hasn't been home in years."

"That must be hard on the family," she said.

"It is. My mom, especially. He sends emails and calls, but we can go months without hearing from him. He's involved in secret, covert missions."

Shane tried to imagine the friend he'd known eighteen years ago as a soldier. "If you talk to him, tell him I send my best."

"I will."

The door to the waiting room opened and

143

a blond-haired woman entered. Shane thought she looked kind of familiar and realized she was Kent and Ford's mother.

The woman smiled with obvious relief and pride. "It's a girl," she said happily. "Skye is six pounds, fourteen ounces and couldn't be more perfect. Montana and Simon are ecstatic and I have another granddaughter."

Annabelle drove onto the Castle Ranch and felt a sense of belonging. Silly, really. She didn't belong here. She was Heidi's friend and Shane's client, but little else. Still, a girl could dream. There was something about the expanse of land, the quiet, the various animals. It wasn't a life she'd ever known, but she sure got the appeal. Plus the ranch was close enough to town that company and a good margarita were only a few minutes away.

She parked and got out. Priscilla stood by the tree, looking fierce and protective. She'd heard about the feline family she'd connected with and hoped it all worked out. There was an obvious size difference — which could get in the way of any meaningful friendship.

Shane had moved two pregnant mares to the fenced area next to the elephant enclosure. Maybe she would bond with them as well and have an even bigger herd. In the past couple of days, she'd done some research on elephants and the females were extremely social. Poor Priscilla had been lonely since her move to the ranch.

She turned toward the barn and saw Shane walking toward her. For a second, she enjoyed the view. A tall, good-looking cowboy in a hat. He was more silhouette than form, the sun behind him. She had to shade her eyes to take in the details, but it was worth it. The man looked good in jeans.

She had a brief thought that he would probably look just as good out of jeans, but decided it was best not to go there. While she'd enjoyed their brief kisses, she wasn't sure how she felt about them. It's not like she and Shane were dating. They were barely friends. As a rule, she didn't get involved physically without some kind of relationship. Still, he could sure get her pulse into an aerobic state without even trying.

"Right on time," Shane said as he approached.

"I'm a big fan of punctual," she told him.

His gaze shifted from her face to something behind her and he groaned. She didn't even turn around. She just waited until she felt the familiar vibration that was Khatar trotting toward her. She held out her arms. He stepped in front of her and she cradled his head.

"Hey, baby. How are you?"

He nickered softly. She scratched behind his ears, causing him to stretch out his neck and roll back his lips.

"You like that, don't you."

Shane shook his head. "I've told him to have a little pride, but he won't listen."

She laughed. "That makes two of you because he thinks you should volunteer to be my sacrifice for the ceremony."

"No, thanks. I've already had one woman cut out my heart."

She suspected he meant the words to be light, but there was something about his tone. She leaned against Khatar.

"That doesn't sound good. Have you heard from your ex lately?"

He took off his hat and slapped it against his thigh. "Nope and I'm good with that. The last thing I need is more drama around here. I have plenty."

"You sure you're not missing her?"

His dark gaze settled on her face. "I took Rachel back too many times already. The first couple of times I told her no, it nearly killed me. Now it's easy. Talking about her reminds me that men do stupid things for a woman."

She wanted to point out that not every woman was wild and unfaithful. She wasn't. She was looking for permanent and meaningful. As long as the man in question was willing to love her with all he had. She was done settling.

"She cheated," he said flatly. "More than once and probably a dozen more times than I know about. When I'd finally had enough and filed for divorce, she begged me to let her come back. I did and she took up with my boss. That was the end for me."

"I'm sorry."

"Me, too. And I'm done talking about it. Want to look at my kitchen plans so I can get a final okay to Jocelyn?"

She smiled. "There you go with the sexy invitations."

He chuckled. The sound was a little forced, but some of the bleakness faded from his eyes.

"I've got the plans in the barn," he said, pointing the way. "So your boyfriend doesn't get his panties in a twist by you going into the house."

She laughed. "But he's so handsome, aren't you, Khatar? And royal. I'm practically dating a prince."

"He'll never drive a fancy car."

"I don't care about that. He's better than a fancy car."

"A woman who knows what she wants. I like that."

For a second he stared at her the way a man stares at a woman he desires. With purpose and invitation. Then it was gone and she was left feeling all tingly on her own.

As she followed him to the barn, she thought about Rachel and how she'd taught Shane not to trust. Which meant he wouldn't like feeling out of control. Not sexually and certainly not emotionally.

She figured he was attracted to her — he wouldn't have kissed her otherwise. But he didn't have any faith. Not in her or himself. He'd learned to be careful. Maybe even to keep his heart out of reach. She wanted messy and he wanted safe.

An intelligent woman would keep things friendly and nothing more. Everyone claimed Khatar was dangerous, but the truth was Shane could do a whole lot more damage. Broken bones would heal. Broken hearts could be scarred forever.

CHAPTER SEVEN

Shane signed the receipt and handed the clipboard back to the delivery guy. As he pocketed the yellow copy he'd kept for himself, he saw Annabelle drive in and park by the barn.

"Have a good one," the delivery guy called.

"You, too."

Shane felt his attention straying to where Annabelle had climbed out of her car. She wasn't due for a lesson anytime soon and, as far as he knew, she usually worked on Tuesday mornings. So what was she doing here?

He walked toward her, skirting around the truck. The driver backed up, turned and left. The now-empty trailer bounced over a bump in the driveway and a few loose pieces of hay drifted to the asphalt.

"Morning," Shane said as he approached.

"You're busy," she said with a sigh. "I

149

should have called."

"Just a hay delivery. It's collected and signed for."

"Hay?"

"Winter's coming."

"It's the middle of summer."

"In six months there'll be snow on the ground. There are a lot of animals to feed. We get a price break if we take the hay as soon as it's baled. That way we're paying the storage costs rather than the company. They like that."

She wore a dress, one of the flirty, fitted ones that hugged curves and promised sin. To someone else, he reminded himself. Because wanting was one thing, but taking was something else. At least, that's what he told himself when he was in control of his hormones.

"I've made a decision," Annabelle told him. Her green eyes glittered with determination.

"I don't like the sound of that."

"You don't know what my decision is."

"That doesn't have any bearing on how I'm going to feel about it."

She grinned. "Ah, a wise man who's spent a fair amount of time around women."

He drew in a breath. "I'm braced. Go for it."

She nodded and stared directly at him. "I've decided we should be friends."

He waited for the second part of her statement, but there didn't seem to be one. "Aren't we friends now?"

"I'd like us to be, but you don't trust me. Because I remind you of Rachel."

He held in a groan. "It's not that simple."

"It should be. I'm not a bad person and I'm nothing like your ex-wife."

"How do you know? You've never met her." He held up both hands. "You know what I mean."

"I know you're a good guy and she let you go. My first husband was a jerk. It took me a while to figure that out. If he'd been a good guy, I'd still be with him."

He didn't like thinking about her married to someone else, so he stopped.

Annabelle shrugged. "We can't really be friends until you trust me and right now you have no reason to. Yes, your horse is in love with me, but I don't think you see him as much of a character reference. So this morning I'm going to show you my world. And I hope that when you see it, you'll understand me a little better, maybe start to trust me and then we can be friends."

She almost made sense, which made him more than a little nervous. What he couldn't tell her was he didn't *want* to like her. Not more than he already did. That not trusting her allowed him to be distant. Okay, he would admit it. Safe. Because Annabelle was trouble and danger and everything bad in one petite, sexy package.

He told himself to say no. That he'd already done enough by agreeing to help her learn to ride. He'd been neighborly, even accommodating. Now he could politely tell her to go away.

"I'm busy," he began.

Her green gaze settled on his face and he could feel her disappointment all the way across the yard. Then her chin came up and she marched determinedly around her car. Once there she held open the passenger door.

"I don't think so."

He knew he could force the issue. Be blunt. But in getting his way, he would have to watch the bright light go out of her eyes. He would see her slim shoulders slump and know he was the cause. Damn it all to hell, he didn't think he could stand that.

Yet another testament to how bad he had it for her. Women, he thought with a sigh. What had God been thinking?

He walked around the rear of her car and slid into the passenger seat. She grinned and closed the door, then got behind the wheel.

"You won't regret this," she promised. "I'm a very safe driver."

It wasn't her driving that had him worried, he thought as she started the engine. It was the proximity. The sweet scent of her surrounded him, teasing and delighting. The car was small, the space confined. He could see too much. The slight dip in the top of her dress when she sat that exposed the swell of her breasts every time she drew in a breath.

Trying to find something safer to focus on, he dropped his gaze only to find the skirt had ridden up some, exposing half her thigh. Not the good half, but still. It was enough to make him wonder if she had the heat cranked on or what.

"Technically I'm not working today," she said as she headed out of the ranch and onto the main road. "Summer hours and all that. So I use the extra time to visit some of our shut-ins. Obviously when we get the bookmobile we'll have regular hours. Right now I call ahead and make sure my visits are convenient."

He rolled down the window, wishing he could stick his head out like a dog. At least that would be a distraction. "What happens in winter?"

"It depends on how bad the snow is and when I can get away. We're open longer hours, but usually someone will cover for me so I can get out to see those who can't come to us."

If he hadn't bought Khatar he could have simply given her the money for her bookmobile and been done with it, he thought grimly. Maybe he could talk to Rafe about borrowing a hundred grand for a few months. Anything to avoid the torture of being trapped in a car with her.

"The first stop is up the mountain. Three brothers bought land together. To be honest, I'm not sure how they've made a living all these years. Someone said they'd sold trees to lumber companies, but that's not something you can do every year. It takes time for new trees to grow. I've heard whispers of a gold mine and someone else said she thinks they're growing pot, but I have my doubts."

She chattered on about the brothers and their connection to the community and how Alfred loved mysteries but Albert was more into books that made him cry. Always a challenge for her. That Alastair had died two years ago and the other two brothers still hadn't gotten over the loss. The wives didn't seem that interested in reading, disappearing into the house when she arrived. She'd tried to make friends, but they were apparently only tight with each other. Like sisters.

"I'm an only child," she said. "When I was growing up, I always wished I had a brother or sister. You're lucky."

"In many ways," he muttered, trying not to look at her bare legs. He sucked in a breath and forced himself to focus on the conversation. At least it would be a distraction.

"My brothers and I have always been close." He thought about Rafe and Clay. "At least I've gotten along with both of them. They've had some trouble."

"Why?"

"Our dad died when we were kids. Rafe's the oldest. Mom depended on him to help her out. Probably more than she should have. He worried, did the brunt of the chores. I remember he was always so serious, so determined."

He glanced out the window. They'd turned off the highway and were now driving up the mountain. Trees crowded the road and shaded them from the bright sun.

"After Dad died, there wasn't much money. Mom worked as a housekeeper for the old bastard who owned the Castle Ranch. He didn't pay her squat, instead promising he would leave her the ranch when he died."

She glanced at him, then turned her attention back to the road. "I thought May and your brother only came here a few months ago."

"They did. After the old guy died, he left the ranch to some relatives back east. We were turned out in a matter of days. Rafe was happy. By then he hated the ranch and couldn't wait to get anywhere that wasn't here. I hated leaving and vowed when I grew up, I'd buy my own place and no one would ever tell me to get out again."

"Which you made happen."

"It took some work, but yes, I have my land."

"And your very fancy horses."

"Very fancy horses."

"What are you going to do with Khatar?"

"Train him, get him well known, then breed him."

"Such a life. Am I getting in the way of the training?"

"No. I'm spending a lot of time getting the new stables ready. I was going to work with him this winter."

She smiled. "He's really not a bad horse.

He's very gentle."

"For you."

"You have to admire his taste."

"I kind of do."

Their eyes met for a second, then she looked away. But not before he saw a flicker of what could only be called interest. Desire hit him square in the gut . . . and lower. He swore under his breath. He reminded himself that the safest thing was to keep his distance. But right then, he couldn't quite see the logic of not having that which he wanted most.

Fortunately, she turned onto a dirt road. Her car rattled and moaned in protest.

"You can see why all-wheel drive would be helpful," she said as she bounced in her seat. "I can't get through to see them in winter. That's a long time to go without a book or a movie."

"Do they get to town?"

"Some."

While he liked country life, he enjoyed being able to get out whenever he wanted. Being cut off for winter wasn't his idea of a good time.

The dirt road narrowed and the trees seemed to move in.

"Did you tell them we were coming?" he asked, picturing a bunch of old guys with rifles and questionable vision.

"Yes. They'll have phone service until the weather gets bad."

The dirt road curved, then widened. As they drove around, the space opened up onto a cleared flat area with three small houses clustered together. The houses were nearly identical, with peaked roofs and plenty of windows. Big porches wrapped around each of them and a pair of rocking chairs sat to the right of the front doors. Five of those chairs were occupied by the oldest people Shane had ever seen.

Two wrinkled little men and three wrinkled little women stared at them. They looked like those apple-head dolls, all brown and bent, with raisin eyes and old-fashioned clothes.

As the car came to a stop, all five of them rose. The women ducked into the house and the men slowly, very, very slowly, stepped off the porches and headed toward them.

"Annabelle!" the wizened little men yelled as one.

She got out and hurried toward them where she was hugged and her cheeks pinched. Shane wasn't sure, but thought maybe the old guy on the left patted her butt.

He was introduced and shook hands. He

was careful not to squeeze too hard.

Albert, or maybe it was Alfred, followed Annabelle to the back of the car, where she had a dozen or so books in a small box.

"So, you're a friend of Annabelle's," Alfred, or maybe Albert, said to Shane. "She's a pretty lady."

"Yes, she is."

Beady dark eyes stared into his. "You best not take advantage of her, boy." Thick, white eyebrows twitched menacingly. "She's special and while my brother and I aren't as young as we used to be, we can still shoot a squirrel a quarter of a mile away. You get my drift?"

Shane nodded, not sure if he should believe the old guy, but not willing to test the theory.

"Unless you intend to marry her," his new friend said with a tooth-gapped guffaw. "Which I'd say makes you a lucky bastard. She's a looker. And has good taste in reading. Don't know if she can cook, though."

Shane held up both hands. "Annabelle and I are friends."

"Bullshit. There's a man and a woman and there's being dead. Not much in between. My Elizabeth and I have been married seventy-two years. You think we save ourselves for Saturday night?"

That clear definition of too much information was accompanied by an elbow nudge and a wink. Shane took a step back, tried to smile and wondered if anyone would notice if he simply turned and jogged down the road, back to town. It was maybe ten or fifteen miles. He should be motivated enough to do that with no problem.

"Albert, come look at what I brought. I found a new author I think you're really going to like."

Twenty minutes later, his stomach protesting the moonshine Alfred had insisted he sample, Shane leaned his head back against the passenger seat of her car and closed his eyes.

"How did you find them in the first place?" he asked.

"They called the library one day last summer and asked if someone could bring them some books. That there was too much traffic in the city for them to feel comfortable driving there."

"Sure. Because Fool's Gold has what? Eight traffic lights?"

She laughed. "It's probably a lot to them. I think the brothers come down the mountain three or four times a year. It's a different world, but they're good people."

Easy for her to say. She hadn't been

160

threatened by a horny man pushing a hundred.

"I don't think I want to meet any of your other library patrons," he told her.

She laughed. "Don't worry. You'll like Ava. She's lovely. A computer programmer who has MS. She gets to the library when she can, but when her MS acts up, it's easier for me to bring books to her."

"A computer programmer who doesn't read ebooks?"

"Some people prefer the feel of paper in their hands. It's a tactile thing."

He could relate to being tactile, but not about a book.

Annabelle held out the small gift bag she'd brought with her. "I know casseroles are traditional, but I'm not the greatest cook so bringing one was risky."

Montana held open the front door to her house and laughed. "If you could see my freezer, you would so not be apologizing for anything that isn't edible. Seriously, we have enough food to last until 2021. I had to send casseroles home with both my sisters and my mom." She hugged Annabelle. "Thanks for coming."

"Thank you for inviting me."

Montana glanced in the bag, then looked

up, her brown eyes bright with excitement. "Really?"

"Her new summer trilogy on audio. I thought you could listen while you did the baby thing."

"You're so thoughtful. Thank you. Please — come in."

Annabelle stepped into the large house. Sunlight poured in front of the second-story window above the double door. Hardwood floors gleamed. The foyer led to a large living room, with a dining room big enough to seat twenty off to the left. Even so, the house had a homey feel. Despite the size of the rooms, Annabelle sensed there was plenty of love to fill every corner.

Montana led her past the formal living room, through a restaurant-size kitchen and into a bright family room. Little Skye lay in a bassinet, her tiny hands waving when she saw her mom.

Annabelle felt her chest tighten a little at the sight of the infant. She didn't consider herself overly maternal, but she'd always thought she would have a family someday. Her divorce had put those dreams on hold. Now she had to figure out a way to resurrect them again.

"How's motherhood?" she asked as Montana got each of them a glass of iced tea.

"Are you sleeping?"

"No, but I'm napping, so that helps."

They walked into the family room and settled on the large sectional. Montana stared at her daughter and smiled.

"The new mother thing is terrifying, but just when I think I can't take it or don't know what to do, someone stops by to visit or calls and gets me through it. Mom is great. She had six, so if anyone knows what she's doing, it's her."

Annabelle nodded, doing her best to only feel happy for Montana and not sad for herself.

She always heard that during a divorce, parents argued about who was allowed to see the children more. In her case, her parents had fought about who got stuck with her. Neither had wanted custody and she had a feeling if there had been a way to return her to sender, they would have done it.

The baby waved her arms again. Montana glanced at Annabelle. "Want to hold her?"

"I'd love to."

Montana carefully picked up her daughter and handed her over. Annabelle took her gently, supporting her head and cradling her body.

Skye was bright-eyed, with a perfect

rosebud mouth and tiny little hands. She was small, barely weighing anything at all. "She's so precious. I would spend my whole day staring at her."

"I do," Montana admitted with a laugh. "I've become one of those annoying women who only wants to talk about her child. To me, she's a miracle. Simon is just as crazy about her. He races home to see her. Cece, our poodle, is totally in love with her, too. Skye gets greeted first when Cece comes in with Simon."

Annabelle knew that Cece was more than a pet. The toy poodle was also a service dog who worked with children receiving medical care at the hospital. Because of her lack of dander and ability to be kept clean, she was allowed in the burn ward, where Dr. Simon Bradley worked his magic.

"You have the perfect family," Annabelle murmured, gently rocking the little girl. Big green eyes stared up at her.

"I do." Montana relaxed back against the sofa. "Simon and I are so lucky. We both want to have more kids, but first we're going to enjoy every second we have with Skye."

Annabelle lightly touched the baby's perfect, tiny hands. "How could you not instantly fall in love with her?"

"Feeling the twinge?" Montana asked. "I've been getting that from a lot of people."

"Some," Annabelle admitted. "I was married before and I figured we'd have kids. When the marriage ended, I was glad we didn't. But now . . ."

"Would it be tacky to ask about Shane? I'm hearing rumors."

Annabelle hoped she didn't blush. "There's nothing much to say. We're friends. He's teaching me to ride for the Máa-zib ceremony fundraiser. The Dance of the Horse."

"He's a good-looking cowboy. That's kind of irresistible."

Annabelle smiled. "Maybe. A little."

He was also an excellent kisser and sometimes, when he looked at her like she was the last woman on earth, her knees went more than a little weak.

"He would be an easy guy to fall for," she admitted.

"Is that bad?" Montana asked.

"I don't know. He has issues, but then, so do I."

"Love is worth the risk."

"So speaks the woman who has it all."

"Trouble in paradise?" Rafe asked.

165

Shane stared at Priscilla. He wasn't much of a pachyderm expert, but if he had to guess, he would say she wasn't happy.

"I don't know," Shane admitted. "She's not interacting with the pregnant mares anymore."

"Maybe it was a fling." Rafe chuckled.

Shane narrowed his gaze. "You want to be responsible for her? Because I'm happy to tell Mom you volunteered."

Rafe raised his arms in a gesture of surrender and took a step back. "No, thanks. You're doing a great job."

"I figured you'd say something like that." He turned back to the trailer, where not one, not two, but four horses were being unloaded, and held in a groan. As promised, Mayor Marsha had come through with animals suitable for riding.

He'd tried to get out of the purchase, but when he'd balked, his mother had simply written a check. Now the horses and gear were being delivered. Horses he didn't want for him to teach little girls he didn't know how to ride.

"You'll be fine," Rafe assured him.

"I don't think so." He squinted as a fifth animal was led down the ramp. "Hold on a damn minute. What the hell is that?"

Rafe glanced toward the trailer and chuckled. "Looks like a pony to me."

"I said no ponies. I hate ponies. Mean-spirited little shits." He stalked toward the guy leading a small brown pony down the ramp. "Stop. There's no pony. I didn't buy a pony."

"I know," the driver said cheerfully. "You're getting him for free."

"I don't want him."

"He's actually a pretty good guy. Name's Reno."

Shane assumed the guy meant the pony rather than himself. "No ponies," he said between gritted teeth.

The driver grunted. "Okay. If you insist."

"I do."

The man tied Reno to the fence and walked toward the other four horses. "Where do you want them?"

"Over here. I'll keep them close to each other while they get settled." He'd prepared four stalls in the barn.

Rafe joined them. It didn't take long for them to get the horses settled. Shane compared the items delivered with the invoice and carefully crossed off the line about Reno being "thrown in for good measure." He and Rafe then waited while the truck driver called his office.

"You got to admit, the pony's funny," Rafe said.

"Not to me."

"Good thing Mom's not here. She would insist he stay."

"Then I'm glad they left for Tahoe this morning." He glared at his brother. "She's not to know about this."

"That you're turning out a poor, old, homeless pony? What's he supposed to do now? Who's going to take care of him?"

"The guy who owned him in the first place."

No way Shane was going to back down on this one. He'd never met a horse he couldn't handle, but ponies were another matter entirely. As far as he was concerned, they were vicious animals who terrorized kids and took great pleasure in their actions. He'd been six when a pony had thrown him, then tried to trample him at a local farm. Rafe had been the one to pull him from beneath the sharp hooves.

Rafe glanced back toward the stable. "You're taking on a lot."

"The riding lessons?" Shane shrugged. "I couldn't figure out how to say no. It's a few lessons. How much time could it take?"

"Not a question you want to ask," Rafe told him. "It's this town. One minute you're minding your own business, the next it's sucking you in. Look at me. I'm moving my whole company here. Dante's not happy."

"He'll get over it. He's a lawyer. He lives to compromise."

Rafe chuckled. "He'd prefer to win, but he's dealing. He's driving over in the next week or so and we're going to find a suitable space. Anything we buy will have to be remodeled which means commuting or renting something temporary."

Shane knew his brother nearly as well as he knew himself. "You'll rent close," he said confidently. "Heidi likes having you around."

Rafe nodded. "I like being around her, too."

Because making his bride-to-be happy was what Rafe lived for. Shane could remember when his brother had lived for the deal. Much like Dante, he wanted to win. But all that had changed when he'd fallen in love.

Shane had acted the same way. Maybe it was part of the Stryker DNA. Their mother had mourned the loss of their father for decades. Until she'd met Glen, over twenty years later. He didn't want to be like that — waiting that long until he was willing to trust again.

The delivery guy ended his call and

walked toward him. "Okay, I've been cleared to take back Reno. Where'd you put him?"

Shane glanced toward the fence line, where the pony had been last. The animal was gone.

"We didn't move him."

The other man shook his head. "I tied him up myself. He couldn't have gotten away."

"Evidence to the contrary," Rafe murmured.

"This is just like a pony," Shane said, looking around. He didn't see him by the barn or the house. Not in the garden or the —

Rafe nudged him. "I think you've got a problem, bro."

Shane turned and saw that Reno had made his way to the elephant enclosure. Priscilla stood right by her fence, her trunk slipping between rails as she rubbed Reno's bony back in a gesture even a human could tell was an invitation to be friends.

Beside him, Rafe started to chuckle.

Mayor Marsha had been right. The cats probably weren't enough companionship for a social animal like Priscilla. The mysterious Wilbur hadn't arrived yet and the mares hadn't bonded with the elephant. Which meant he couldn't turn away the pony, no matter how much he wanted to.

"Well, damn," he said, then turned to the

delivery guy. "Just leave him."

"You sure?"

No. He wasn't sure. This was hell. He'd been happy to be coming back to Fool's Gold, to buy land and start his breeding program. What he'd gotten for his trouble was a bunch of animals he didn't want, a woman he couldn't forget and a sense his life was being managed by forces he couldn't understand or control.

Rafe patted him on the back. "Reno is one of us now, Shane. You'd better get used to it."

CHAPTER EIGHT

Annabelle parked by the house on the ranch and quickly got out. She hurried to the corral where four unfamiliar horses waited. Shane carried saddles out of the barn. As usual, the sight of him doing something tough and manly set her girly hormones humming in appreciation. She ignored the quiver in her tummy and the desire to feel his mouth on hers and focused on the more important question.

"Is it true?" she asked when she saw him. "Did Glen and May really elope?"

He put down the saddles. "They phoned last night to say it was a done deal."

Annabelle had gotten the call that morning. Everyone in town was buzzing about the romantic news. "So the trip to Tahoe wasn't just a getaway."

"I guess not."

She thought it was romantic, that the older couple had found happiness together, but maybe May's children didn't see it the same way.

"Are you doing all right with this?" she asked. "Is it weird to think of your mom as married?"

Shane walked closer. As he approached, he removed his hat and she could see his dark eyes. They glinted with amusement.

"They've been sleeping in the same bed since I got here," he told her. "I've had to deal with their whispers and giggles, not to mention all the stuff they're doing that I don't want to think about. Marriage is pretty tame by comparison."

"Okay, sure. That makes sense. Still, it's pretty romantic. Them running off and not telling anyone." The fact that Glen and May had found each other gave her hope that love could pop up when least expected.

She glanced at the new horses.

"For the lessons?" she asked.

"Yes. Right after you." He didn't look happy as he spoke.

"You should get business cards printed up. You know, for the riding school you're starting."

"Thanks for the support."

Before she could say anything else, Khatar came strolling around the barn. He was already saddled, but judging by the reins hanging to the ground, she would guess he'd been tied up.

"You're so smart," she said, holding open her arms. The horse walked up to her and nuzzled her cheek.

Shane muttered something unintelligible under his breath. "I don't know how he always gets free."

"He's a good boy." She rubbed and scratched behind his ears. "So you've accepted that I'm going to ride him in the ceremony."

"I know when it's time to stop betting against the house."

She turned toward the saddle and noticed the pony in with Priscilla.

"Oh, look. She has a new friend."

"I don't want to talk about it."

"What do you mean? She's adorable. So tiny."

"He. His name is Reno."

"Look at those little hooves. What a cutie."

Shane was muttering again. The few words she could make out didn't sound polite.

"Don't you like Reno?"

He laced his fingers together for her to use as a step. "No."

She put her boot into his hands and grabbed the saddle. Khatar obligingly went perfectly still.

"But he's just a pony."

Shane lifted her into the air. She swung her leg over the saddle and settled easily into place. After gathering the reins, she leaned over and stroked Khatar.

"I hate ponies," Shane said darkly. "I never wanted Reno in the first place. The guy who owned the riding horses sent him along as a bonus. Before I could send him back, Priscilla had decided she liked him."

Which meant Reno got to stay. Annabelle did her best to hide her smile. Shane might have his flaws, but at heart, he was one of the good guys. Between the pony and the little girls who wanted to learn to ride, not to mention caring for his mother's menagerie and Khatar's insistence that he was Annabelle's one true love, Shane didn't have much say in his life anymore. But instead of trying to get his way, he did what was best for everyone else.

He handed her the reins. She took them and urged Khatar forward. He went easily, walking directly through the gate, into the corral where Shane led them through walking, then trotting.

"Let's go through the first part of the dance," he said, motioning to the center of the corral.

She'd given him a few books that described Máa-zib rituals, specifically the Dance of the Horse, and had offered her suggestions for what she and Khatar could do. It was all simple stuff, with a few crossover steps and a couple of turns. Just enough to intrigue the crowd until the final moment when she pretended to cut out the male sacrifice's heart. She figured that was enough for a big finish.

About an hour later, they were done. Khatar had quickly learned the next steps in his dance. Annabelle realized her main job was to sit on the big guy's back and let him do his thing.

"I think he might be smarter than me," she admitted, swinging her leg over the saddle and sliding to the ground.

Shane stepped up close behind her. He put his hands on her waist and guided her down. When she turned, he was standing very close. Close enough that she had to rest her fingertips on his shoulders to steady herself and tilt her head back to gaze into his eyes.

They were almost touching. Almost but not quite and she found herself wanting to move that last inch or two toward him. She wanted body against body, his arms around her, drawing her nearer still until they had no choice but to kiss.

Her gaze dropped to his mouth and she would swear she felt her own lips tingle in anticipation.

Shane sure knew how to kiss. She had a feeling he knew other things, too, and imagined his work-roughened hands against her bare skin. The visual was clear and powerful. Her breasts started to ache and she felt both restless and unable to move.

Bad idea, she told herself firmly, looking back into his dark eyes where sexual fire tempted. Bad, bad idea. While she liked Shane and respected him, he had relationship issues. He wanted tidy and sensible, she wanted messy. He'd been burned and she'd yet to feel what she would consider fire. Sleeping with him would be dangerous because she didn't think she could give her body without at least a little of her heart tagging along. And then what? A night of great sex wasn't worth the pain. Even a night of spectacular sex wasn't enough, although it and he were a temptation.

A car pulled up next to the stable. At the sound of the engine, Shane drew back and she turned to Khatar. Seconds later doors opened and four young girls came racing toward them.

"We're here! We're here!"

177

"Is that one of the horses we're going to ride? She's so pretty."

"Will I fall?"

"Can we go really fast today?"

The questions came on top of each other as the girls came to a halt in a circle around Shane. He looked harried and trapped, which made Annabelle smile.

"You girls look very ready," she said, taking in their shiny new cowboy boots and worn jeans. They were adorable. All excited about a new adventure.

"We are," Mandy told her, the girl's hair fastened into a braid. "Oh, I brought you this." She dug into her front pocket and pulled out three worn dollar bills. "I helped my dad clean out the garage over the weekend. I was thinking I would save the money for a new computer game, but then I started thinking about all the kids who want to read and can't get books. So I'm giving it to you for the bookmobile, instead."

Annabelle smiled at her. "You're very generous." She didn't really want to take the girl's money, but knew that learning to give to others was an important lesson. "I'll use this to buy a book," she promised. "I have bookplates that say who donated the book. Would you like to come in and sign the bookplate, so everyone who reads the

178

book knows it came from you?"

Mandy nodded vigorously. "That would be fun. Thank you."

Mandy's mom walked up. "Hi. I'm Darlene. You must be Shane."

They shook hands. Darlene turned to Annabelle. "Thanks for organizing this. The girls are really excited about the chance to learn to ride." She glanced back at Shane. "At the risk of being one of 'those' mothers, it's safe, right?"

He nodded. "The horses we'll be using are gentle and well trained. I rode them all personally to make sure they're suitable."

Mandy gazed up at Khatar. "Is he one of them?"

"No. In fact I'll be putting him away now."

"But he's so pretty."

"I like how he's almost shiny in the sun."

The little girls swarmed around Khatar. Shane lunged for the reins, but the girls were quicker. Not that it mattered. Khatar stood quietly, accepting all the attention. He lowered his head so the little hands could stroke and pat him.

"That's a horse who loves the ladies," Annabelle said.

Shane stared. "It's the dam — um, darnedest thing I've ever seen."

"It looks like you have everything under

control," Darlene said. "I'll wait in my car. I have a new book and this is a perfect excuse for a little reading time."

Shane rounded up the girls and herded them toward the waiting horses. "We're going to start with a few rules on safety," he said.

Annabelle touched his arm. "I'll take care of Khatar."

"Why? I'm sure he'll take off his own saddle and brush himself, if you ask."

She laughed. "Bitter because he loves me more?"

"No, but he really is a dangerous horse."

"I can see that." She found herself caught up in his dark gaze. "I know you didn't ask for all this." She lowered her voice. "The riding lessons and the pony and everything. But thank you for helping the girls."

He shifted uncomfortably. "Yeah, well, it's fine. If I can teach a bunch of teenage boys how to rope a calf, I can teach ten-year-old girls how to ride a horse."

She wanted to point out she wasn't admiring his skill set so much as his character, but decided not to go there. Where Shane was concerned, she was already in a weakened state. Better that he not know the power he had over her.

■ ■ ■ ■

Late Friday afternoon Shane found himself in town. He'd finished his chores for the day and had driven into Fool's Gold without a particular destination in mind. He parked and got out, then stopped on the sidewalk, not sure where to go. Jo's Bar was off limits. Too many women and not enough sports. Rafe was with Heidi, so he couldn't hang with his brother.

He wandered through the main part of town, stepping around tourists going in and out of the stores. Morgan's Books had a big crowd for a signing for Liz Sutton's latest mystery. He thought about buying a copy for his mom, but didn't want to wait in the line.

He couldn't figure out what was wrong. He *should* find a quiet bar, get a beer and watch a game, then call it a night. Instead, he checked his phone for messages — there weren't any — then kept walking.

About a mile later, he stopped in front of an unfamiliar house. It was small, with a nice yard and well-tended flowers. He hadn't been there before, but somewhere he'd picked up the address. He knew who lived there and he was clear on what would happen if he knocked.

He wasn't indecisive. He knew exactly what he wanted. What kept him from acting was the consequences. Because sex complicated everything. The better the sex, the bigger the complications. Because wanting Annabelle was driving him crazy but having her might be another level of hell.

Still not sure what he was going to do, he stood on the sidewalk and stared. After a couple of minutes her front door opened and Annabelle stepped out onto the porch.

It was light enough for him to see the details. She wore white shorts and a green T-shirt. Her feet were bare, her long red, wavy hair was loose. She looked young and pretty and sexy and he knew then he had to have her. There was no longer a choice.

"One of my neighbors phoned. She said there was a strange man staring at my house and asked if I needed her to call the police."

He glanced around and saw an old lady peering at him from behind a half-drawn curtain. He waved and she drew back into her house.

"Didn't mean to frighten you," he said.

"What did you mean to do?"

"I haven't figured that out yet."

Annabelle watched Shane watching her. He

looked good, standing there. Tall and male, his hair still damp from a recent shower. She read the intent in his eyes and knew why he'd come by.

It would be so easy to tell him no. To simply say she was busy and go back inside. He was the kind of man who would accept her polite no. If that was what she wanted.

There were a hundred reasons not to give in. At least a dozen scenarios that would result in having her heart broken, her life disrupted and her living with regret for a long time to come. But she also knew that Shane had a good heart. And if she never took a chance with another guy, especially one who made her knees weak from his kindness *and* from raw desire, where would she be? Stuck in the same rut.

The man was her personal fantasy. Was one night really so bad? So dangerous? Surely she was strong enough to understand what was happening and deal with the consequences.

She turned and walked back into the house, leaving the door open behind her. Once she'd crossed the threshold, she had a quick decision to make. She doubted there would be much idle chit-chat once he followed.

She paused in her living room, then

decided there was no reason to be subtle.

She walked down the short hallway to her bedroom. It was still light out and the afternoon was warm. She pulled the shades closed, flipped on the air conditioner, then turned to pull down the covers on her bed. Only she never got that far.

Shane stood behind her. He put his hands on her shoulders, then turned her toward him. She went easily, willingly. Their gazes locked for a single heartbeat, then he was pulling her close or she was surging forward. She wasn't sure which and it really didn't matter. Not when he kissed her.

His lips were firm yet gentle, taking and offering equally. Anticipation sweetened the moment as she kissed him back, moving her mouth against his. His arms came around her, holding her tight. Safe.

She rose on tiptoe, wanting to press herself against him. He was all hard muscles and warm body.

He kept the kiss chaste, then drifted to her cheek, then her jaw. He nibbled his way down her neck, exciting her with each contact of lips and teeth. Goose bumps broke out on her skin as heat began to pour through her.

He reached her collarbone, then retraced his steps, finding the sensitive skin behind her ear. He nipped the lobe and then licked that spot, before returning his attention to her mouth.

She parted the second she felt him kiss her again. He swept his tongue inside, circling, tracing, teasing. She met him stroke for stroke, feeling her stomach clench and wanting so much more than just a kiss.

As if he'd read her mind, he began to move his hands up and down her back. They slipped under her T-shirt and she felt strong fingers against her spine. He paused at the curve of her hips, then slid down until he cupped her butt.

Both hands squeezed gently. She sank into him, letting her breasts nestle against his chest, her tummy pressed against his erection.

She pressed her fingers into his shoulders, hanging on as her legs trembled slightly. Wanting made her insides melt and swell. She knew that whatever happened later, there was no way she could have resisted Shane. Not after that first kiss. That first touch. She was practically quivering with need and he'd barely gotten to first base.

He drew back from their kiss and stared into her eyes.

"You're so beautiful," he murmured.

Sex talk, she thought. Not that it wasn't

nice. "I have freckles."

His mouth turned up in a slow smile. "I look forward to discovering them. One by one."

She shivered. "Me, too."

He wrapped both arms around her waist and lifted. She shrieked as her feet came off the ground, then hung on tightly to his neck.

He held her securely, still smiling that sexy smile. Instinctively, she wrapped her legs around his waist, bringing her center in direct contact with his arousal. Hard to soft. Aggressive to yielding. He shifted his hands to her butt, holding her in place. Their eyes locked, she rocked against him.

Her breath caught. His escaped with a hiss. Heat flared in his eyes. She rocked again, pushing harder, wishing there weren't the layers of clothes. Wanting to be naked with him touching her everywhere. Wanting him inside of her, riding her harder, faster, until she had no choice but to surrender and be taken.

"Shane," she breathed.

He was already on the move.

Still holding her, he crossed the distance to the bed in two easy steps. He lowered her to the mattress. The second she was sitting, he released her and jerked up her T-shirt. She raised her arms, wanting to help him undress her. The shirt went flying.

Her bra followed, then he was easing her onto her back. His mouth found hers in a deep kiss even as his hands settled on her curves.

He rubbed every inch of her breasts before taking her tight nipples between his fingers. The tandem ministrations made it difficult to concentrate on anything but how good he made her feel. He kissed her over and over before breaking away and bending down to take her left nipple in his mouth.

The hot, wet kiss left her breathless. She gasped as he sucked in her sensitive flesh and caressed her with his tongue. She ran her hands up and down his back, then tugged on his T-shirt so she could feel skin rather than fabric.

He straightened enough to pull off the T-shirt, then kicked off his boots and pulled off socks. Her shorts and bikini panties followed in one quick tug, leaving her bare. Before she could blink, he was on his knees, his hands parting her thighs and his mouth against her in an unexpected but intimate kiss.

She gasped as he found her swollen center on the first try and flicked it with his tongue. She went from hungry to desperate in the space of a second and was ready to beg for more. He circled her, then brushed her with his tongue again, causing her to pull her legs back and open, resting her heels on the edge of the bed.

He settled into a rhythmic cadence, circling, brushing, licking, each movement arousing her more than the one before. He stretched up his long arms and settled his hands on her breasts. She lay there, open, vulnerable, caught in his sexual web and happy to stay forever.

His mouth continued to move against her and she pulsed her hips slightly, urging him on, feeling herself surging toward her release. Heat filled her. Every inch of her skin was sensitive, nerves crying out for his touch. And then there was his tongue. Back and forth, pushing her higher, taking her beyond control until she had no choice but to give in.

She felt the tension building and sucked in air. Release hovered for a second before racing through her. Her muscles contracted over and over, spasming as she groaned softly, losing herself in the pleasure.

He continued to touch her, carrying her through her orgasm. When she was finally done, he stood, pulled a couple of condoms out of his pocket and shoved his jeans and briefs to the floor.

His erection was as large as the rest of him. She stared at him, imagined him inside of her and knew she was in for the ride of her life. Then she shifted back on the bed, so he could slide in next to her.

He joined her and drew her close. She pushed him onto his back and grinned. "I've got this one."

One eyebrow raised. "You sure?"

"Oh, yeah. I've been taking lessons."

The second eyebrow joined the first.

She smiled. "First you prepare your mount."

"Annabelle," he began, but she ignored him.

She shifted to her knees, then bent down to press her mouth to the middle of his chest. His skin was hot and smooth, every muscle defined. She traced a line to his right nipple, then his left. After licking both, she moved down his chest, toward his belly. Her long hair tickled his body as she moved. He grabbed her wrist before she could reach the promised land.

"You don't want to do that," he said, his voice low and thick with tension.

She raised her head. "Why not?"

"Let's just say my control is a little more shaky tonight than usual. I can't promise I'll last through to the main event."

She eyed his arousal then sighed. "All right. But next time I'll be in charge."

"Whatever you say."

She tilted her head, still watching his face. "Let's see. What happens next? Oh, right. Equipment." She leaned over him to grab one of the condoms.

As she did, he reached up and briefly cupped her breasts. "Did I mention the beautiful part?"

"Yes, but that's the sex talking."

"No, it's not."

She ripped open the condom wrapper, then shifted back so she could slip it on him. The thin layer had to stretch a bit to fit him and she was careful to roll it down to the base of his penis.

"I need to make sure there aren't any creases or loose straps," she said, running her hand up and down the length of him.

He closed his eyes and groaned. "Of course you do."

"Then I climb on from the left."

She lifted one leg across so she could straddle him, then reached between them to guide him inside.

"Then I settle into a comfortable position."

His eyes opened as she eased down, taking him into her.

He was bigger than she'd imagined, filling her, stretching her. She consciously relaxed as her body surrounded him. When he was all the way in, she leaned forward and braced herself on the bed.

Her hair tumbled around her face and brushed against his chest. Shane reached for her hips and shifted her slightly. Instantly she felt an answering quiver deep inside as he rubbed some aroused part of her.

"Like that?" he asked, surging up a little more.

She gasped. "Exactly like that."

The slow, sexy smile returned. "Good to know."

She began to move, up and down, his hands guiding her. She had planned this part of the evening to be about him, but found herself caught up in what she was feeling. Every stroke pushed against erotic nerves and left her breathless. He went deeper and she found herself moving faster. In a matter of seconds, she was unable to think about anything but the tension building inside of her, of the need and the release that would sweep through her.

More, she thought, moving up and down, her eyes sinking closed. There had to be more. His steady hands helped her find the best pace, to reach for that one spot, to ride him until she was closer and closer and . . .

Her orgasm exploded deep inside, making her cry out. She couldn't stop, couldn't breathe, could only feel the exquisite thunder that vibrated through her. She was vaguely aware of him pulsing within her, of his moan and his hands holding on tighter. They strained toward each other. On and on until there was nothing left, until she was boneless and weak and shattered by what her body had done.

She collapsed on him. He caught her gently and guided her until she was on her side, facing him. He got up and disappeared into her bathroom, then returned, got back in bed and pulled her close.

Sanity returned and with it a sense of "Oh, crap, what did I just do?" She'd suspected sex with Shane would be good, but she hadn't thought it would take her to a new section of the universe. What exactly was she supposed to say now?

He kissed the top of her head. "You're a surprise."

"Mmm" was the only response she could think of. At the same time, she was hoping he couldn't feel her blushing.

"I'm trying to think of the right word," he told her. "*Amazing* doesn't cut it. *Spectacular.* I think that works."

She risked glancing up at him and saw the contented expression of a very satisfied man.

"Don't get a big head about this," she told him.

He winked. "It wasn't my head you liked."

She groaned. "If I had the strength, I would so punch you."

"I'd let you and even pretend it hurt."

"Quite the gentleman."

He smiled at her then and she felt everything shift back to where it was supposed to be. This was Shane, she reminded herself. One of the good guys. He wasn't Lewis. He wasn't interested in making her feel small or broken. He didn't use sex as an emotional tool to hurt. He didn't play games. He mostly said what he was thinking.

"Spectacular, huh?" she asked.

"More than. I'll come up with a better word."

Happiness bubbled inside of her. She got out of bed and dashed to her closet to pull on her robe. There was wine in the refrigerator and she could dig up a few snacks. They would get their strength back and then try it all again. And to think she'd planned an evening of catching up on her favorite cooking show. Those who could did, those who couldn't watched it on TV.

"Be right back," she said and headed for

the kitchen.

She got the white wine out of the refrigerator and found some cookies that only needed to bake for twelve minutes. After turning on the oven, she got out cheese and crackers, and debated slicing up a peach. She'd just finished washing the fruit when Shane came out of the bedroom.

Dressed.

"You're leaving?" she asked, standing there holding a dripping peach.

"I'm going to let you get on with your evening." He leaned in and kissed her.

"I don't understand."

He drew his eyebrows together as he glanced at the food she'd put on the counter. "Were you thinking I would stay?"

She dropped the peach into the sink and wiped her hands on her robe. "No. Of course not."

Wariness invaded his expression. "Annabelle, this was just sex, right? Getting it out of our system?"

She supposed the mature response was either to agree or calmly point out that no, she hadn't realized she was a booty call. What she said instead was, "Oh, really? So now that you've had me, you're free to get on with your life?"

He took a step back. "I wouldn't put it

like that," he said cautiously.

"Sure you would." She grabbed the peach and flung it at him.

He stepped to the side and it went flying past him to land with a thunk on the carpet in the living room. She reached for the plastic-wrapped cheese.

"You had an itch," she said, her voice rising, "so you came here to get it scratched."

"It wasn't like that."

She threw the cheese as hard as she could and then followed with a box of crackers. He ducked both.

"You're upset."

"Me? Why would you think that? You show up, have sex with me, then run as fast as you can. Because hey, it's out of your system now, right? What's not to like? Make sure the door doesn't hit you in the ass on your way out."

She glanced around for something else to throw and saw a heavy frying pan on her stove.

"Annabelle, don't," he began.

She reached for the pan. "If I were you, I'd be running right about now."

"We can talk about this. Be rational."

She had to use both hands to lift the pan. "Do I look rational to you?"

"Annabelle," he said, backing up as he spoke.

"Get out, Shane," she yelled. "Get out now."

He turned and left.

She waited until he was gone to drop the pan back on the stove, then sucked in a breath and told herself she wouldn't cry. No matter what, he wasn't worth it. No guy was. Not ever.

CHAPTER NINE

Shane woke up early. Not much of a stretch, considering he hadn't slept well the night before. He'd kept thinking about his evening with Annabelle, trying to figure out where it had all gone wrong.

Going over there was a start, he thought as he dressed and headed down to the kitchen. She was a temptation and he'd given in. That didn't come without a price. And maybe he should have explained things more thoroughly before they got started.

He reached the kitchen. Heidi was already up. She milked her goats early and was usually the first one to make coffee.

"Morning," he said as he walked into the room and headed for the pot.

She regarded him steadily.

He reached for the handle, but she stepped in front of him.

"I don't think so."

He stared at her. "Excuse me?"

197

"I don't think so," she repeated. "If you want coffee, or anything to eat, you'll have to go to town."

"Why?"

"Because you're a jerk and I don't make coffee for jerks."

His sleep-deprived brain slowly clicked into place. Right. Heidi and Annabelle were friends. Annabelle had been upset. She'd probably called her friend to talk, because that's what women did.

He took in Heidi's angry glare, the determination in her stance and nodded. "I'll go into town."

"You do that."

Thirty minutes later, he felt as if he'd slipped into an alternative universe. He'd managed to get coffee at the Starbucks, but when he'd gone by the feed store to place an order, the manager had told him he would have to go elsewhere.

"My wife knows Annabelle," the man had told him. "Darlene volunteers at the library. She said you weren't welcome here anymore."

Shane gaped at him. "This is your business, isn't it?"

The man gave him a pitying look. "Dude, have you ever been married?"

"Yes."

"Then you should know better."

Shane wasn't sure if he meant for asking the question or messing with Annabelle in the first place.

"It wasn't what they're saying," Shane protested.

"You didn't tell her you'd slept with her to get her out of your system?"

Shane swallowed. "I might have said something like that, but . . ."

The other man waited.

Shane drew in a breath. "Right. I'll leave."

"You're going to have trouble all over town," the man called after him. "This is Fool's Gold. You can't mess with one of the women and then act as if it didn't happen."

"I'm starting to see that."

Shane stepped out into the still cool morning and looked around. There weren't a lot of people on the street but those who were fell into two camps. The men ignored him and the women gave him the evil eye.

Still holding on to his coffee, grateful the Starbucks was part of a national chain and not a local place or he wouldn't have been served coffee at all, he walked toward his truck.

He wanted to stop and tell everyone he wasn't the bad guy. That he and Annabelle had jointly agreed to have sex and the fact that he didn't want to marry her when it was over didn't make him a jerk. All he'd done was . . . was . . .

He stopped in the middle of the sidewalk and swore. He'd told her he'd used the experience to get her out of his system. As if she were some kind of virus he had to get over. They'd had amazing sex and then he'd walked out. With her throwing things at his head.

He hadn't meant it the way it had come out, but he didn't get points for being stupid, either. He looked back at the feed store, then shook his head and walked to his truck. He'd stepped in it big-time. The question was, what was it going to take to fix things?

Annabelle checked the invoice against what had been ordered. Adding new books to the library's inventory usually made her happy. Today it was less about the thrill and more about whether or not she could concentrate. The fact that she could focus on work would be enough of a win, she told herself. Happiness would follow with time.

The good news was Shane might have been a jerk, but he hadn't broken her heart. They hadn't been together long enough for that to happen. So while she had a bruised ego, she wouldn't have scars. She felt a little foolish for having misjudged him, but everyone got to make a mistake now and then. It was what she did about the mistake that would speak to her character.

She turned away from her computer and stared out the window. What bothered her the most was that she'd been so wrong about him. She'd been going around all happy that Shane was one of the good guys — nothing like her ex. But in the end, he'd been a lot more like Lewis than she wanted to admit. He'd used her for his own purposes, not once thinking about her feelings.

Someone knocked on her office door. She glanced up and said, "Come in," at the same time, only to realize Shane was standing in the doorway.

Immediately her heart began to pound and very specific parts of her body cheered in anticipation. Her stomach clenched, her thighs felt a little quivery and the sense memory of how he'd felt inside of her made it difficult to think about anything else.

All right. Maybe she wasn't as over him as she should be.

"Do you have a second?" he asked.

He looked good, she thought bitterly. All tanned and strong, wearing those worn jeans, the ones that were faded and soft looking. Why couldn't he have grown a hump in the past two days? Or a second, small but unattractive head?

She motioned to the chair across from her desk and laced her fingers together on her lap.

"Is this a library issue or something else?" she asked.

"Something else."

She waited. Whatever he had to say, she would listen, then answer and send him on his way. She was calm. She was controlled. She would gather her strength from the spiritual remnants of the powerful Máa-zib women who had first come to this part of the country. And if that didn't work, she would go crying to Charlie. Because she was pretty sure Charlie could beat up Shane. Or at least give it a good try.

"I'm sorry," he said. "I behaved badly."

She stared at him. "Really? In what way?"

He drew in a breath. "Come on, Annabelle. You know what I'm talking about. After we had sex I said I was leaving because I'd gotten you out of my system."

The words were just as harsh the second time around, but she told herself not to react.

"I didn't mean it like that," he said. "Not exactly."

She continued to wait. If he wanted to find his way out of this mess, he was going to have to do it alone.

He ran his hand through his hair then looked at her. "I've been obsessed with you from the first second I saw you dancing on that damn bar."

Her chin came up. "You saw that?"

"Oh, yeah. I walked into Jo's Bar one of my first nights back and saw you dancing. It was like taking a bolt of lightning to the gut. I couldn't stop thinking about you. It was all I could do not to pull you over my shoulder and carry you off somewhere." He gave her a sheepish smile. "They arrest guys for doing stuff like that."

"So I've heard."

"I got out of there as fast as I could, but you were in my head. So I asked my mom to find me a nice girl. Someone . . . boring and not very exciting."

His reaction to seeing her dance on the bar had gone a long way to making her feel better. But now all those good feelings fizzled. "You mean someone like a librarian?"

He nodded sheepishly. "She mentioned you and you seemed safe, but then you showed up and I was lost." He leaned forward. "I've told you about Rachel and that you remind me a little of her. But it isn't you, it's me. That feeling that I have to have you. It was bad with her, but it's worse with you. Hell, even my horse has a crush on you."

He sounded desperate, but she wasn't going to trust him again easily.

"I've wanted you from the first second I saw you," he told her. "Night before last, when I came over, and you let me come in, I needed you more than I needed air. Afterward I thought I would be free of you. That's what I meant. That we could go back to being friends."

"Oh, sure. Because I want to be friends with someone who assumes sleeping with me once is a lifetime cure."

He fell back in the chair. "I'm saying this all wrong again, aren't I?"

"Pretty much." But she was beginning to understand his twisted male logic. Unfortunately it confirmed everything she'd been afraid of. She wanted love with all its complications and Shane wanted safe. Not a good combination.

"You assumed that being with me couldn't possibly be as good as it was in your mind," she continued. "Because you're fantasizing about something that doesn't exist. Like being with a movie star."

He nodded slowly. "Maybe," he admitted, sounding both cautious and wary.

"So when we were done, you felt you'd lived the fantasy and now you could return to your regular life."

"Something like that."

"So walking out right after had nothing to do with me at all."

He shifted in his chair.

She smiled. "I mean you weren't thinking about me. It wasn't personal. You weren't leaving me, you were dashing toward potential freedom."

"Yes. I thought I was over you."

"But you're not?"

The question popped out without her considering what she'd just put on the table. And once out, the words hung there in the small room.

Shane straightened. "I'm not. I want to be, Annabelle. I won't lie. But maybe I should simply accept reality. You're someone who will always have the ability to get my attention when you walk in a room. That doesn't excuse what I said or how I acted and I'm sorry."

For the first time in a long time, a man had left her speechless and not in a bad way. He was admitting that there was chemistry and he couldn't control the fact that he wanted her. It was kind of a nice thing to hear. On the downside, it put her firmly back in the category of his ex-wife. She would forever be the kind of woman he wouldn't or couldn't trust.

Obviously an intelligent woman would choose this moment to end things.

"I accept your apology," she said.

"Thanks."

"I'm sorry you're so obsessed with me."

He grinned. "No, you're not. But I'll deal with it. I like your idea of being friends. Can we go back to that or is there too much damage?"

She would rather stay lovers. Being with him had been amazing. Two days later, she was still enjoying aftershocks. But they wanted different things. Different endings after an amazing night together. Friends might not be sexy, but it prevented her from once again wasting herself on someone who didn't understand who she really was or want what she did.

"We can be friends," she told him. "Did you mean what you said before? About looking for someone quiet?"

"Sure. Boring sounds good. I don't like the drama, but I seem stuck with it."

"I'm not dramatic."

"You were dancing on a bar."

"I wasn't drunk," she said primly. "I was demonstrating the dance of the happy virgin."

"Uh-huh. Sure you were. Face it, Annabelle. You're one of those women destined to drive men wild. Accept your destiny."

His words made her feel like some kind of sexual goddess, which was impressive considering she'd grown up believing no one would ever care about her. Not that sex was caring, but at least it was sort of in the same family. Or it could be.

Lewis had used sex to make her feel small. He complained if she didn't want to make love and when she did, he told her she wasn't a lady. Most of the time he hadn't cared about her pleasure, and every once in a while he "allowed" her to have an orgasm.

Until him, she'd enjoyed the few lovers she'd had, even if the guys had been lousy at relationships. But Lewis had been the first man to claim he loved her. So she took the good with the bad and hoped the relationship would improve. Over the years, she'd realized that she wanted, no, needed more than someone who made her feel smaller than she was. So she'd walked away from him. He'd vowed she wouldn't see a penny from him and she'd been fine with that. She'd taken her clothes and whatever personal belongings could fit in her car. That had been plenty.

She looked at Shane. She wanted to tell him that she wasn't anyone's idea of a goddess, except maybe his. It was nice to know she could move him in that way. In bed, he'd been a caring, giving lover, healing several of the wounds her ex-husband had left behind. They might never be romantically involved, but she appreciated what had happened between them.

"I'd like to be friends again," she told him.

"Good. Me, too."

"I'll call off the town."

He chuckled. "Seriously? Because I can't buy so much as a nail around here."

"Never forget Fool's Gold is, at heart, a matriarchal society."

"You gotta love that."

"I do."

They both rose. She tilted her head as she studied him. "Do we shake on it?"

"It's that or go for it right here on your desk."

The image filled her head and she found herself wanting to say yes.

He stepped around her desk. "Sorry. I was kidding." He leaned in and kissed her cheek, then stared into her eyes. "I am sorry. I was wrong and I hurt you. There's no excuse for that."

"Thank you."

He walked away.

She sank back in her chair, relieved to know that her initial assessment had been right. Shane was one of the good guys. Everyone screwed up. It was how the mistakes were handled that defined who a person was. He'd taken responsibility and made amends. Which made him just about perfect.

Except he wanted safe and boring. The exact opposite of what she did. Friends, she reminded herself, was a much better solution. It wasn't as if they were going to be tempted into bed with each other again . . . right?

Annabelle parked by the house on the Castle Ranch and watched yet another horse being unloaded from a trailer. She had a feeling this one was just a little fancier than the riding horses Shane had collected for the girls' lessons. One clue came from the trailer itself. Not only did it look new and expensive, but there was some kind of heating and/or cooling unit on top. No AC via an open window for these horses.

The horse itself was beautiful. A light

brown with a darker mane and tail. His legs were long, his muscles sleek. His head was well-shaped. Shane walked with him down the ramp.

Heidi came out of the house and walked over.

"One of the expensive ones," she said with a grin. "I can't remember his name."

"He looks gorgeous," Annabelle admitted.

"He should. He's worth a ton. Probably not millions, but plenty. He's a racehorse. Resting here on his way to Del Mar."

"Del Mar as in racing? Horses on the surf and all that?"

Heidi grinned. "Sure. Shane has a dozen or so horses out racing. Didn't he tell you?"

"Not really. He mentioned something about racing and I knew Khatar was valuable."

Heidi's grin broadened. "Yes, the horse you're planning to paint."

"It washes off," Annabelle said defensively. "Besides, Shane said I could."

"Of course he did. You could tell him to wear a tutu and he'd agree."

"I'm less sure of that. Although Khatar probably would. He's a very sweet horse."

"To you."

"And the girls who are taking riding lessons."

"Maybe."

They watched Shane lead the horse into the barn.

"I'm practically expecting him to get that horse a Sleep Number bed," Heidi grumbled. "Only the best for his precious racehorses. Not that I can really complain. He knows what he's doing. One of them came in second at Belmont."

"He mentioned that. The one that's part of the triple crown, right?"

"I think so. Rafe said something, but I was looking at bridal magazines and not really listening. Does that make me a bad sister-in-law-to-be?"

"No. It makes you human."

Heidi laughed. "Thank you. Now I feel better. Come on. Shane's going to be a while. In the meantime, we can go check on Persephone. She's restless. I think she's about ready to give birth. Cameron swears she'll be fine, but I can't help worrying."

"Cameron's the vet?"

"Yes. His large-animal practice sure took a jump when we showed up here. Between my goats, Shane's horses and May's menagerie, he's one busy guy."

They walked around the side of the house, toward the goat pen. During the summer, Heidi's goats fed on the wild bushes and grass. They came into the goat house once a day for milking.

"You're keeping Persephone close?" Annabelle asked, not seeing the very pregnant goat outside.

"I brought her in a few days ago. Rafe teases me about how much I worry, but she's one of my girls. I can't help it."

"You're a good goat mom."

"I hope so. Oh, did you see the pig?" Heidi pointed toward Priscilla's enclosure. "Wilbur showed up a couple of days ago. He's smaller than we thought, but seems nice. Priscilla likes him and he and Reno are getting along fine."

Annabelle turned and saw Priscilla the elephant walking in a group with a pony and a pig next to her. "Somewhere in the tree in the corner is a cat with kittens," she murmured. "That's got to be the weirdest thing in the world. I love it."

"Me, too."

"Am I too late?" May asked, flinging herself out of her car.

Shane shook his head. "Seriously, Mom? You came home from your honeymoon because one of Heidi's goats is giving birth?"

Glen got out and gave him a pitying look.

May glared at Shane. "I care about those goats. They're practically family. And based on how you and your brothers have been doing so far, probably the only thing close to a grandchild I'm ever going to get. So yes, I'm here for the birth."

She flounced past him.

Glen followed, pausing long enough to murmur, "You really need to figure out women, son," before following his new wife into the goat house.

"What did I do?" Shane demanded.

Rafe patted him on the shoulder. "You look so bright, too."

Shane swore. "This isn't fair."

"So little is, bro."

Shane shook off his hand. "It's a goat."

"Come on. I'll buy you a drink."

Shane followed his brother back to the house. Rafe pulled two bottles from the refrigerator and popped the top on both of them. They took their drinks into the living room.

"It's a goat," Shane repeated.

"You know that and I know that, but what Heidi or Annabelle or Mom would say is that you're showing you don't care about the goat."

"No, I'm saying it's a goat. She was born knowing how to give birth, just like the horses and nearly every other animal. Sure, you want to check in because there can be a problem, but they're gathering like it's some kind of miracle."

"Uh-huh. Glen's right. You really need to figure out women."

Shane wanted to protest that he did, but he had a failed marriage and his most recent fling proved otherwise.

"You know what happens once there's a birth," he said instead.

"I know."

"Heidi's going to want to get pregnant."

"We've already talked about it."

Shane eyed his brother. "You're calm."

"We both want kids."

"Right away?"

"We're going to wait until after the honeymoon to start trying, but yeah. We'll get going soon."

"You're good with that?"

Rafe grinned. "I love Heidi and I'm damned lucky to have her. Of course I want kids. As many as she wants."

"At least that will get Mom off the rest of us."

"Yup. I'll be the hero. Again." Rafe sighed loudly. "It gets old."

Shane chuckled. "You've got quite the ego."

"Is that what we're calling it?"

Shane glanced out the window and saw Charlie arriving. Apparently word had gone out about Persephone.

"You realize this is going to happen every time one of the goats gives birth," he said.

Rafe nodded. "Worth it at twice the price."

Because his brother loved Heidi. Goats and whatever else his bride wanted would be fine with him.

He wanted to feel pity for Rafe. The once-powerful businessman was a slave to his heart. But he didn't exactly look unhappy. And when he saw Rafe and Heidi together, the love was palpable. There was nothing there to mock. If anything, Shane was the odd man out.

"You got lucky," Shane told him.

"That I did. With Heidi, I'm always sure I'm right where I belong."

Something Shane had never been able to say in his first marriage. He hadn't been sure of anything. Not if Rachel was coming home that night, or how long it would be until he saw her again. She'd lived life on the edge and because he'd wanted to be with her, he'd accepted that.

For him, love and pain were intertwined. Now, with time and distance, he realized what he'd had before hadn't been love at all. Which meant what? That with the right person he could have a sure thing? That passion could also be a haven? He didn't know the answers to those questions — and he wasn't convinced that finding out was a risk he was willing to take.

CHAPTER TEN

"I'm walking," Annabelle said with a grin. She'd already had one margarita. Going for a second was definitely going to give her a buzz, but this was a party.

"Rafe is driving back into town to get me," Heidi said with a sigh, holding up her empty glass. "So I'm good."

"I'm walking," Charlie grumbled. "Although I'm insulted you'd even ask."

"I didn't," Jo said, standing by their table, obviously amused. "I simply said the special tonight was the mini tacos you all like and that I could bring another round of margaritas. Not even a hint of a question."

"You're so smug now that you're in love," Charlie said with a scowl.

Jo leaned close. "The sex is amazing. You should try it some time."

Charlie quickly turned away, but not before Annabelle saw the flash of pain in her friend's eyes. Jo had no way of knowing about Charlie's difficult past — the date rape and the ridicule that had followed.

Heidi also caught the look and smiled brightly at Jo. "We know you're always looking out for us and we appreciate it. Another round please, and yes to those delicious mini tacos. I think two plates will be enough."

"Sure thing." Jo scribbled on a pad. "Still toasting the goat?"

Heidi winced. "I assume you mean that in a 'raising a glass to' kind of way."

"Yes. I know you don't roast your precious animals."

"Did you know goat is actually the most popular source of animal protein in the world?" Annabelle asked.

Heidi's eyes widened in horror. "You didn't just say that."

"It's true, but heartbreakingly sad," Annabelle said quickly. "I'm sorry. It's one of those weird factoids I carry in my head. I think I learned it on Oprah."

"I miss Oprah," Heidi said.

"She's already drunk." Jo sounded disgusted. "One margarita. I'm never getting rich off you guys."

"I'm not drunk. I'm buzzed. There's a difference."

Jo shook her head and left for the bar.

When the three of them were alone, Heidi turned to Charlie.

"She didn't mean anything by the sex comment," she said in a low voice.

"I know." Charlie picked up her glass and swallowed the last of her margarita. "I usually don't react to people talking about stuff like that. Tonight's different. I guess I'm in a mood or something."

"It's Persephone," Heidi told her. "The baby thing."

"I love your goat, but she's not affecting my life."

"Montana's baby could be," Annabelle offered. "I know I'm hearing a faint ticking sound."

"Me, too," Heidi said.

"Yes, but you have a man," Annabelle reminded her. "A man who loves you and wants to marry you. I'm guessing you've already discussed starting a family."

"We have." Heidi looked blissful. "I don't know what I did to get so lucky, but I'm really grateful. And you have Shane."

If Annabelle had been drinking, she would have spit. "Shane and I aren't an item. We're friends."

Charlie rolled her eyes. "Say that all you want. No one is fooled."

"He's teaching me to ride."

"Sure he is."

Annabelle knew she couldn't deny the sex part. Not after telling her friends what had happened when he'd left. From there, word had gotten spread around, creating trouble for Shane. At the time, she'd been angry and hurt, so she hadn't minded getting a little back at him. Now she realized there were consequences.

"That was a one-time thing," she said primly. "We won't be having sex again. We've come to an understanding. We're friends."

"Keep saying it," Charlie told her. "One day it might be true."

Annabelle glanced around to make sure no one was sitting too close, then leaned toward her friends and lowered her voice. "I have to admit, I do like him a lot. Maybe more than a lot. We want different things though and he doesn't trust me."

"Why doesn't he trust you?" Charlie asked. "You didn't do anything wrong."

"It's his ex," Heidi explained. "I never met her, but I heard stories from Rafe. Apparently she's a real byotch."

Charlie snorted. "You did not just say that. Seriously?"

"I'm hip," Heidi said with a sniff. "Is that the right word?"

Annabelle grinned. "If you have to ask, then the answer is probably no."

They were still laughing when Jo returned with another round of margaritas and more chips.

"Change in topic," Annabelle said when she'd left. "How are things going with the wedding planning? Shouldn't we have another meeting soon?"

"Maybe next week." Heidi grabbed a chip. "I'm still pulling together my guest list. Our friends from the carnival are coming. Did I tell you that? We got confirmation a couple of days ago."

Heidi had grown up on the carnival circuit. Her parents had been killed when she'd been little and she'd gone to live with her grandfather. Heidi had always been surrounded by people who adored her. Now they would come to see her happily married, making an already special day even more so.

"That's great," Annabelle said. "With the wedding being held at the ranch, the size isn't much of an issue."

"That's true," Charlie said with a grin. "A couple hundred extra hamburgers won't matter much."

Heidi rolled her eyes. "We're not having hamburgers."

"Too bad. Nearly everyone likes them and they're fun food. Weddings are too serious, if you ask me."

"Then serve burgers at *your* wedding."

"Maybe I will. Not that I have any great plans to get married."

"You could start dating," Heidi told her. "Go slow. Pick someone you don't really care about."

Annabelle raised her eyebrows. "Yes, because you want a relationship with a man who doesn't matter."

Charlie picked up her refilled margarita. "She's saying that when it goes badly, I won't be hurt."

Heidi winced. "I didn't say that. I just meant then you could practice without worrying about your heart."

Charlie smiled. "I know you meant it with love. It's okay. Maybe I should find some guy to take me through the steps I missed before. Get a skill set to use on someone I do care about."

"I love it when a plan comes together," Heidi said with a sigh. She turned to Annabelle. "What about you? I say you give Shane a chance to see you're nothing like his ex."

Annabelle reached for a chip. "No, thanks," she admitted.

"Why not?" Charlie asked. "According to you, he's all things good. Handsome. Sexy. A god in bed."

"I didn't say that, and no. We're just friends."

"Uh-oh. It's trouble when you start lying to yourself," Charlie told her.

"No. I'm keeping my heart firmly out of play this time." Maybe it was the margarita kicking in, or the fact that she trusted her friends. Either way, she drew in a breath and spoke a painful truth. "My parents were never in love. My mom got pregnant while they were dating, so they got married. They were never happy and they made it clear I was a complication for them. I tried to be the perfect child, but neither of them was interested in having a kid."

She glanced at Heidi. "I envy you growing up the way you did."

Heidi looked surprised. "Moving around all the time? Never having a home without wheels?"

"No, being in the middle of a group that really loved you and looked out for you. I wanted that so much. But I couldn't find it. I had friends, of course, but not a place to feel safe. My boyfriends were a series of disasters. When I finally met Lewis, I thought he was the one."

"The ex-husband?" Charlie asked.

Annabelle nodded. "He's a writer, so I thought wow, creative. He's a little older, which I took to mean stable. But it turned out he was never actually interested in me as a person. It was more about what I represented. He liked to control me. Emotionally, I mean. He didn't hit me or anything."

"Sometimes fists are easier to understand," Charlie said quietly. "Mind games can be damaging, too."

"I see that now. Lewis saw me as a possession, not a person. It took me a long time to figure out I wasn't wrong to be unhappy and even longer for me to leave. But I got out and found Fool's Gold and now I have a home." She sniffed. "I swear, I'm not going to cry."

Heidi's eyes were already bright. "You can. It's okay."

"No, it's not," Charlie grumbled. "Stop it. She's here, she's fine, she's having sex with Shane. Where's the bad?"

Annabelle grinned and her tears faded. "I've told you. The sex was a one-time thing. I'm not going to fall for a guy who doesn't get me — and who doesn't want all the complications of love."

"I believe that. What I don't believe is the

sex not happening again. That's what they all say. No one believes you, kid. You might as well accept that."

Heidi shrugged. "She's kind of right. I know I'm assuming you'll do it again. The Stryker brothers are pretty irresistible."

"You'll see," Annabelle told them, raising her chin. "I have amazing powers of resistance. I'll stand firm."

Charlie looked at Heidi. "Twenty bucks says she doesn't last a week."

Heidi picked up her margarita. "Sorry. No way I'm taking that bet!"

"If you tell anyone, there's going to be trouble," Shane muttered, leading Reno toward the barn.

"I assume you're talking to him," Charlie said. "Because if you're talking to me, you're absolutely right. There *is* going to be trouble."

Shane wondered if hitting himself with a two-by-four a few times would make the day go better. Now he was being threatened by a woman. This had to be the low point of his life, because he couldn't imagine it getting much worse.

Charlie was tall, only a couple of inches shorter than him, and strong. She had plenty of muscles. Still, he knew he outweighed her and was significantly stronger. However, she was female, which meant she would have an inherent advantage in any fight. Namely that he couldn't fight back. It was how he'd been raised.

The pony trotted along beside him, calm and curious, ears forward. So far the animal had been friendly and a faithful companion to Priscilla.

He tied Reno to a post and grabbed a brush. "You sure about this?" he asked Charlie, deciding that ignoring her threat was the safest course of action. "Depending on her age and size, one of the horses would be better."

"You're a pony hater, which makes you unlikeable," Charlie told him, collecting a second brush and starting on Reno's other side. "Trust me. He's the better choice. A horse would be too hard for Kalinda to get on. More important, if something goes wrong, we can just pull her off."

He didn't like the sound of that. "Are you sure this is a good idea?"

"Yes. She needs to get out into the world. To experience things in a safe way." Charlie glared at him, something she did a lot. "I've told you about the burns."

"Yes. 'Don't be shocked, don't stare. Just act normal.' I'm not an idiot."

"That's yet to be seen."

What he didn't tell her, mostly because he wanted to keep his head firmly on his shoulders, was that he liked this side of Charlie. The sweet side that worried about a kid.

When she'd called that morning and asked if she could borrow Reno, he'd agreed. She'd shown up and explained the pony was for a ten-year-old burn victim. The previous summer, a gas barbecue had exploded, causing burns over forty percent of Kalinda's body. All this time later, she was still having surgeries and healing.

Priscilla called from a nearby corral. She hadn't wanted Reno to leave, so they'd compromised by bringing her closer to where Kalinda would ride. At least Wilbur and the cat family had been content to stay in Priscilla's enclosure.

"My life used to be normal," he muttered, dropping the blanket on Reno's small back, then reaching for the saddle.

Charlie grinned at him. "If you wanted normal, you never should have moved back here. Didn't your brother warn you?"

"I think he tried, but I didn't believe him."

They finished saddling Reno. Charlie grabbed the bridle and slipped in the bit. The pony didn't protest and almost seemed happy with the process.

They'd barely finished when a car drove into the yard. Charlie waved and walked toward the vehicle. Shane stayed by Reno.

He reminded himself not to stare. The girl had been through enough. But Charlie's warning hadn't prepared him for the sight of Kalinda slowly, obviously painfully, getting out of the car.

Her face had scars that twisted red. Only her startlingly blue eyes were undamaged. They stared at him solemnly, as if expecting judgment. She wore a long-sleeved shirt over jeans and had a surgical glove on one hand.

Charlie walked toward her unhesitatingly. "Hey, kid. You made it. Wait until you meet Reno. He's a cool pony. I think you're going to like him."

A pretty woman in her early thirties got out. She was blonde like her daughter, on the small side, with a worried frown pulling her eyebrows together.

"Hi, Charlie," the woman said. "I'm not sure this is a good idea."

Charlie put her arm around the mother. "Let's see how it goes, Fay."

"If you say so."

The group approached. Shane smiled at Kalinda. "Hi. Welcome to the Castle Ranch.

This is Reno and I'm Shane."

"Hi, Shane," the girl said in a soft voice. "I'm Kalinda."

"Fay," the mother said, stepping toward him and holding out her hand. "Thanks for doing this. We're —" Fay's eyes widened and she screamed. "Oh God! What is that?"

Shane groaned, wondering if Khatar had somehow gotten out again. He turned to see Priscilla walking toward them.

"My mother's elephant," he said. "Priscilla."

"I'll get her." Charlie walked toward the large animal.

"Your mother has an e-elephant?" Fay stepped closer to her daughter, her mouth hanging open.

"It's a long story." He glanced at the girl, expecting to see the same amount of fear, but Kalinda was smiling.

"That's so cool," she whispered. "An elephant."

"It's more complicated than that," Shane admitted. "My mom bought her without knowing much about elephants. Now that we've done research, we've learned female elephants are social. Which means Priscilla needs friends. We've been trying different animals to keep her company." He patted Reno. "So far, this little guy is her favorite."

Kalinda giggled. "They'd look pretty funny together."

He found he liked that happy sound and wanted to hear it again. "There's more. Back in her enclosure is a pig named Wilbur and a cat family. Priscilla watches over them."

Kalinda grinned. "For real?"

"Yup. I'll show you when we're done here." He patted the saddle. "Okay, let's get you on this pony."

They discussed the best way to get her on Reno. Her burns went down her front far enough to make bending difficult. So Shane simply picked her up and put her on the pony.

He was shocked by how little she weighed and how small she felt in his arms. Once she was settled in place, he showed her how to hold the reins in her good hand, then led her into the corral. He released Reno to close the gate, then turned back and found the pony was slowly walking around the ring. He would swear the animal was being extra careful not to jar his delicate rider.

Charlie and Priscilla moved closer to watch. Fay joined them, eventually moving close enough to cautiously stroke the elephant's shoulder. Shane walked along with Reno, although he quickly realized the pony was very much in tune with his rider.

By the house, Persephone and her baby enjoyed the warmth of the sun. Khatar dozed in the shade of a tree. The llamas and sheep grazed. In this crowd, his racehorses weren't even close to the most unusual animal around.

As Reno carried Kalinda carefully around and around the corral, Shane moved back to the fence and watched. Fay smiled at him, tears in her eyes.

"Thank you," she whispered as her daughter laughed. "She needs more things like this."

He watched the girl move. "She's doing well. After a few more sessions on Reno, she could move to one of the smaller horses. I have one in mind. He's a good guy. Very gentle."

"That would be great," Fay told him. "I want to sign her up for lessons."

Charlie leaned around Fay and punched him in the arm.

"What?" he asked, staring at her.

"You did good, cowboy. With all of this."

"Thanks," he said, consciously not reaching up to rub the spot that now burned like a sonofabitch.

Priscilla turned her massive head and if

he didn't know better, he would swear the elephant smiled at him.

"We need music," Annabelle called over her shoulder as Khatar cantered across the open land. With the wind in her hair and the sun bright overhead, it was a wonderful day. She was free, on the open range and loving life.

The powerful stallion moved smoothly, his muscles moving in an easy rhythm. When Shane had suggested they do more than ride around the corral, she'd been nervous, but now she got the appeal. She felt like she was in a movie. All that was missing was the soundtrack.

Shane, on Mason, moved up next to her. "My place is that way," he said, pointing.

She glanced to her right and saw construction equipment, what looked like part of a foundation and the beginnings of a stable. Before she could figure out how to turn Khatar, the horse was already moving in that direction.

"You're so good," she said, leaning over to pat him.

He picked his way down a slight rise and came to a stop by what would be the house. It was Saturday and the crew wasn't working, so the equipment was quiet. She couldn't imagine how loud it would be midweek, with all the engines doing their thing.

Shane dismounted and came around to help her. While she could have gotten down by herself, she liked the idea of sliding into his arms. If she were a better actress, she might feign an injured ankle or something, so he had to hold her. As it was, she had to content herself with his hands briefly settling on her waist, then a quick moment of body contact as she turned toward him. Then he stepped back and motioned to the house.

"Want a tour?"

"Sure."

They left the horses in the shade of a couple of trees. She followed him across a graded area of cleared land toward the foundation.

"Front door," he said, pointing. "Entryway, living room beyond that. We'll go around back."

"Just like the hired help."

He chuckled. "I'll be coming in from the stable. The back door makes more sense."

He led the way into a surprisingly large room. She could see where the door would be.

"The mudroom?" she asked.

He nodded. "Sink over there, with a

counter. Lots of storage for boots, jackets, slickers."

They went into what would be the kitchen. She pressed her hands together. "You listened and moved the wall."

"I did. You made a good point."

"What you're thinking is, I'm pretty smart for a girl."

"I would never think that."

They went into the formal dining room and the oversize family room.

"Guest rooms that way," he said pointing to the left. "Study in front of us and master down the other way." He lightly put his hand on the small of her back. "There are more changes out here."

They went back toward the stable.

"I'm clearing more land and expanding the barn. For the riding horses."

She glanced up at him. "Really?"

"What the hell. I can't get out of it now."

She wasn't fooled by his faux growly voice. "You like the kids and you like giving lessons."

"Maybe." He looked at her and grinned. "Okay, yeah. I do. Did Charlie tell you about Kalinda?"

"She mentioned the girl had been by. I know who she is. When she has to stay in the hospital for her surgeries, I take her books. She's come a long way."

"I heard."

"The recovery has been difficult. She nearly died a couple of times. Her parents have been through so much. Charlie said she really liked riding."

"Reno was great with her," he said. "Patient. It was as if he understood her physical limitations. I've been doing some research online. About how riding helps kids with physical challenges. I've been thinking about getting a couple more horses, training them to work with kids who are handicapped. I don't have a business plan yet, but it makes sense to offer something like that here."

Well, crap. The last thing she needed was Shane acting like some hero, she thought, turning away so he wouldn't see her going all gooey at the thought. He was hard enough to resist when he was a regular guy. If he did this, how could she stand a chance?

"Would you have time?" she asked.

"I'll make time. There's a guy in town, Raoul Moreno. He has a camp for disadvantaged children."

She smiled. "I know Raoul. He's a very handsome former football player."

"He's married. With kids."

Her smile turned into a grin. "Jealous?"

"No."

"You look jealous."

His dark eyes brightened with amusement. "You're reading too much into the information."

"I don't think so. Anyway, you've talked to Raoul?"

"I had a quick phone call with him after Kalinda left. Charlie gave me his number. I'm going to go see him in the next week or so. We might see if we can work together. Maybe some of his camp kids could work on the ranch."

"Horses as therapy," she murmured.

Was it her imagination or had he just moved a little closer? Or maybe it was her. She could be the one moving. Because honestly, out here, in the quiet and beauty of nature, with Shane being all manly and irresistible, she was having trouble concentrating on what he was saying.

"We could do a lot of good."

"Yes, you could."

He cupped her cheek with his hand. "You're trouble, you know that, right?"

"No, I'm not."

"You are to me."

They were friends, she reminded herself. Just friends. Nothing more. Anything else would be dangerous, not to mention foolish.

"I do like that there's not a lot of drama," he admitted. "Despite the fact that you dance on bars."

"It was one dance and you're right about the drama. I avoid it. I like my life calm. Predictable even."

"Then you probably already know I'm going to do this."

He dropped his head and pressed his mouth to hers.

The kiss was soft. Tender. With just enough hint of passion to add a little tingle to the moment. She leaned into him, angling her head and wrapping her arms around his neck. His mouth moved back and forth, as if he wanted to remember exactly how it had been when they'd kissed before.

He drew her close. He was as strong and warm as she remembered. She let her eyes drift closed as she parted her lips and got lost in the easy flow of passion washing through her.

His tongue moved against hers, exciting her. She touched him back, enjoying the dance. Wanting grew as did the heat. Need followed. There wasn't a part of her body that didn't long to be near him.

She thought about what had happened

before. How great the lovemaking had been and how difficult after. There was also the issue of protection. She sure didn't have any condoms with her and hoped he didn't, either. Because she didn't want him to be the kind of guy who was always prepared.

He drew back slightly, then rested his forehead against hers.

"You're a complication, Annabelle."

"Me?"

He straightened and put both hands on her shoulders. "If you knew how much I wanted you," he began.

She shivered in anticipation.

"But," he began.

"I know. We're friends."

"Oh. Right. I was thinking more practically. You know, about protection. But yeah. We're friends."

Still humming with desire, she managed to smile. "The friendship thing was a mutual decision."

"Going to rub my nose in it, are you?" he asked.

"Sure."

"I respect that."

He put his arm around her and led her back to the horses. When they were standing by Khatar, he stroked her cheek with his index finger.

"Maybe we could renegotiate our terms," he offered. "Interested?"

More than he could begin to guess, she thought. Sex only, she told herself. No emotional engagement. "I might be."

He grinned. "You're not easy, are you?"

"Where's the fun in that?"

They rode back to the ranch. Once they were there, she wondered if it would be foolish to invite him back to her place right then, or if she should hold out until that night.

But before she could decide, she spotted an unfamiliar car by the house.

"Company?" she asked, pointing.

"Not that I know of."

The car was a Mercedes, but a different model than Rafe's. Just as big, just as powerful. Just as expensive.

She followed Shane toward the car only to come to a stop when the driver stepped out. He was of average height, slim build. Light blue eyes and graying blond hair. Well-dressed, in expensive clothes.

She stared. No, she told herself. She was wrong. It couldn't possibly be . . .

"Lewis," she breathed.

Shane turned back to face her. "Who?"

"Lewis," she managed to say. "My ex-husband."

Lewis started toward them and held out his hand. "Hello. I'm Lewis Cabot. Annabelle's husband."

"Ex," she corrected. "Ex-husband."

Lewis looked at her and smiled. "No, Annabelle. That's what I came to talk to you about. We're still married."

CHAPTER ELEVEN

Annabelle felt the earth shift off its axis. Married? *Still* married?

"That's not possible," she said. "We're divorced. We worked out a settlement."

He hadn't wanted to. For a long time he'd refused. But in the end, she threatened to take him to court. He'd realized that any judge would give her a percentage of his earnings for the time they'd been married. While he'd always found fault with her, the truth was, their marriage had been good for his career. He'd written two of his bestselling books while they'd been together.

Rather than give her a piece of that, he'd agreed to the divorce. Her lawyer had tried to talk her out of the deal, but she'd explained she would rather be free than rich. After all, they didn't have kids and she was perfectly capable of supporting herself. Let Lewis keep it all. Being away from him had been worth any price to her.

"Apparently there was a bit of trouble with the law firm," Lewis said cheerfully. "We're still married." He turned to Shane. "I'm a writer. You might have heard of me. Lewis —"

"No. Sorry."

Annabelle risked glancing at Shane, but there was no way to tell what he was thinking. Still, she doubted it would be good. After all, this moment would qualify as drama by anyone's standards.

His dark gaze moved from Lewis to her and back. "You two probably want to talk about this," he said, edging back toward the barn.

"No!" Annabelle said quickly. "It's fine. I'm leaving. I have to go . . ." She stopped, realizing she didn't know what to do next. Panic had seized her brain, making it impossible to think.

Lewis, here. In Fool's Gold. The one place she'd always felt safe.

The back door of the house opened and Heidi stepped out.

"There you are," she said. "Annabelle, I really need to talk to you. Can you give me a second?"

Annabelle nodded and started toward her.

"We have to talk, as well," Lewis said urgently.

No, they didn't. They'd given up the need to talk the day they'd agreed to the divorce.

"I have to help Heidi," she said, already moving toward the house.

Lewis sighed heavily. "I can see you're as difficult as ever. That's fine, Annabelle. I know how to win you over. I'm staying in town at Ronan's Lodge. I'll be in touch."

She hoped he was lying, but didn't think her luck was that good. She looked at her friend and let Heidi's supportive gaze guide her to safety. When she reached the back porch, Heidi took her arm and led her inside.

"How long has he been here?" Annabelle asked.

"Nearly an hour. Were you really married to him?"

"Unfortunately."

"Don't get mad, but he's kind of a pompous jerk."

"It took me a while to figure that out."

"At least you did." Her friend hugged her. "Poor you. He thinks you're still married."

"I got that part. He has to be wrong. We signed papers. We had lawyers. That's the only thing I took from him, the legal fees to get out of the marriage. I liked the irony of it."

Her head spun and she couldn't seem to

catch any of the thoughts zipping by. She figured she would go her whole life and never see Lewis again. How could he be in Fool's Gold? And why now?

Married? He had to be playing some kind of game, but why?

She stared at Heidi. "I don't know what to do."

"You have a legal problem, then you get legal advice." She pulled a business card out of her jeans back pocket. "I hope it's okay, but I called ahead. Trisha is expecting you in her office right now."

"Trisha Wynn? The lawyer who helped you with the ranch?"

"Yup. She's great. You'll like her." Heidi hugged her again. "This is all fixable. You were divorced before, you can be again."

"Shane is not going to understand this," Annabelle murmured, accepting the comfort.

"What do you mean?"

Annabelle straightened. "He was just saying he likes the lack of drama in my life. Finding out I might still be married doesn't exactly qualify me for calm person of the week. If Lewis is right and we're not divorced, Shane is going to think the worst. That I'm a liar or an attention-seeker."

Heidi's eyebrows rose. "I see. And this

concerns you?"

"Of course. I don't want Shane to hate me."

"Or think badly of you. Because you're friends."

"Yes, we're friends."

Heidi bit her lower lip. "Be careful. It sounds like you've crossed the friendship line."

"No. I'm fine. I like Shane, nothing more. I'm not in love with him."

Heidi didn't look convinced, but she smiled and said, "I'm sure you're right. Besides, you have enough to deal with right now. Let's get rid of Lewis before we take on any other problems."

Annabelle had seen Trisha Wynn in court when the other woman had been helping Heidi, so she was prepared for the tight-fitting, low-cut, sexy clothes. Despite the fact that Trisha was probably in her sixties, she barely looked forty-five. Why she dressed like a woman in her twenties, Annabelle didn't know, but she wasn't in a position to be picky. Not when her marital freedom was on the line.

Trisha nodded as she listened to the phone call she'd been having. "Yes, of course," she murmured. "Understandable.

Disappointing, but understandable. Uh-huh. You're sure." She paused. "Thank you. I'll check my email right now."

She hung up the phone and smiled at Annabelle.

"Good news. The final documents are being emailed to me right now. I'll get back to them with your current address and my current address. On behalf of lawyers everywhere, I'm embarrassed to tell you, it's true. The final paperwork was never filed with the court."

Annabelle clutched the arms of her chair and told herself however bad she felt, she had to keep breathing. Passing out wouldn't solve any problems.

"No," she said with a moan. "That can't be true. I can't still be married to him. I didn't like it the first time. What if he won't let me go?"

Trisha smiled at her. "It's not his decision. The paperwork is being hand-delivered to the court right now. Once it's filed, it's only a matter of a few days, maybe a week or so, until the divorce is final." Her smile faded. "You haven't married anyone since the divorce, have you?"

"No!"

"Then there's no problem."

There were several problems, she thought

246

as Trisha clicked on something and then started the printer. The biggest of which was still being married to a man she never wanted to see again. Her second biggest problem involved Shane and what he must be thinking. So much for her not having drama in her life. Right now there was plenty.

"I wonder how he found out," she said, more to herself than Trisha. "And why he came to see me instead of getting in touch with his lawyer?"

"You're the one who wanted the divorce."

"How did you know?"

"Years of experience. You're the one coming to see me, not him. If he'd been upset, he would have done as you said. Gone to his lawyer and gotten it taken care of. You would have heard through legal counsel. Did he fight you for the divorce?"

"A little," Annabelle admitted. "He didn't understand why I was leaving."

"When the wife walks out, the man is always surprised. Plus they find it so inconvenient to have to suddenly take care of themselves. They're shocked to discover that clean clothes don't magically appear in drawers and dinner doesn't cook itself." Trish shrugged. "Not that I'm bitter."

"I can see that."

"Let's just say I have a lot of experience being married. These days, I want a lover, not a husband. Legally, it's a lot less messy."

She put on reading glasses, got up and walked to the printer. "Here are copies of the final papers." She flipped through the sheets. "I see. You really did want out, didn't you? There's no alimony, no divisions of assets." Trisha looked at her over her glasses. "Did you have legal representation?"

"Yes, and I'm fine with the settlement. I wasn't interested in Lewis's money. He earned it, not me."

"You facilitated him earning it. You could have gotten at least a small percentage of it."

"No, thanks," Annabelle told her. "I would rather not be married. We didn't have kids and I can take care of myself."

"I see. A person with principles. How annoying." She passed over the paperwork. "Make sure I have a number where you can be reached. I'll be in touch as soon as the courts process the paperwork and the divorce is final."

The Fool's Gold Mountaineers were a short season A-league baseball team with a reasonably good win-loss record. Or so Shane overheard as he waited with Rafe. The stadium was on the small side, but recently refurbished, with an enthusiastic midweek crowd.

"I told you," Rafe said, pushing Shane toward the ticket collector. "It'll be good for you."

"I don't have time for a game. I have work to do."

"You're moping. You need to get out."

"Get off me."

Shane really wanted to say something else, but there were too many old ladies in the crowd, not to mention kids and just ordinary people who probably wouldn't appreciate him swearing loudly in public.

Damned good manners, he thought grimly.

"She's already talked to a lawyer and had the paperwork filed," Rafe said, handing over his ticket, then accepting the torn half back.

"I don't know what you're talking about," Shane insisted, following him into the stadium.

"You're acting like you're five. Annabelle. I'm talking about Annabelle. The petite redhead who's got you seeing stars?"

Shane looked past him. "It's weird. There's a buzzing sound in my head. Like an annoying fly or something."

Rafe chuckled. "You can pretend you don't care all you want but I know the truth. You're pissed. I'm just saying, she didn't do anything wrong. She really did think she was divorced, the papers have been filed with the court and then it'll be done. Some lawyer in North Carolina screwed up. You shouldn't blame her for that."

"Did I say I wasn't talking about this?" Shane asked, wondering why Rafe was trying so hard. Heidi must have put him up to it. After all, Heidi and Annabelle were friends.

Just when he was starting to trust Annabelle, too. He'd begun to tell himself that despite having seen her dancing on a bar, she wasn't into drama. He already knew that she could go fifteen minutes without needing to be the center of attention. But the minute he let down his guard, her ex showed up, insisting they weren't divorced.

His gut told him it was okay to trust her. His head reminded him that he'd been fooled before.

Once inside the stadium, Shane looked around. The ads on the inside of the fences were the old-fashioned painted kind. Only the scoreboard was electronic. There was a handful of vendors set up by the stairs to the seats and an old guy in a yellow T-shirt selling programs.

"Over there," Rafe said, pointing.

Shane glanced in that direction and saw a group of men sitting together. Ethan Hendrix was waving at them. Shane saw Kent next to him. There were a few other guys he recognized. Josh Golden, the former world champion cyclist, was talking to Raoul Moreno.

"That guy on the end is Tucker Janack," Rafe told him. "His company is building the casino and hotel just outside of town. Next to him is Simon Bradley."

"The doctor. Right. We met him when Montana's baby was born."

"The man on the other side of him is Finn Andersson," Rafe continued. "You know Cameron."

Shane nodded at the local vet.

They walked up to where the other men sat. There was a lot of handshaking and backslapping. The oldest one of the group was Max Thurman, boyfriend of the Hendrix mom.

Shane found himself seated between Cameron and Kent. The beer vendor was waved over and a fight nearly broke out as everyone offered to pay. Shane chuckled as Raoul and Josh tried to arm wrestle for the privilege of picking up the tab and he figured the guy selling beer probably walked away with a fifty-dollar tip.

Kent passed him a beer. "You getting settled okay?"

Shane nodded. "I'm having a place built on the land I bought. Until then, I'm staying with my mom, Glen, Heidi and Rafe. The house is a little crowded."

Kent chuckled. "I won't make fun of you, dude. I stayed with my mom when I moved back."

"When was that?"

"Last year." Kent sipped his beer. "I'm a math teacher at Fool's Gold High School."

"No way. Seriously?"

"Yup." Kent chuckled. "I never expected that to happen. But in college, I really enjoyed math. The summer between my sophomore and junior year, I worked at an academic camp for middle school kids in Colorado. That was it for me. When I went back to college that fall, I changed my major, got my credentials and now I'm a math teacher."

"Sounds like you enjoy your work."

"I do. I teach a range of classes, including the advanced students, studying calculus, and the kids who can barely add. Both are satisfying, in different ways."

"Not just the smart kids?"

He shrugged. "The smart kids are probably going to do well regardless of who's running the class. The ones who are having trouble need me. When I can take a kid who hates math and then get him or her to understand a few principles, they light up. Suddenly they realize they *can* be good at something difficult. It's not that they're dumber than everyone else, it's that no one took the time to help them. With the fundamentals in place, the world opens up."

Kent shifted in his seat. "I get carried away."

"Impressive," Shane admitted. "You're the teacher everyone wants to have."

"I like what I do. I'm also the assistant baseball coach in the spring, but that's only part-time. Math is my thing." He glanced at the field where the players were warming up, then back toward Shane. "Too bad being a math teacher isn't exactly a chick magnet."

Shane grinned. "Is that a problem? Aren't there plenty of single women in Fool's Gold? I keep hearing that." Although he was really only interested in one. Unfortunately, nothing about Annabelle was easy.

"I guess." Kent took another sip of his beer. "I'm not interested in dating, really. I was, ah, married before."

"Me, too," Shane said in a low voice. "Divorce is hell."

"Tell me about it. My parents were in love until the day Dad died. All my sisters are happily married. So is Ethan. The only reason Ford doesn't have the perfect wife is because he's in the military, traveling all the time. Otherwise, I'm sure he'd be married with a couple of kids. Now Mom has Max. I'm the relationship screw-up."

Shane wanted to offer comfort, but he was in no position to do so. It wasn't as if he had figured out his personal life, either.

"You've got a kid," he pointed out instead. "That's something."

Kent nodded. "Reese is great. I'm lucky to have him. It's just . . ."

He looked around, as if making sure everyone else was busy with their own conversations. "It's been over a year and I still miss her, you know?"

"Your ex?"

"Yeah. Lorraine was 'the one' and now she's gone. I keep thinking she'll come back. That she'll realize she needs us. But I'm kidding myself. She doesn't need anybody. It's hard on Reese."

"Doesn't he see his mom?"

Kent shook his head. "She walked out on both of us. She's never around, never calls.

He doesn't say much, but I know he misses her."

Shane swore under his breath. He couldn't imagine a woman acting like that when it came to her own child.

"Have you started dating?" he asked.

"No." Kent shrugged. "My mom's been on me about it and my sisters mention it now and then. Even Reese says I should move on. But why? So I can date someone I'll never care about? What's the point?"

The point was to heal and then have a life. Kent sounded like he was caught up in the past and that was never good.

Sure, Shane had suffered through a tough divorce, too, but he'd managed to move forward. It wasn't as if his ex still got to him. He didn't use her to define the other women in his . . .

He tightened his hold on his beer as the uneasy truth settled on him. He wasn't as different from Kent as he would like. The truth was that Rachel was the yardstick by which he'd carefully measured Annabelle. All of Annabelle's actions were judged according to what his ex would have done. The two women had never met, had almost nothing in common, yet in Shane's mind, they were exactly the same. Hardly fair to any involved party.

"Attention, everyone," Josh said as he rose. The group went quiet.

"This is the first time we've all been together without the women around," he said with a grin. "Not that we don't love our ladies."

"Charity deserves a whole lot better than you," Ethan yelled.

Josh laughed. "Yes, she does, but she loves me. Which makes me the luckiest man here." He held up his plastic cup of beer. "Every man who got some last night, raise your glass."

Shane and Kent groaned as all the married men, and Rafe, lifted their beers.

"And that, gentlemen," Josh said to Shane and Kent, "is why it's good to be married."

Cups were raised and toasts accepted. Shane patted Cameron on the shoulder. "Beats looking after goats or giving cats vaccinations, doesn't it?"

Cameron grinned. "It's nice to get away, but by the time the game is over, I'll be happy to get back to my girls."

"How old is your daughter?"

"Almost nine."

"So you're a long way from worrying about her dating."

Cameron winced. "I hope so. I was dreading that. Most teenage girls don't want their dads tagging along on the date and that's pretty much the only way I was going to let her go out. Now Rina can help keep me calm."

"Fool's Gold is a great place to raise kids. I grew up here," Shane said.

"Rina and I are looking forward to having children together and Kaitlyn is very excited about being a big sister." Cameron drew in a breath. "When my wife left, Kaitlyn was a newborn. I was terrified. What did I know about taking care of a baby? But I got through it and Kaitlyn and I became a family. Then Rina came along and she made everything complete. Life is funny that way. Little miracles show up when we least expect them."

The players moved to the baselines and the announcer asked everyone to stand for the national anthem. Shane rose, along with his friends. They sang together.

When the last notes died, everyone cheered. The players took their positions and the game began.

The Mountaineers' pitcher struck out the first three at bats. The first hit for the home team was an over-the-fence home run. Shane yelled with everyone else, enjoying the home team's skill. Josh and Raoul joked about who was more famous in town. Ethan offered Shane advice on the house Shane was having built. Simon and Cameron talked different breeds of dogs with Finn. Tucker and Kent debated mathematical averages in trying to beat the house in casino gambling.

Shane enjoyed the afternoon, the game and the company, but in the back of his mind, he couldn't stop thinking about Kent and Cameron and the women in their lives. Both men had suffered through disastrous marriages. Kent was stuck — still hurt, still waiting for Lorraine to return. He had his kid and his work, but was he happy? Was there contentment, or just a sense of longing for what he would never have again?

Cameron had gone another direction. He, too, had dealt with a child as a single father. But instead of retreating, he'd opened his heart to Rina and was now happily married. He'd let go of the past — something he had to do before he could move on.

Shane knew he could go in either direction. He could stay lost in anger and bitterness, remembering what had happened until he didn't have room for anything else. Or he could let go and move on. The choice was his, and whatever he chose, there would be consequences.

Chapter Twelve

"You must really love her," Shane said as Khatar tossed his head after flawlessly executing the complicated step sequence they'd been working on.

The horse pranced a couple of paces to the left, then went to the right, starting the steps over again.

"You don't need me here, do you?" Shane asked. "You can do this all on your own."

Khatar moved closer and gently butted him. Shane rubbed the horse behind the ears.

Since falling for Annabelle, the once-difficult stallion had become a friendly, easygoing animal. Shane wasn't about to turn him loose in a playschool, but the change was remarkable. He wondered if Khatar's previous trainers had simply assumed he would be difficult and had treated him accordingly before he'd had a chance to prove himself. He'd reacted to their assumptions. Or was he giving the horse too much credit?

He led Khatar across the yard, toward the large pen next to Priscilla's. After a morning of hard work, Khatar deserved a little freedom in the big one-acre fenced area.

A black Mercedes drove up by the stable and came to a stop. Shane recognized the vehicle and the man who stepped out of it. His good mood faded and he was ready to put his fist through something. Or someone.

"Good morning," Lewis called. "I'm here to see Annabelle."

Shane felt Khatar tense. The horse raised his head, as if trying to appear even bigger.

"Right back at you," he muttered to the horse, then glanced over at Lewis. "She's not here."

Lewis raised his eyebrows. "She doesn't live here?"

"No. She has a place in town." He was about to say she worked at the library, but decided he wasn't going to give the other man any more information.

"Interesting. I thought . . ." Lewis gave him a quick, meaningless smile. "Thank you." He turned his attention to Khatar. "Amazing animal."

"He is. Do you ride?"

"Me? No. Never been one for outdoor sports."

"Annabelle does."

Lewis blinked at him. "Excuse me?"

"Annabelle rides Khatar."

"You must be mistaken."

Khatar chose that moment to lunge for Lewis. When Shane held him back, he rose on his back hooves, front legs pawing toward the other man.

Lewis scuttled back for safety. "That horse would kill her. How can you allow it?"

"It wasn't my decision."

Shane hadn't been pleased to see Lewis, but he suddenly found himself enjoying the conversation. Still, he didn't want Khatar to hurt himself, so he led the horse over to the closest corral and secured him behind the gate.

"I'll be back," he told the horse in a low voice. "Then you'll have your afternoon of running around."

Khatar ignored him and glared at Lewis.

Shane walked back toward the man hiding behind his car.

"I can't imagine what she enjoys about being here," Lewis said with a sniff. "She's not the outdoor type."

"How long were you married?"

"Two years." Lewis paused. "Closer to

four now, what with us still being married."

"How did you find out the divorce wasn't final?"

"My lawyer bought into another practice. In the process of moving, he went through his files and realized we'd never received the final paperwork from the clerk."

"So you came to see her rather than let her know by phone?"

Lewis smiled. "I knew that by now Annabelle had to be regretting the divorce. She doesn't belong in a place like this. Fool's Gold." His lip curled in a sneer. "What a ridiculous name. Have you seen the town? Like something out of a 1960s TV show."

"I wouldn't know. I wasn't around then."

Lewis bristled. "I'm simply pointing out that it's hardly a regular sort of place. Not anywhere Annabelle would be happy."

"You two lived in North Carolina?"

"Yes. Raleigh. I have a lovely house. Very quiet and spacious with good light. I'm a writer."

"You mentioned that."

Shane studied the other man. He was probably in his early forties. He dressed like he had money and he'd paid plenty for the car. Shane wondered if Annabelle had been impressed by either. He would have said she was more interested in character, but he'd been wrong before.

"Divorce is tough," Shane said. "Mine was ugly."

Lewis seemed to relax. "Ours was very civilized, but unnecessary. I see that now. Perhaps I could have been more attentive, although it's difficult when I'm working. Writing demands everything. Annabelle was always there for me. Taking care of things. She handled my schedule, kept up the house. When she was gone, there was no one."

Like when the staff quits, Shane thought, but didn't say.

Lewis stared past him, as if seeing something Shane couldn't. "She's so beautiful. I'd forgotten that part. I have pictures, of course, but they don't capture the life in her. I always admired that about her."

"She's a librarian here," Shane told him.

"Yes, Annabelle did always want to keep her little job. This time, I'll make her understand her work gets in the way."

"You're expecting her to come back to you?"

"Yes. That's why I'm here. We're still married. Her place is with me."

He wanted to point out that Annabelle had ties to the town, that she was eager to raise money for her bookmobile. But what if he was wrong? What if she was having second thoughts about her marriage?

Lewis glanced around. "If she's not here, then I won't take up any more of your time."

"No problem."

He wanted to say more, to announce that there was no way that Annabelle was going anywhere with that guy, but he wasn't sure. And not knowing left a gnawing sensation in his gut.

He waited until the other man had left, then walked Khatar over to the fenced acre and let him loose. Then Shane got in his truck and drove to town. He had a few questions of his own and he knew the best place to get them answered.

"Haven't seen you around for a while."

Annabelle looked up from her computer to find Shane standing in the doorway of her small office. As always, the sight of him in worn jeans and a long-sleeved shirt set her heart racing.

She motioned to the chair on the other side of her desk and saved her work. "I've been dealing with a few personal issues," she said. "You might have heard. My ex-husband isn't as much an ex as I would like."

"I have heard." He stayed where he was,

as if waiting for something. Obviously whatever it was had to be more than an invitation to take a seat.

She drew in a breath. "At the risk of falling into the 'too much information' column, I would like to state for the record that I thought the divorce was final, I wanted it to be final then and I still want it to be final. Lewis was a mistake and I'm glad our sad marriage is behind me."

For a second, nothing happened. Then Shane gave her a slow, sexy smile. "I was wondering," he admitted as he walked into the room and took the chair she had offered.

She smiled back, trying not to sigh with relief. "His arrival was a shock and not a welcome one. I like things to go according to plan. Sign divorce papers, get divorced. Surprises are highly overrated. I've talked to an attorney here," she continued. "The last of the paperwork has been filed with the courts. The divorce will be final in a matter of days."

"Lewis will be disappointed."

"How do you know?"

"He came to the ranch this morning. Looking for you."

She groaned. "Tell me you're lying."

"Sorry. The car is nice."

"If you're into cars."

"You're not."

She managed a smile. "You've seen what I drive. Not exactly fancy. Some of it is my budget, but most of it is I've never been much of a car person."

"I'm a truck guy, myself."

"I noticed. It's the horse thing. Not that Khatar wouldn't look great in a BMW."

"It would have to be a convertible," he said with a wink.

She laughed. "I can see him now, flirting with all the ladies." She leaned forward, resting her hands on her desk. "Lewis really came by?"

"Yup. He thought you were out at the ranch."

"He doesn't know about the horseback riding lessons."

"He thought you lived there. He seemed surprised when I mentioned you were riding Khatar. Said you weren't one for the outdoors."

"I have my moments. The horseback riding is fun." She hesitated, not sure how to delicately ask the obvious. "How obnoxious was he?"

"Not too bad. He's, ah, confident."

"That's one way of putting it." She thought about the man she'd been married to. "I was younger, obviously, when we met. Less sure of myself. Just out of college. My parents weren't exactly warm and fuzzy and I never felt as if I belonged anywhere. When I met Lewis . . ." She paused, not sure how to explain.

"Older guy?" Shane offered. "Charming? He paid attention."

She wasn't sure if she should be pleased or horrified that he'd figured it out so quickly.

"Pretty much. He was giving a guest lecture at the college. I went to hear him and thought he was smart and funny. I'd been invited to the reception that followed and was introduced to him. He asked me out to coffee. It was flattering."

More than flattering. At the time she'd half expected him not to show up or to call and say he'd been joking. But he'd come and he'd been more interesting than anyone she'd met.

"He'd traveled so many places and he wrote books." She smiled. "I was a library science major, so meeting an author was pretty thrilling. He asked me out and it sort of went on from there."

"Sounds normal," Shane said.

"It was. I fell in love with him." She considered her statement. "No. I fell in love with what I thought he was. With the man I wanted him to be. In truth, Lewis never saw me as a person. I was as much an object to him as the rare books he collected. He wanted a wife who was attractive and smart. More than that, he wanted someone he could control, who would take care of him."

She ducked her head. "It wasn't all him. I have some responsibility in why the marriage failed. I didn't tell him what I wanted. I didn't stand up for myself. By the time I was able to say I wanted a partnership, it was too late. He expected me to be his secretary, housekeeper and sexual party girl and I expected something else. We couldn't come to an agreement, so I left."

"Good for you."

"It's hardly action worthy of praise."

"You left a comfortable situation to go out on your own."

"I wasn't in the marriage for the money."

"Some people would have stayed because of it."

"I don't know about that. Besides, I'm more than capable of taking care of myself. By the time we'd worked out the details of our divorce, I knew I'd mistaken gratitude for love. It made it easier to leave."

She didn't go into details about the split. There was no point in mentioning that

Lewis hadn't wanted her to go. That he'd fought her, resisting even getting a lawyer. Finally economics had won out. When she'd said she wouldn't ask for anything, he'd signed the papers.

"Seeing him again," she continued, "has reaffirmed my decision. No regrets. Well, my lawyer not doing his job is one, but that's all."

Shane studied her for a few seconds. "I know you're busy. I just wanted to say hi."

She stood, as well. "Thanks for stopping by."

They stared at each other. For a second she thought he was going to kiss her. She would have liked that. His arms around her, his mouth on hers. Being with Shane always felt good. Right.

But he only smiled before leaving.

"Typical man," she muttered, then laughed. Ironically *not* being kissed by Shane was still more exciting than any kiss by Lewis.

Charlie sat in the shade, under the big tree in Dakota's backyard. She held baby Jordan Taylor in her arms. The afternoon was warm, the breeze light. If the best part of life was made up of perfect moments, she was living one right now.

Dakota sat across from her on the big, tattered blanket they'd spread out on the grass. Hannah leaned against her mother, her toddler fingers clutching a big, chunky puzzle piece. She tried fitting it in several spots before finding where it went. When the piece slid into place, she looked at her mother and laughed with delight.

"You are such a smart girl," Dakota told her, then kissed the top of her head. "Look at that! You're doing the puzzle all by yourself."

"You're good with her," Charlie said, enjoying the exchange while fighting a stab of envy.

"Thanks. I will say, for the record, that despite the fact that I have a degree in child psychology, not one of my classes prepared me for what it's really like to be a parent. I've been thinking of sending the university a letter and asking for a refund."

Charlie chuckled. "I'm sure they'll get a check right out to you."

"I hope they will. I'll put it toward the kids' college funds." Dakota glanced at her over Hannah's head. "But that's not why you came by, is it?"

"No." Charlie had called a few days before to set up the meeting with Dakota. She hadn't explained what she wanted to talk

about. Now she wished she'd said something so she wouldn't have to figure out how
to deal with it now.

"Just blurt it out," Dakota said gently. "I
doubt you can shock me."

"I used to be a man," Charlie told her.

Dakota laughed. "I don't believe you."

"Okay, that's not it, but I was hoping for
a better reaction."

"Sorry to disappoint."

She glanced down at the baby in her arms,
then looked back at Dakota. "I'm thinking
of adopting and I wanted to talk to you
about that."

Dakota touched her daughter's shoulder.
"Okay, that's surprising, but in a good way.
I think adoption can be wonderful, but I'm
biased." She tilted her head and tucked her
shoulder-length blond hair behind her ears.
"Have you been thinking about adopting
for a while?"

"A few weeks. For a long time I didn't
think I wanted a family. Kids, I mean. I
thought I was one of those people who just
never had any desire to be a mom. But
lately, I'm feeling different about the subject." She wanted to belong. To be important
to someone, to be there, no matter what.
She wanted the connection, the responsibility, the joy.

"Not to get too personal, but there are more traditional ways to have a baby. I assume you know where they come from."

Charlie grinned. "I've heard, yes. Storks."

"If you put in your reservation early . . ." Dakota looked at her. "No man in your future?"

"I don't think so."

Because she couldn't imagine being with a man that way. Not after what had happened. Besides, you couldn't miss what you've never had, right?

"What if you fall madly in love? That's what happened to me. I was so sure that I would never find the one. I moved forward on my own and look what happened."

"If I meet some guy, that's okay, too," Charlie said, figuring the odds were slim.

Dakota studied her. "This is about your past." She wasn't asking a question. "You're not worried you won't find someone and fall in love. You've already decided you don't want to try."

Charlie gently rocked the baby. "Your psychology degree can be annoying."

"You're not the first person to tell me that. I'm not prying."

Charlie looked at her. "You can't pry. I came to you. I'm not mad. I just . . ." She looked past her to the flowers reaching for the sun. The garden was beautiful. Alive. Safe.

"I want to be like everyone else," she murmured. "You know. Normal. But that's not going to happen. I'm not that girl. Which means I look for alternatives. Like adoption."

She glanced back at her friend, half expecting Dakota to scold her. Instead the other woman smiled.

"Makes sense. You've always been the type to take charge of your destiny. This is one more way of doing that. There are a lot of considerations when you're adopting a child."

"I know," Charlie said quickly. "My work. I'm gone twenty-four hours at a time. That's going to be tough. But I'm already talking to people about day care. I'd get someone to live in. Or take the baby to someone's house."

Dakota grinned. "Okay, I was actually talking about the reality of a single woman adopting. But sure, dealing with day care is important too."

"You adopted when you were single."

Dakota smiled at her daughter. "I did. I went international because I thought I'd have more luck. I have information on the organization and the orphanage, if you want it. One thing to consider is age. Do you want an infant or an older child? If you want a child over five or six, I would suggest you look in this country first. There are a lot of kids available to adopt. The odds go up if you're not picky about ethnicity. You could also start as a foster parent. You know, for practice. In addition, there are private adoptions. However, I think you'll have more trouble competing directly with couples."

"I've thought about that, too," Charlie admitted. "I hadn't thought of an older child." That might be better for her. Once a child could walk and talk, he or she would seem less breakable. Plus, the kid could tell her when she was messing up. That could be good.

"I need to think about this more," she said, staring down at Jordan Taylor. "It's complicated."

"But worth it," Dakota told her, hugging Hannah. "Aren't you, baby girl?"

Hannah squealed and fell back into her mother's arms. They tumbled onto the grass, Dakota tickling her daughter, who shrieked with delight.

Charlie watched them and knew she would figure out a way to have a family of her own. And if that family didn't include a man, that was going to be okay, too.

■ ■ ■ ■

Annabelle hung on to the saddle and did her best not to scream. "I can't," she said, hoping she didn't look as scared as she felt.

"You're perfectly safe. You're not going to fall."

"Easy for you to say," she told Shane. "You're standing on the ground. I know. We'll trade. You sit up here while Khatar stands on his back feet and I'll watch. Then I for sure won't fall."

Shane turned away, but not before she saw him smile.

"You think this is funny?" she demanded. "It's not. Nothing about you trying to kill me is funny."

"I'm not trying to kill you. I was giving the dance a fancy finish. I thought the crowd would like it."

"No. What the crowd would like is me cutting out your heart. Let's practice that."

"I'm not your male sacrifice."

"You seem to be heading in that direction."

"Annabelle, you're a good horsewoman. You have to have a little faith in yourself."

"I do. It's gravity I'm not so keen on."

She didn't understand. Somewhere between the last time she'd seen him and today, Shane had lost his mind. He'd started talking about what he'd been working on for the festival and how Khatar would rise up on his back legs right before the male sacrifice. Which sounded great. Until she'd realized she was supposed to be on the horse's back when he did it.

"Do you know how high up I am already?" she asked.

"You'll be fine."

"You're right. Because I'm not going to do it."

Shane had removed his hat. It sat on the top of a post. So she could see his whole face, including the amusement dancing in his dark eyes.

"Just once. To try."

"No!"

She should have known something was up when she'd seen that Khatar was already saddled. Half the time she rode the horse bareback.

"Think of the children," he said quietly. "The children who don't get to read all winter. And the shut-ins. Albert and Albus."

"Albert and Alfred," she corrected automatically. "You're not going to make me feel guilty."

"Want to bet?"

She glared at him, but dammit, he was right. She did have a responsibility and a big finish to the dance would help bring in more money. Maybe even get people talking enough that they wanted to see the dance again next year, thereby ensuring an income stream.

Her already upset stomach made a few threatening noises, but stayed in place. She glanced around, looking for escape. Only there wasn't anywhere to go.

"I should have said I'd ride Priscilla," she murmured. "That would be easier."

"You're going to be fine. Khatar will do all the work. You're just along for the ride. What if you like it?"

"Why do you suddenly sound like a teen-age boy trying to convince me to have sex?"

He laughed. "That would be your twisted mind at work, not mine. Come on. Grab hold of the saddle. Use both hands, if you want. You'll feel better. Just don't let the reins hang. We don't want Khatar tripping."

"You got that right," she said, reaching for the front of the saddle. She gripped it as tightly as she could, then squeezed her legs for good measure and tried not to close her eyes.

"Good." Shane turned his attention to the horse. "All right, big guy. You can do it."

He led the horse through the steps, then moved back. "Tug back and up. Like I showed you. But not too hard."

She whimpered as she did as he instructed. Khatar took two steps to the right, then left, finishing by rising up on his rear legs.

It was as if the back of the world fell away. One second gravity was her friend, the next she was in danger of tumbling out of the saddle, most likely to her death. She did her best not to scream, while holding on with hands and thighs.

Khatar hung suspended for what felt like six or eight years before landing lightly on all four feet, then taking a slight bow. When he was still, she released the breath she'd been holding and leaned forward to hug him.

"You're very talented," she told the horse. "Let's never do that again."

Shane walked over and patted Khatar's shoulder, then reached for her.

"See," he said triumphantly. "Nothing to it. You did good."

"Yes, not getting dead is always a victory." She swung her leg over the side of the horse and slid to the ground.

When her feet hit, her knees buckled. Shane caught her easily and drew her against him. She hung on, both because touching him was always nice and also because she was still shaking.

"You okay?" he asked, frowning at her.

"What part of 'I was scared' is confusing to you?"

He touched her cheek. "I meant it, Annabelle. I wouldn't let anything bad happen to you."

"Sure. You say that now."

She stopped talking, mostly because she couldn't remember the rest of what she wanted to say.

His dark gaze locked with hers. She knew he was going to kiss her about two heartbeats before his mouth touched hers. His lips claimed hers with a gentle insistence. Immediately heat surged through her, making her toes curl in her boots and her insides start to melt. His arms came around her, drawing her close, and she went willingly into his embrace.

She loved the feel of all his muscles, she thought hazily, tilting her head and letting her eyes drift closed. He was a man who worked hard for a living and it showed. His strength protected those he cared about.

A really interesting intellectual subject for later, she thought as his tongue touched her bottom lip and she parted for him. But right now, the kissing was far more important.

She gave herself over to the erotic dance of their kisses. She met him stroke for stroke, enjoying the fire that followed. She leaned in more, wanting to feel her breasts against his chest. Between her thighs she was both hot and swollen. Ready.

Something hard bumped her from the side. She broke the kiss as she staggered to her left. When she turned, she saw Khatar glaring at both of them.

"Oops," she said, patting the horse's shoulder. "Was that uncomfortable to watch? Sorry. We should be more sensitive."

"Horses don't kiss," Shane told her.

"All the more reason for us not to do that in front of him." She leaned toward Khatar. "We'll be more careful next time," she promised in a whisper. "Don't tell you-know-who."

"I can hear you," Shane told her, sounding more amused than exasperated.

She smiled at him. "I have no idea what you're talking about."

"You're crazy. You know that, right?"

"I've heard rumors."

He shook his head, then put his arm around her. "Come on. I'll take off his saddle and you can brush him. That will make him feel better."

"You're a very good horse parent."
"Owner. I own him."
"Don't say that. You'll hurt his feelings."
"He already knows."

Chapter Thirteen

Annabelle's good mood lasted through the rest of the morning. Khatar enjoyed his grooming and she enjoyed talking to Shane. Now she headed home, prepared to shower and change, then go to the library for a few hours of paperwork. She wasn't technically on the schedule, but sometimes she preferred to simply get work done on her own time.

She pulled into her driveway about two seconds before she saw the Mercedes parked on the street. Lewis, she thought, the lingering effects of Shane's kiss deflating like a popped balloon.

She climbed out of her car and waited while Lewis got out of his.

She remembered when she'd first met him. How impressed she'd been by his intelligence and his worldliness. He'd traveled, met interesting people, knew obscure facts about countries she'd barely heard about.

She'd loved how he'd been a writer — someone who could take an idea, thoughts, and turn them into a story that could make her laugh and cry and check under her bed to make sure no one was lurking there, waiting to kill her. She'd mistaken admiration for love. Probably because she hadn't known what love should feel like.

They'd both been at fault, she thought sadly. Lewis had wanted to be adored and she'd wanted to be rescued. Neither of them had actually wanted the work of being married.

Now she watched Lewis approach. He was a handsome man, in a controlled, urban kind of way. He didn't have Shane's rough edges or muscles. He was the kind of man you went to an art museum with, whereas Shane . . . wasn't.

"You should be hearing from your lawyer shortly," he said when he was a few feet away.

"The divorce is final?"

He nodded.

"That's good news."

"Is it?"

She saw the sadness in his eyes. And the questions. Aware that her neighbors were attentive at best and nosy at worst, she led the way to her front door.

Once in her small living room, she motioned for him to take a seat. She settled across from him, in an oversize chair. She knew that good manners dictated that she offer him something to eat or drink, but she couldn't quite bring herself to say the words. Encouraging Lewis didn't seem like a good idea.

He studied her for a minute or so, then spoke. "This is what you want?"

She wasn't sure if he was asking a question. "The divorce? Yes. It's what I want."

"Because you're with Shane."

With him? Not in the way Lewis meant. "There were unfixable problems in our marriage," she said instead.

He leaned forward and laced his fingers together. His pale gaze settled on her face. "I miss you, Annabelle."

"I'm sorry," she said automatically.

"Are you? Do you think of me at all? Or have you completely moved on?"

Okay, the conversation had officially shifted to awkward. "We've been apart longer than we were together," she began. "I've made a life for myself here. I'm happy."

"I see. What if I said I'd changed? That I was willing to compromise?"

"I think that it's for the best that we don't revisit the past," she said gently.

"You don't believe me."

"That you've changed?" She shrugged. "I don't know. I think growing as a person is a good thing. But would it make me want to try again? No. I'm sorry."

"We were good together," he insisted. "Don't you remember?"

What she remembered was never feeling enough for him. That his words could be cruel. "You wanted me to be like a china doll," she said slowly. "Something to occupy you when you had time. Something to show off."

"No, that's not true. I might have been a little demanding, but as I said, I'm different now. I've learned how to be more of a partner. There must be things you miss."

She stood. "Lewis, I appreciate you letting me know about the paperwork on the divorce. It's final now and we can both move on. It's for the best."

He rose. "You're simply going to walk away? Just like that? Without trying at all?"

It wasn't in her nature to be cruel. She would go out of her way not to hurt his feelings, but he was starting to bug her. She drew in a breath.

"This entire conversation is an example of why I left," she said quietly, knowing that getting angry wouldn't accomplish anything.

"I've told you what I want, what is important to me, and you aren't interested. You're pushing back without consideration for anyone but yourself. When you don't like what I say, you tell me I'm wrong and then you try to make me feel guilty. I'm not wrong and I won't take responsibility for how you feel now. We're divorced. I'm not proud of that, but I accept it. I've moved on and you need to do the same."

She braced herself for the explosion. Lewis didn't like being told he was at fault and he rarely reacted well when that happened. But instead of getting angry, Lewis seemed to shrink a little.

"I see," he murmured. "It's truly over."

"Yes."

He stared at her, then turned toward the door. "Goodbye, Annabelle."

"Goodbye."

"You'll regret this, you know. Regret losing me."

She pressed her lips together and waited until he left.

She walked to the window and watched him drive away. With a little luck, he would leave town and she wouldn't see him again.

When they'd first met, she had been so sure he would be the one to rescue her. Since then, she'd learned the only person who could take on that job was herself. She had learned the painful lesson in the weeks after she'd left him, when she'd been alone and scared and emotionally broken.

Time and hard work had healed her. Now she was ready for a real relationship between equals. Someone who loved her as much as . . . She smiled. Someone who adored her with the same devotion as Khatar. Without being a horse.

She wanted that to be Shane. He was smart, funny, sensible and calm. His biggest flaw was comparing her to his ex-wife. She knew she wasn't anything like her, but she wasn't the one who needed convincing. Until he saw the difference, she would have to be careful about protecting her heart. Because she was determined not to make a mistake again. This time, when she gave her heart, it was going to be forever.

"You gotta stop," Shane said, not looking up from the bottle he shook. "I mean it. Get back to where you belong."

The riding horses he'd reluctantly taken possession of had come with their own tack. All the leather was in decent shape, but old and dirty. He'd decided to take the afternoon and clean everything. Not only to keep it in good working order, but because, well, his students were girls. Not that he would admit that to anyone, even under threat of torture.

So he'd lined up the equipment by the barn, set up a comfortable work station in the shade of one of the big trees and prepared to spend a few hours listening to the Dodgers-Giants game on the radio.

Sometime into his second hour, he'd become aware he wasn't alone anymore. A small brown nose had poked its way under his arm, much like a dog wanting to be patted. Only it wasn't a dog. It was the damn pony, Reno.

Khatar's ability to escape from nearly any enclosure had been passed on to Reno. Or maybe the pony had shown up with the ability. Shane wasn't sure, but he didn't like it. Worse, when Reno got out, he was careful to make sure his girl tagged along. Which meant not only was the small pony loose, but an elephant was now strolling around the property.

"Explain to me why the only one who stays where she's supposed to is the cat," Shane muttered, putting down the leather cleaner and staring at the pony.

Reno curled back his lips in what Shane could only assume was silent equine laughter.

"I get it," Shane said. "You think you're tough stuff, don't you. A new girlfriend and an instant cat family. You're practically the quarterback of the football team."

Reno butted Shane in response.

"Annoying twit horse," he muttered, scratching the animal behind the ears.

He got up and walked toward the barn. There was a new shed on the other side. One with a metal door, secured by an industrial strength padlock. It wasn't kept locked with a key . . . yet. So far the twisting metal mechanism had proven to be animal secure, but Shane was fully prepared to use a key if necessary.

He went inside and shoved a couple of apples in his pockets, then picked up two watermelons and walked out. Reno trotted right behind him, already sniffing at his jeans.

"Get away," he grumbled.

Priscilla stopped exploring the flower garden and strolled along, back toward the enclosure. Reno glanced over his shoulder, as if making sure his lady love kept up. They walked back into their home and faced Shane.

"I mean it," he told them. "This has got to stop. Don't make me get a more complicated gate and lock. I will if I have to."

They stared at him with shared amusement. Shane sighed.

"Back in Tennessee all I had to worry about was fifty or so racehorses," he told them. "That was easy. You guys are hard."

He lowered the watermelons to the ground, then took out one of the apples and used his pocketknife to slice it and feed it to Reno. While he did that, Priscilla delicately picked up the watermelon and chopped it.

"That's quite a collection you have there."

Shane turned toward the voice and saw Lewis approaching. At the sight of Annabelle's ex, he felt his hackles rise and wished they were keeping something more aggressive than a small pony and a few goats on the grounds. Idly, he wondered if Priscilla was in the mood to charge.

Reno ate the last of the apple. Shane gave him a quick pat, then let himself out and secured the gate.

"Annabelle's not here," he told Lewis, leading the way back to the house.

"I know. I saw her earlier. At her place." Lewis adjusted his sunglasses. "I'm going back to North Carolina."

"Because the divorce is final?"

Lewis turned away. "Yes. Because the divorce is final."

Shane could almost feel sorry for the guy.

He'd obviously had second thoughts about losing Annabelle. He'd shown up, hoping to win her back. Although from his point of view, Lewis hadn't done all that much to make himself the good guy in all this. A woman like Annabelle had to be wooed. Made to feel special.

"She wanted me to stay," Lewis said, glancing back at him.

Shane couldn't see the other man's eyes. His sunglasses were in the way. But he would bet a considerable amount of money they were shifting all over the place, proof of the lie.

"Did she?" Shane asked.

"Thought we should get back together. She said she'd regretted the divorce. I considered the offer. I mean, who wouldn't? She's an amazing woman. But fool me once and all that. She's really not . . ." He looked away again. "I'm done with her. In case you were wondering."

He wanted to point out Annabelle hadn't seemed like she was regretting anything except having Lewis show up in the first place, but where was the win in that? Kicking a man who was already down wasn't his idea of sport.

"She gets under your skin," Lewis said quietly. "Once she's there, she's hard to get rid of." He cleared his throat. "I won't say I wasn't tempted, but this is for the best. That's what I wanted to tell you."

"I appreciate the information."

Lewis gave a brief wave and walked to his car.

Shane watched him go. He wasn't sure why Lewis had stopped by. It wasn't to gloat. After all, he hadn't gotten what he'd come for. Maybe the other man didn't have any friends and he'd needed to share the loss with someone. Even if the information had been cloaked in lies.

Heidi came out of the back of the house. "Was that Lewis?"

"Yes. He's heading back to North Carolina."

"Good," his future sister-in-law said. "Annabelle wasn't happy to have him show up. You know that, right?"

"I figured it out."

"I'm glad he's gone."

"Me, too."

Annabelle sipped her latte. "How many?" she asked.

Nevada rolled her eyes. "Five. Can you believe it? Five puppies. If I didn't love my sister, I would so be killing her. Do you know how many times a night Tucker and I have to get up to feed them?"

"How old are they?"

"Six weeks. Thank goodness. The first week was the worst. They were so tiny then. Only three weeks old. Now they're bigger and Cameron —" She paused to sip her iced Frappuccino. "Cameron says we can start transitioning them to regular food this week. I'm checking their teeth. Making sure there are enough for them to handle the kibble. Which I'm soaking in hot water."

"They must be adorable."

"They are," Nevada admitted. "Come see them."

"I don't think that's a good idea."

"Afraid you'll want one?"

"More than a little."

"Tell me about it," Nevada said with a grin. "Tucker and I are doing our best not to keep any of them. That's the danger of fostering an animal. You get attached. Plus, they're puppies. How am I supposed to resist? I tell myself it's good practice for when we have a baby. At least now I know what it's like to get up several times a night for feeding."

The puppies' mother had developed a fatal infection and died. Montana had roped her sister into caring for the litter until they were old enough for "forever" homes.

"I think a couple of my guys are thinking about adopting them," Nevada told her. "I've been taking them to work with me, which is great. I get help with the feeding and there are plenty of volunteers to play with them. These are incredibly socialized puppies."

Heidi walked into the Starbucks and waved. "Let me order and I'll be right there."

Heidi had called earlier to say she was running into town for groceries. She'd wanted to know if Annabelle had time for a quick coffee. Annabelle had run into Nevada on her way over and had invited her along.

Heidi collected her latte and joined them. They sat by an open window, the light afternoon breeze just cool enough to be pleasant.

"How are the wedding plans?" Nevada asked. "Have you reached the crazy stage?"

"Yes. I'm frantic." Heidi touched Annabelle's arm. "I have help, so that's good. I can't imagine what it was like for you and your sisters. A triple wedding? On New Year's Eve?"

Nevada smiled. "It was a lot to organize, but there were the three of us and our mom, so that helped."

"I'd be lost without Annabelle and Charlie," Heidi admitted.

"I'm happy to help," Annabelle told her sincerely. "I'm less sure about Charlie's motivation but she's good at intimidating people and that can come in handy."

"She got me a great price on the tents," Heidi said. "I have a dress. There are a few more details, then it's just the work part. You know, counting heads as people RSVP, that kind of thing."

"We're here to help," Annabelle told her.

"I know. Thanks."

"The shower is in a couple of weeks," Nevada said. "I got my save-the-date card tucked into my calendar."

"We're planning lots of fun and special stuff," Annabelle said with a laugh.

"Are there going to be games?" Nevada asked casually. She picked up her latte, then sighed. "Okay, I'll admit it. I love the games. Especially the one with all the stuff on the tray you have to memorize. Or coming up with words from the spelling of the bride's and groom's names? Silly, but they're fun."

"I'm surprised," Annabelle said. "And delighted. There will be games and champagne."

"The little Jordan almonds?" Heidi asked. "Can I put in a request?"

"You bet. In your wedding colors. Only

the best for the bride-to-be."

She and Charlie had a planning meeting tomorrow. Annabelle made a mental note to mention the games and Jordan almonds.

Heidi looked at Nevada. "How's work? I drove by the construction site the other day. I can't believe how much has been done on the casino and hotel."

"The grand opening is next spring. I'm not much of a gambler, so I'm not that interested in the casino, but I can tell you the hotel is beautiful. The spa is going to be gorgeous. I might have to try it out for something." Nevada ran her hands through her short hair. "Maybe extensions."

Annabelle grinned. "That'll be the day."

"It would shock Tucker, that's for sure. He likes my low-maintenance style."

Annabelle had seen Tucker look at his new wife and knew the word *like* didn't come close. He was a man who was well and truly in love. When Nevada was around, the rest of the world didn't exist. Which was as it should be, she thought with only a tiny bit of envy.

"Speaking of husbands," Heidi said and raised her eyebrows. "Guess who stopped by the ranch yesterday?"

They both looked at her.

Heidi turned to Annabelle. "Lewis."

Annabelle groaned. "My ex," she explained to Nevada. "He's been in town for a few days. There was a legal complication with the divorce." She drew in a breath. "I heard he stopped by the ranch on the way out of town."

"I know that he talked with Shane for a couple of minutes. Then Lewis left."

Annabelle didn't like the sound of that. Not Lewis with Shane or her having to find out what he'd been discussing.

A couple of older women entered. Nevada waved at them, then leaned back in her chair. "Does anyone else think it's strange that in a town like Fool's Gold we don't have one of those cute local coffee places? Not that I don't love Starbucks, but don't you think we need one?"

"We do," Heidi agreed. "Maybe a coffeehouse art gallery."

Annabelle grinned. "Or a place that has poetry readings."

"Really bad poetry," Nevada added.

"Of course. It's the best kind. Or performance art. A woman brushing her hair for an hour or someone setting up a plant we could all watch grow."

They laughed together.

"Don't say anything to Mayor Marsha," Nevada advised. "Trust me. The second she gets the idea that you're the right person for the job, she'll be on you and you won't stand a chance."

"I'm a believer," Annabelle said. "Shane had no plans to teach those girls to ride horses and now he has horses for them and is scheduling regular lessons. It's pretty funny."

"She has more power than any of us can imagine," Nevada said. "You have to respect that."

Heidi and Nevada continued to talk about the mayor, but Annabelle found herself caught up in thoughts of Shane. He had resisted the horseback riding lessons, but in the end, he'd surrendered to the inevitable. The irony was, he was good with the girls. Patient and gentle with their delicate sensibilities. For all his macho attitude and developed muscles, he was kind of a pushover and she found she liked that in a guy.

With her divorce final and Lewis gone, maybe she and Shane could look forward to a little quiet time together. A chance to get to know each other better. Maybe in a room with a big bed and a lock on the door, she thought with a smile.

He was special, the kind of man worth hanging on to. She knew he was attracted to her. More important, he liked her. Now all she had to do was make sure there weren't any more surprises.

CHAPTER FOURTEEN

"Relax," Shane said patiently.

Annabelle tried to loosen her grip on the saddle. The good news was these days she was able to hang on with only one hand instead of both. That was progress.

She enjoyed the dance Shane had choreographed for Khatar. The steps were mostly easy, with swoops to the side and a couple of spins. It was the big finish, with the stallion coming up on his back legs, that still made her sweat. If only he weren't so tall. She didn't think having Reno make the same move would be so frightening.

"Okay," she said, and drew in a deep breath. "Let's go through it."

Shane gave a three-tone whistle. As soon as she heard the sound, Annabelle nudged Khatar into place. The stallion knew what came next and easily worked through the steps. She guided him into a quick turn to the left, one more to the right and gripped him hard with her thighs as he rose into the air.

She leaned forward, going with the movement rather than fighting it, and tightened her stomach muscles to keep her from falling back. Her right hand held the reins and her left hovered over the saddle. At the last second, she raised her left arm so her fingers were nearly shoulder level. Khatar returned all four hooves to the ground and she shouted a cheer.

"Did you see?" she asked Shane as she patted the stallion. "I didn't hold on."

"I saw. That was great. You'll do even better next time."

She glanced at him. "Now you're treating me like one of your students."

"You *are* one of my students."

"You know what I mean. You get that teacher voice."

"You don't like my teacher voice?"

"I've had your tongue in my mouth, so no."

He crossed to her and helped her down. She slid to the ground and turned to face him, only to find him standing very close.

"No teacher crushes in high school?" he asked, his dark eyes crinkling with amusement.

"My teachers were all women, Shane.

What about you?"

"Oh, my eleventh grade algebra teacher was hot," he admitted. "Married, but hot." He lightly touched her cheek. "About my tongue in your mouth . . ."

She grinned. "Yes?"

He glanced past her. "Maybe later. You know how he gets."

She turned and patted the horse. "Are you jealous, Khatar? Not to worry. I love you best."

"Figures," Shane said. "Beaten by a horse."

"He's prettier than you. I'm sorry to be the one to tell you that, but it's the truth. He's one handsome guy."

Later, when Khatar was back in his corral, Shane walked her to her car.

"What's your schedule like at the library?" he asked. "Could you get a couple of days off?"

She leaned against her door. "That could be arranged. Why?"

"Deadline's Dream is in a race in Del Mar on Saturday. I was going to go down and watch him run. I'd like you to come with me."

"The Del Mar racetrack?"

"That's the one. Have you been? It's one of my favorite places to go."

302

Excitement started at her toes and worked its way up. Tingles joined in and she did her best not to break into the happy dance.

"I haven't been. It's by San Diego, isn't it?"

"Yes. It'll take us most of the day to get there. I thought we'd drive down on Friday, spend Saturday watching the races, then head back Sunday."

A weekend away. With Shane. In a hotel. Her day was getting better by the second. She'd been thinking she should ask Shane what Lewis had said when he stopped by earlier in the week, but suddenly that wasn't important. Shane wanted to spend the weekend with her. Alone.

"I know a great hotel," he said. "On the water." He shifted his weight from foot to foot. "I'm not assuming anything. We'll get two rooms."

"Will we?" she asked, doing her best not to smile.

"If that's what you want."

"Nice to know." She gazed into his eyes. "And if it's not what I want?"

He cleared his throat. "That would be good, too."

"Just good? Not better than good?"

He cupped her face in his hands and bent down to kiss her. His mouth was hot and demanding, pressing against hers in a way that left her breathless.

"Better than good," he murmured as he straightened.

Her heart pounded hard in her chest. Need made her insides clench. The man had a way about him, she thought hazily.

"Then one room should be plenty," she told him.

"I'll pick you up at eight Friday morning," he told her.

"I'll be waiting."

"I've never planned a bridal shower," Charlie whispered as she leaned across the table. "Or been to one. Should I have gotten a book or something?"

"You'll do fine," Annabelle told her. "Think of it as a regular party."

"Because I host so many of those?"

Annabelle handed her a pad of paper. "Okay, then think of it as we're having a bunch of Heidi's friends over for dinner. The good news is, we're not even cooking." One of the advantages of taking over the newly opened banquet room at Jo's Bar was the cooking would be done by someone else.

"That I can handle," Charlie said. "But what about the rest of it? Mayor Marsha stopped by and asked about games. I don't know any games."

Annabelle did her best to hide her smile. "Don't forget the Jordan almonds. Heidi said she wanted those for sure."

"What the hell is a Jordan almond?"

Annabelle laughed. "How about this? We'll order the food and the cake and the champagne today. We'll go get the decorations and party favors next week. I'll handle the games and you can order the flowers. Nothing fancy, just a nice arrangement for each table."

"I'm free Saturday. Want to go then?"

"I'm, ah, going out of town this weekend."

Charlie stared at her. "Since when?"

"Since yesterday. I'm doing to Del Mar."

"Aren't we fancy?" Charlie reached for her lemonade, then stopped. "Isn't there a racetrack in Del Mar?"

"I've heard there is."

"Doesn't Shane own racehorses?"

Annabelle batted her lashes. "He might."

"You're going away with him for the weekend."

She wasn't sure if Charlie sounded outraged or impressed. Either would work.

"Yes," she said in a low, conspiratorial voice. "I'm spending the weekend with a gentleman friend."

"Interesting. So things are going well with

the gentleman friend."

"They are. I like Shane. He's a good guy, which is rare."

"Tell me about it," Charlie said with a growl.

Annabelle drew in a breath. "Oh, no. I'm sorry. Does talking about this bother you?"

Charlie rolled her eyes. "No. I'm jealous, not upset or hurt. Okay, not jealous because, no offense, Shane doesn't do it for me. It's just you're going away with a guy. It's no big deal." She smiled. "I don't mean that in a slutty way."

"No offense taken."

"Good." Charlie drew in a breath. "You're normal. Sometimes I would like to be normal, too."

Annabelle knew that Charlie's first time had been so traumatizing, she'd yet to make a second attempt. "Have you talked to anyone about what happened?"

"I'm talking to you."

"I mean —"

"I know what you mean," Charlie said quickly. "A therapist. Yes. A few years ago. It didn't help."

"Did you give her a chance or did you get pissed off during the first session and never go back?"

Charlie sniffed. "I went to two sessions

before she pissed me off."

"As long as you didn't give up."

Her friend picked up her lemonade, then put it back down. "Fine. Maybe I should talk to someone. But not right now. When I get home, I have to go online and figure out what a Jordan almond is."

The Del Mar Oceania Resort was one of those gated places with plenty of lush foliage and a guard. Shane pulled up behind a Lexus.

"You think if we'd brought my truck they would have turned us away?" he asked with a grin.

"Very possibly," Annabelle said, trying not to look too impressed by the luxury villas she spotted just inside the fence line.

Instead of driving his truck, Shane had "borrowed" his brother's car. Not Rafe's, which would have involved simply asking. Nope, he'd taken Clay's brand-new Cadillac CTS-V coupe, a fancy two-door model with enough power to leave mere mortal cars in the dust. Or so it had seemed when Shane had demonstrated the car's speed on a relatively quiet part of the interstate.

"You sure Clay is going to be okay with this?" she asked, running her hands along the smooth leather seats.

Shane grinned. "My baby brother asked me to take good care of his car and I am."

"I think he meant for you to park it in the garage, not drive it to San Diego."

"Details."

Shane drove forward and gave his name to the guard, who checked a list, then waved him through. They followed the main drive around the villas and pulled up in front of the hotel.

The car was instantly swarmed by uniformed employees. One opened Annabelle's car door and welcomed her to the Del Mar Oceania Resort. Another collected luggage, while a third took the keys from Shane and handed him a small card in return.

Palm trees and tropical flowers provided lush landscape. Annabelle inhaled the scent of jasmine and honeysuckle. She could hear running water, but couldn't see the pond or stream. The air was just warm enough to be pleasant, but not too hot and smelled sweet, with a hint of the ocean.

They walked into the hotel. The lobby was large, with lots of big windows and plenty of open space. The tropical theme continued, in an understated elegant kind of way. A bellman trailed after them with their luggage.

Check-in took only a few minutes, then

they were on their way upstairs in the elevator. Annabelle found herself fighting unexpected nerves as she followed the cart down the hall to a door at the end. Anticipation battled with the reality of going away with a man. She hadn't done that since her marriage and look how that had turned out.

Still, this was Shane. He was always sweet to her and she should remember that. As to the fact that they would be sharing a bed, that was only good news.

The bellman pushed open the door and stepped back to allow them to enter. Shane rested his hand on the small of her back and guided her inside.

Her first impression was that there had to have been a mistake. This couldn't be a hotel room.

They'd stepped into a living room larger than her entire house. There was a balcony with a view of the Pacific, two sofas, a couple of smaller chairs and a dining table over to the left. Fresh flowers spilled from half a dozen vases, lightly scenting the air.

"The bedroom is this way," the bellman said, pointing to the right.

She went through the open double door to find an equally large bed in the center of a huge space. Another balcony offered an impressive view of the sparkling blue water.

She wandered around the bed to the bathroom that was all done in marble, with double sinks, a walk-in shower and a tub for maybe six. While she recognized the name on the carefully packaged bath products, she'd only ever seen them in magazines.

She'd been expecting a basic kind of room, maybe with a little sofa by the window. Not the latest version of "Rich people in Del Mar." She waited until the bellman had left before turning to Shane.

"It's a little unexpected," she told him.

He grinned. "I asked for a nice room with a view. They listened."

"Impressive."

"Intimidating?" he asked.

"A little."

He moved toward her. "Remember, I'm the guy who takes care of horses and an elephant. But every once in a while, it's good to mix things up."

He was also a successful, wealthy businessman. Something easy to forget when he was surrounded by those horses and that elephant.

"You're a little more complicated than you seem, Shane Stryker," she murmured.

"In a good way?"

"The best way."

He moved closer, or maybe she did. Suddenly the size of the room didn't matter and the view was a whole lot less interesting than the man taking her in his arms. What appealed to her most was the feel of him, the strength and the heat. The way he held her and how he claimed her mouth in a kiss she never wanted to end.

She tilted her head and parted her lips, wanting him to deepen the kiss. He obliged with a sweep of his tongue. She sank into him, resting her fingertips on his shoulders, as much to be close to him as to stay standing.

His tongue brushed against hers. She circled, teasing him. The intimate kiss sent alerts to nerve endings throughout her body. Low in her belly, she felt heat and pressure. Need circulated everywhere. The room itself seemed to retreat until there was only this man and how he aroused her.

He moved his hands up and down her back. She'd worn a sundress and high-heeled sandals. When he moved against the zipper, her stomach clenched. But he didn't lower it. Instead he rested his hands on her hips.

She found herself wanting to nudge him higher or lower. Either would work. Or kiss her more. Or take off his clothes. Anything.

She must have transmitted her eagerness because he pulled back slightly and chuckled.

"Impatient?" he asked before lightly kissing her jaw.

"A little."

"I was trying to take it slow. You know, be the good guy."

He kissed and nibbled his way down her neck. Everywhere he touched, she felt shivers and desire.

"Being good is highly overrated," she whispered, arching her head back so he could do more.

"If you're sure."

"I'm sure."

For a second nothing happened. Then he put his hands on her shoulders and drew her close again. When he kissed her this time, there was no teasing, no gentle seduction. He plunged into her mouth with a force that left her breathless. His hands moved unerringly to her zipper and had it down in less than a second. With one quick tug, the dress fluttered to her feet. His fingers unfastened her bra just as quickly, then his hands were on her bare breasts.

She couldn't seem to catch her breath, but that was okay. Given the choice between what he was doing to her and breathing, she didn't have a tough decision to make.

As they kissed, she met him stroke for stroke, but concentrating was difficult. Especially with the way he touched her breasts. He explored every inch of her, then turned his attention to her tight nipples. He caressed them, rubbing, squeezing, teasing, until he'd created a direct line between them and the very center of her being.

She was already swollen. She could tell by the heavy, aching sensation that pulsed in time with her rapid heartbeat. Anticipation quickened her blood. She wanted more.

She drew back enough to nip his bottom lip. Shane responded with a quick laugh, then bent down and gathered her in his arms. The unexpected lack of contact with solid ground had her clutching at him. One sandal went flying and she managed to kick the other off before he deposited her in the center of the bed.

He knelt over her, tenderly brushing her hair from her face.

"You're so beautiful," he murmured, before leaning down to take her left nipple in his mouth.

Her eyes sank closed as she got lost in the sensation of wet heat and swirling tongue. He licked and sucked, drawing her breast deeply into his mouth. She grabbed his shoulders, half rising into a sitting position. He switched to her other breast, repeating his tender ministrations before reaching for the tiny bikini panties she'd worn.

The scrap of silk and lace that had in fact cost more than her dress slipped down her legs. He tossed it away and shifted so he was kneeling between her legs. She parted her thighs more, watching him watch her.

"Take your time," he whispered, then parted her swollen center with his fingers before bending down and kissing her intimately.

The first long, slow stroke of his tongue had her digging her heels into the bed. The second had her pushing her hips toward him, wanting — no, needing — so much more of this. Her breath caught as she got lost in what he was doing to her.

He moved purposefully, setting up a steady rhythm designed to make her lose control. He kissed her sensitive center, circling around and over, then did it again and again. Everything felt so perfect, she thought, aware of her body straining toward release even as she tried to hold back and make it last.

It had been like this before. Him taking control of her body, carrying her along until there was nothing for her to do but accept the ride. She was —

He moved his hand. Fingers pushed inside of her, then withdrew, mimicking the act of love. The added sensation made her groan. He repeated the action, this time curling his fingers slightly, finding that one spot deep inside of her. As if he were caressing her clit from both sides. She pushed toward him, needing all of what he offered.

Control was impossible. If he did that again, if he continued to touch her like that . . .

She came with a scream. Pleasure poured through her as she shuddered her release. He continued to touch her with his tongue, his fingers moving in and out. She convulsed around him, tightening and straining, every muscle contracting as her orgasm went on and on. When she was finally done, he settled next to her, his large hand splayed across her stomach.

She waited for her heart to return to something like normal, then turned her head and opened her eyes. Shane watched her, his dark gaze bright with passion and satisfaction.

"You're good at that," she whispered.

"You inspire me."

She reached for him, but he caught her hands in his.

"Not so fast."

She glanced down at the erection straining against his jeans, then back at his face.

He grinned. "I'm not saying I don't want to, but I thought we could have champagne first." He motioned to the bottle resting in a silver ice bucket. "If you wouldn't mind bringing it, I'll open it."

There was something about the way he was looking at her. Something provocative. As if he had specific expectations about what was about to happen.

"I don't understand."

"I'd like you to get the champagne. Naked."

She raised her eyebrows. "As the champagne isn't wearing clothes, is this about me walking across the room without my clothes on?"

"Oh, yeah."

She wanted to offer a disclaimer about her thighs and very possibly her butt, but this wasn't the time. Besides, the man had already seen her naked. If he didn't like the view, he wouldn't have asked for more of it.

She got out of bed and walked around to the other side. As she approached the ice bucket, she decided if this was what he wanted, she would give him the best she had. She moved behind the ice bucket and faced him.

"This champagne?" she asked, lightly touching the top of the bottle.

"That's the one."

"What about the ice?" She picked up a small square of ice and held it in her hand. "Want this?"

Interest sparked in his eyes. "What are you suggesting?"

She pressed the ice against her throat and slowly ran it down to her belly. The ice was freezing and immediately began to melt. Water dripped down between her breasts. Her already hard nipples tightened even more.

Shane sat up and began to unfasten his shirt. He worked quickly, his gaze never leaving her.

"Anything else?" he asked, ripping off his shirt. He moved to the side of the bed and pulled off his boots and socks.

She wasn't sure what to do next. Her lone experience with porn had been a badly done movie she and her friends had watched in college and, honestly, she hadn't seen the point. She knew men were visual, so maybe some kind of sexy dance. Only she wasn't the sexy dance type. Maybe she could try the dance of the happy virgin or something.

Pathetic, she thought, getting desperate

and cupping her breasts. She really needed to do some research on the subject. With Shane, it could be fun.

She'd barely raised her breasts in her hands, when Shane was on his feet and his jeans and briefs were falling. He crossed the room in two long strides, and grabbed her wrists. He had her back on the bed before she could catch her breath. Then the condom was on and he was inside of her.

He pushed in deeply, groaning quietly, his entire body tense. All of ten seconds later, he was done. She blinked up at him.

"Really?" she asked before she could stop herself.

"Sorry."

"No, it's fine. I'm just surprised."

He pulled out and rolled off her. She shifted toward him, supporting her head on her hand.

"Shane?"

He grimaced. "I'm like a teenager. It's what you were doing. I couldn't help it."

"Five seconds with ice and then cupping my breasts?"

He turned to face her. "You do it for me. What can I say?"

That maybe she didn't need a sexy dance after all. "I like that I do it for you. You do it for me, too."

He grinned. "Let's have the champagne. Give me fifteen minutes and I'll prove myself with you."

"Deal," she said, thinking there was nothing to prove.

Like much of Southern California, the Del Mar Racetrack had Spanish influences in the architecture. The grounds were well maintained and lush, the clubhouse impressive and owners and trainers had their own parking.

Annabelle stepped out of the car and smiled at Shane. He looked good. Better than good. A little tired, maybe, she thought with a smile. One of the advantages of being a woman, she thought as he took her hand. She could hide *her* dark circles with concealer.

"What are you smiling about?" he asked as they walked toward the entrance.

"Last night."

"Which time?"

"All of them."

As promised, he'd more than proven himself. They'd ordered dinner in and had spent a long, leisurely evening talking and making love. Later they'd settled into the huge bathtub and explored each other until the water had grown cold.

"Tell me about your horse," she said. "It's a he, right?"

"Deadline's Dream. Yes, a boy."

She grinned. "Is that a colt or a gelding?"

"Impressive. Using technical horse terms."

"I'm learning."

Not just about horses, she thought. But also about Shane. He was wary of her. Slow to trust. But she could live with the flaw. Because he was worth it. He was . . .

She glanced up at him and knew she was in danger. A man like him was difficult to resist. Difficult not to care about. Impossible not to love.

But until he fully believed in her, until he saw her as who she really was, she would have to be careful. Hearts were fragile at best and hers had already been broken once.

CHAPTER FIFTEEN

Shane woke early, just before dawn, judging by the faint light in the sky. They'd slept with the balcony doors partially open and a cold morning fog crept into the room.

He carefully climbed out of bed and closed the doors, then returned to the warmth of sheets, blankets and Annabelle.

She lay on her side, facing him, her eyes closed, her breathing steady. Dark red hair trailed across one bare shoulder and he could see part of a breast.

Wanting stirred. When she was around, it didn't take much. Knowing she was in the room pretty much did it for him. Last night he'd taken her again and again, unable to get enough of her. They'd fallen asleep in each other's arms. Now he watched her and wondered what he'd gotten himself into.

From the first moment he'd seen her, he'd been unable to escape her. He'd tried. But here he was, in her bed. Trapped by a desire he couldn't control and a need he couldn't explain. He should be running, or at least looking for an exit. But he wasn't. He couldn't leave. Not yet.

Was it possible she was who she seemed? She never looked at other men, she was funny, sexy and sweet. Maybe it was time to accept that and give them both a chance.

He got out of bed again and walked into the living room. Once there he strolled behind the wet bar and started coffee. He used the half bath and the spare toothbrush that housekeeping had thoughtfully put into a drawer. When he returned to the bedroom, the main bathroom door was closed. Seconds later it opened and Annabelle appeared.

"Morning," she said with a shy smile. "You know, the hotel provides robes."

"You're not wearing one," he said, taking in the delicious view. Full breasts, a narrow waist and round hips. She was all curves and attitude.

"Neither are you."

"I'm a guy."

Her gaze dropped to his growing erection. "Well, that explains the anatomical differences."

"I made coffee."

She smiled. "See, this is why you're such

a fun date."

They were standing about ten feet apart. He was aware of her body, of the bed and the fact that he wanted her again. He also knew that she was probably tired, sore and not in the mood. Damn.

"Shane?"

"Yes?"

"I know what you're thinking."

"No, you don't."

The smile widened and her eyes brightened. "Yes, I do. I can see it on your face. And other places."

He glanced down. There was no hiding that, he thought, knowing if he got much harder he would explode.

"The coffee is going to take a few minutes," she told him. "Until then, do you remember what happened when you asked me to get the champagne? Back when we first got here?"

He remembered every detail of her walking across the room, turning around and touching herself, first with ice and then her hands. He swallowed.

"Uh-huh."

"That was just my breasts." She moved her hands to her belly and laid them against her soft skin. "Remember?"

His gaze locked on her slow moving

fingers. How they were inching down and down. His breath caught. She wouldn't . . . She couldn't . . .

She did.

Her right hand slipped between her legs and moved in a slow circle. Her gaze locked with his and he saw passion in her eyes.

He didn't remember moving. One second he was on the other side of the room and the next he was pulling her close, kissing her deeply, his hand nudging hers away.

"Me," he insisted, wanting to be the one to feel her swollen, damp flesh.

Then she was urging him toward the bed.

"Touch me everywhere," she breathed, lying down, then opening her arms to him. "Touch me, Shane."

And he did.

Charlie watched the twin girls play with their terrycloth stuffed animals. Rosabel, otherwise known as Rose, sat next to her sister, Adelina, each holding a worn cat.

"I can't believe they're a year old," Charlie said.

Pia Morena leaned back against the sofa. "Me, either. It's going so fast. Peter's already twelve. Next year he'll be a teenager. When did that happen?"

"Kids grow up."

324

"I know and I don't like it." Pia smiled. "I plan to send off a sternly worded letter of protest." She pointed at the twins. "They're walking and starting to talk. I feel like in thirty seconds they'll be dating and borrowing the car."

"You have a little time."

"I hope so. I'm loving the whole 'Mom' thing. I don't want to become obsolete."

Charlie raised her eyebrows. "You're being a little dramatic."

"I know. I have moments when I'm completely normal. This would not be one of them." She sighed. "I think it's because we're getting a family picture taken tomorrow. It reminds me of the passage of time. Plus, we're talking about having another child and while I want that, I know it means the twins are growing up."

"They're a year old, Pia. Get over it."

Pia laughed. "This is why I like you, Charlie. There's no drama. You're a completely rational person."

Charlie knew that wasn't true. She had as many demons as the next person. Maybe more. Which was why she'd stopped by.

Pia's smile faded. "So it is serious."

"What?"

"Why you asked to come over. What's wrong? How can I help?"

Pia Moreno was in charge of the festival calendar in town. She coordinated the million little details that went into making Fool's Gold a tourist haven. Without Pia there would be no Winter Festival or Book Festival. No vendors selling jewelry and lemonade. No rides, no horse-drawn carriages in the winter.

But Pia also illustrated the best of the people in town, Charlie thought. Without even knowing what was going on, she offered to help.

"I'm thinking about having a baby," Charlie said slowly. "On my own."

She paused, to give that information time to sink in.

Pia's eyes widened slightly. "Oh, wow. That's great. You want to know about IVF, right?"

"Yes, and I'm surprised you're not going to try to talk me into waiting for a man."

Pia grinned. "Charlie, you're incredibly capable. If you want to have a child on your own, you'll do great. That whole gruff, crabby thing is just a facade. In case you were wondering, no one is fooled."

"Thanks for telling me."

"You're welcome. Okay, in vitro fertilization. There are needles. I'll warn you up front. Hormones and shots. Your body has to be prepared." She straightened. "Wait. Before that, you need an in vitro. I mean, a fertilized egg. Are you planning to use your own egg?"

Charlie nodded.

"Then you're going to need sperm." She motioned to the twins. "We already had that part taken care of."

Several years ago, Pia's friend Crystal had lost her husband in Iraq. The young couple, aware of what could happen to a soldier in a war zone, had prepared by storing several embryos. After her husband's death, Crystal had decided to implant the embryos, only to find she was seriously ill herself. When she died two years ago, she'd left the embryos to Pia.

It had taken Pia all of fifteen minutes to realize she had to have her friend's babies. Three embryos were implanted and two of them survived. Rosabel and Adelina had followed nine months later.

"I can get sperm," Charlie told her. If not through a volunteer she knew, then through a sperm bank.

"Okay. Then they'll harvest your eggs, about which I know very little and then fertilize them. Once you have a couple of viable embryos, they'll put them back in and then you wait. Dr. Galloway handled it for me here in town."

"I already go to her," Charlie said.

"Good. Then I would say talk to her." Pia tilted her head. "I have to ask. Are you sure you don't want to just have sex with a yummy guy? It would be easier. And cheaper."

"I have savings."

Pia raised her eyebrows in a silent question.

Charlie didn't want to go into her past yet another time. "There are reasons that the old-fashioned way doesn't work for me," she said instead.

"Enough said. Dr. Galloway will walk you through the procedure and then you'll have the information. Once you're actually pregnant, things should go along for you pretty much like they would if you'd done it the regular way."

"Meaning if I weren't a high-risk candidate I wouldn't be doing this in vitro?"

"I'm pretty sure that's right. I had the multiple birth thing, which could be an issue for you, as well. If they implant more than one embryo, it's always a possibility."

Charlie glanced at the twins playing happily together. Two kids? She wasn't sure how she would make that work, but she could figure out a way. It would be worth it. She needed to belong, to give her heart. Hell, having a baby was biological. Why should she have to fight the need?

"Thanks for the information," she said. "I appreciate it."

"You're welcome. And hey, if you want to get in some practice by babysitting, that would be great, too."

"So you and Raoul can have an evening out together?"

Pia grinned. "Of course."

"I may take you up on that. Would I have to stand in line?"

"There are a lot of women in Fool's Gold who do love to babysit. Peter complains he has too many grandmothers. Not that he objects when they show up with cookies."

Charlie knew she would get the same kind of support from the community.

"What's going to happen when you and Raoul want to have one of your own? Are you going to be able to handle four kids and your job?"

Pia slumped back against the sofa. "No, and believe me I'm very aware of the problem. The marketing department at the college has been great about giving students credit when they come work for me. They need three units of actual experience to graduate and I'm now an easy way to get that. So I have two or three interns at any given time. But if I have another baby, there's no way I can be responsible for the town's festivals. We'd have to hire someone else."

Charlie wanted to say she couldn't imagine another person in charge. That it had been Pia the past eight or nine years and that it should always be Pia. But that was unrealistic. Things changed. Look at her. A year ago she would have said she was perfectly happy being on her own. Now she was seriously considering starting a family.

"You don't have to decide today," she told Pia, but speaking as much to herself.

"I don't. And I won't. So there."

Pia laughed. The twins both turned toward the sound, their expressions delighted.

"Mama!" Rosabel said, holding out her arms.

"Duty calls." Pia rose and collected her daughter. When Adelina also raised her arms, Pia turned to Charlie. "Can you get her?"

Charlie picked up the toddler and held her close. Adelina smiled at her. Chubby fingers reached for Charlie's short hair and hung on.

"Not letting me go, huh, kid?" Charlie asked.

Adelina laughed.

The sound cut through her, making her happy and sad at the same time. Happy to be with the little girl and sad about the journey she would have to take to get a child of her own.

But it would be worth it, she promised herself.

"The disco ball is a nice touch," Annabelle said, staring up at the slow-moving silver ball.

"I found it at a garage sale," Jo told her. "It seemed perfect for the party room."

"Not the banquet room?"

"I thought party room sounded better."

"It does."

Annabelle glanced around at the big room. Jo had leased the space next to her bar. Her future plans were to break out a wall and expand the bar itself. For now, she'd cut in a doorway that led to stairs. On the second level was the party room. A big, open area with a view of the town and the mountains beyond. There was a bar in the back, a small stage, a great sound system and plenty of tables and chairs. Rumor had it one of the walls was really a false front, with a big TV behind it, but tonight it was covered up. The bridal shower would provide its own entertainment.

Annabelle and Charlie had spent most of the afternoon setting up. Balloons were tied together in clusters in the corners of the room. Paper tablecloths covered the round tables. Jo was providing all the dishes, flatware and glasses. Charlie had stayed in the room to accept the flower delivery while Annabelle had gone to get the cake. The two-tiered replica of a wedding cake was done in three kinds of chocolate and had a special place of honor near the front of the room.

By the window, a long table held the goodie bags and the supplies for the games. There were scissors and tape and a stapler to make a wrapping paper dress and inexpensive plastic tiaras so everyone could be a princess.

Jo picked up a clipboard from the bar and grabbed a pen. "Okay, just to confirm. You're having champagne as your only liquor. I have twenty bottles chilled, but I'll only charge what you use."

Annabelle laughed. "Twenty? We're only having about thirty people at the shower."

"Uh-huh. Trust me. I'll make sure everyone is either walking or has a ride." She moved to the next item. "The menu. We have lasagna, fried ravioli, raw vegetables with dip so we can pretend to be healthy, garlic bread, cut fruit with melted chocolate, individual cups of tiramisu and cake. The champagne I mentioned along with soda, coffee and tea."

Annabelle looked at the menu. "Where did the fried ravioli come from?"

"I'm trying it. That's on me. I want to see if people like it." Jo put down the clipboard. "I'll be in and out all evening. I know I'm technically a guest, but I'll want to check on the bar, as well. Two servers will be assigned. The sound system is set." Jo went behind the bar and handed her a remote. "Adjust the volume with this. If anyone hates a selection, push the 'next' button and it will skip the song. You know where the bathrooms are, right?"

"End of the hall."

"Then we're good." Jo glanced around at the banner proclaiming "Happy Wedding, Heidi," the flowers, the cake and balloons and shook her head. "I was right to elope."

"Not your style?"

"No, but it looks good on Heidi. Have fun. Call me if you need me."

Jo left. Charlie came in with one of the servers. Both women carried buckets of ice.

"In case," Charlie said.

She'd traded her usual firefighter uniform

for dark wash jeans and a simple long-sleeved blue shirt. The top was fitted, as were the jeans. More so than Charlie's uniform or her traditional casual look of a T-shirt and baggy cargo pants.

Annabelle took in her long, lean legs and narrow hips. Maybe it was nerves about the shower or carrying the ice up a flight of stairs, but Charlie's face was slightly flushed, her eyes bright. The shirt deepened the blue in her eyes.

She had amazing bone structure. Annabelle wasn't sure why she hadn't noticed until now.

Charlie set down the ice and glared. "What?" she demanded. "You're staring at me."

"You look nice."

Charlie grimaced. "Oh, please."

"I'm serious. I never got it before, but you go out of your way to avoid dressing like a woman. You don't wear makeup or act feminine at all. But you're really very pretty."

The grimace turned into a glower. "Don't make me hurt you."

"I'm unimpressed by the threat." Annabelle continued to stare. "You downplay your looks because you don't want attention."

"I'm the tallest girl in the room. Trust me, that's not attention I want."

"I'm short, so I know there's an advantage to being the tallest girl. But you don't use it."

Charlie drew in a breath. "I know what beautiful is. My mother. I'm nothing like her."

"There are all kinds of beauty."

But Annabelle could tell Charlie didn't believe her. Charlie's mother was a petite, graceful ballerina. That could intimidate anyone, let alone a tall, gawky girl. Add the horrible date rape to the mix and it made sense that Charlie avoided anything remotely feminine. But with their guests arriving in the next few minutes, this wasn't the time for that conversation.

They checked on the food, hit Play on the remote to start the music and then suffered through three minutes of "What if everyone hates our party" jitters before Heidi and May arrived.

"It's perfect," May announced, glancing around at the room. "I love it."

"Me, too," Heidi said. "I'm nervous. Why am I nervous?"

"Because you haven't had champagne," Charlie said, giving both women hugs.

One of the servers opened the first bottle

of champagne and started to pour. Annabelle passed out glasses.

In the next twenty minutes the rest of the
guests arrived. The Hendrix triplets were
there, along with their mother, Denise.
Mayor Marsha, Charity Golden, Pia and
their resident famous author, Liz Sutton.
Rina McKenzie, recently married to the local vet Cameron, arrived with Julia Gionni
of the feuding Gionni sisters.

As more women arrived, Annabelle made
sure she was by the door to collect the gifts
and guide guests to the champagne. Conversation and laughter drowned out the music.

Once everyone had their drink, Charlie
proposed a toast to the bride-to-be. The
buffet was set out and people lined up to
get food. The tables filled quickly as everyone settled in for dinner.

Annabelle found a seat by Charity. The
city planner wore her hair in a cut bob with
bangs.

"You've done a great job," Charity said as
Annabelle sat next to her. "I love that Jo's
opened this banquet room."

"Party room," Annabelle corrected. "She's
calling it a party room."

Charity laughed. "Of course she is. I
remember when I first moved here, I was so
impressed by the idea of a bar catering to

women. I wasn't sure she could make the concept last, but she's doing great."

"I know. The first time Charlie and Heidi suggested we have lunch here, I was shocked. I'm not exactly the bar type. But it's great."

Charity's brown eyes widened. "Not the bar type? Really? Because I heard you were dancing on the bar a few weeks back."

"I keep telling everyone," Annabelle said, exasperated. "I wasn't drunk. I was demonstrating the dance of the happy virgin."

"I wish I'd seen that. Will you be doing it again at the Máa-zib festival?"

"No. That will be the horse dancing. I'm just along for the ride."

"Too bad. Because I'm guessing a lot of guys would pay to see the happy virgin dance."

Maybe, but there was only one she was interested in showing it to, she thought.

Charity picked up her champagne, then paused. "Uh-oh. I know that look. Who's the guy?"

"What guy?"

"I don't know. The one making you look . . ." She paused.

Nevada, sitting across from them, looked up. "Sappy," she offered. "Trust me. I know the look. I get it every time I think of

Tucker. It's humiliating, but inescapable."

"There's no look," Annabelle said quickly, determined to think of something other than Shane. "No guy."

"That's not what I heard," Pia called from another table. "I heard there was travel and hotel. A night at a hotel."

Several women hooted.

"Details," someone called out. "We want details."

May winced. "Not too many. We're talking about my son, ladies. There are some things a mother shouldn't know."

"Oh, good point," Pia said. "But you can give us generalities."

Annabelle sprang to her feet. "Oh, look. Heidi's done eating. Let's open presents."

"I'd try champagne," Charlie murmured, standing to join her. "You're more likely to distract them with alcohol."

Fortunately there was a momentary lull in the music so everyone heard Mayor Marsha say, ". . . bought the radio station."

"Who bought the radio station?" Pia asked. "Why don't I get the good gossip anymore? Is it having the kids? They're worth it, of course, but I miss gossip."

Mayor Marsha glanced around the room. "A very interesting man has purchased the radio station on the edge of town. His name

338

is Gideon."

"Oh, like the angel," Heidi said, obviously feeling her champagne.

"Ah, no," the mayor said. "He has an interesting past, though. I'm sure you'll all get to meet him soon enough."

Just then Jo arrived with the dessert and questions about the mysterious Gideon went unanswered.

After everyone finished eating, the tables were pushed back and the chairs drawn in a loose circle. Charlie collected the presents for Heidi to open.

The invitations had gone out with "Bring something Heidi will love" as the gift suggestion. Lingerie was a given, and well represented. Mayor Marsha gave Heidi a beautiful set of antique cheese molds, perfect for a woman with goats and a cheese business. May, Heidi's future mother-in-law, had wrapped two tickets to Paris.

"For your honeymoon," May said happily.

Heidi stared at the gift, then looked up, obviously stunned. "Paris? For two weeks?"

Charlie sighed. "Yes, and before you ask, Annabelle and I have already volunteered to look after the goats. We'll be by in a couple of days for our milking lessons."

Heidi wiped away happy tears as she hugged them all.

Later, while the guests created a wrapping paper wedding gown, Charlie pointed to the collection of empty champagne bottles.

"There are going to be less of those left over than we'd thought."

Annabelle sighed. "I know, but it's been fun. What a great shower."

"Have a little bride envy?"

"Maybe. When I married Lewis, there wasn't any of this. He thought it was silly and I pretended I agreed with him."

"Shane wouldn't mind the party and later he'd want you to try on all the sexy outfits."

"Who said anything about Shane?" Annabelle asked.

"No one has to. We can all see it. You're falling for him."

"I'm not." She sighed. "Maybe. A little."

"Heidi swears Stryker brothers are the best," Charlie told her.

"I don't question his character. He's a great guy. But he has baggage and it makes me nervous."

"Nobody's perfect."

"You're telling me to follow my heart?"

"I'm saying from where I'm sitting, falling in love sounds nice," Charlie admitted.

"Then you could, you know, start dating."

"I don't think so. I can walk right into a burning building without blinking, but going out with a man?" She shook her head. "Not going to happen."

Annabelle reached out and squeezed her friend's hand. Sometimes the solutions were obvious. Impossible, but obvious. Charlie should get off her butt and go out with a guy and Annabelle, well, she was less sure what she should do. Trust Shane came to mind. Believe in him to find his way.

Because Charlie had a point. From where she was sitting, falling in love sounded very, very nice.

CHAPTER SIXTEEN

"Is that a pig?"

Shane didn't bother turning around. What was the point? There was only one answer to the question.

"Yes."

"A real pig?"

"His name is Wilbur."

Giggles exploded from behind him. He flinched like a cat being hit by rain.

"From the book," one of the girls said.

"It's *Charlotte's Web*," another offered. "Shane, have you read it?"

He finished adjusting the saddle and then reluctantly turned around to face his class of beginning riders. "Yes, I know it's a book. Yes, I know the name of it. Yes, I've read it."

Shane's big plan that would give Wilbur a week with Priscilla and Reno had ended the second his mother seen the pig. Once she'd met Wilbur, it had all been decided.

"Let's get started," Shane told the girls.

They stood in line as he gave each one a lift up into the saddle, then pointed to the open gate on the left.

"In there," he said.

They did as he asked, walking sedately into the ring. Before he could follow, his mother burst out of the house.

"Did you tell them?" she asked eagerly.

"Not yet," he answered, over a chorus of "Tell us what?"

"Sorry," May said, not looking the least bit sorry. "I'll be quiet while you tell them now."

Four pairs of eyes stared at him. Shane stood in the center of the corral and suddenly felt foolish. What if they didn't want to be a part of things? What if he couldn't teach them or the horses?

He cleared his throat. "I thought it would be fun for you to be in the parade with Annabelle."

"Really?"

"Can we?"

"That's so great."

"Yay!"

"That was a yes?" he asked, holding in a smile.

They all nodded.

"Yes!"

"Good. I've been working on what you could do on your horses. A few simple steps."

"And there'll be costumes," May added.

Shane turned to look at his mother. "Excuse me?"

"Costumes. For the girls."

There was more cheering. Shane felt the beginning of a headache. "I didn't say anything about costumes."

"That's because you're a man. It's a parade. They need costumes. I've seen what Annabelle is going to wear and I've made a few sketches. Now we just have to find someone who can sew."

"My mom sews," one of the girls offered.

"Mine, too."

May beamed. "See. Problem solved. I'll talk to the girls after their lesson. Annabelle will be so happy."

Words deliberately designed to make him rethink any complaints. Because making Annabelle happy had become a priority with him.

"Now you're fighting dirty," he told his mother.

She laughed. "I do what I have to so that I win. You should respect that."

"Mostly it frightens me."

Still smiling, May waved at the girls.

"Listen to Shane," she called as she walked back to the house. "Don't forget, he's a real cowboy."

"Thanks for the endorsement," he muttered as he turned back to his class. "Okay, let's start practicing being in the parade."

Mandy raised her hand. "Can we wear lip gloss?"

Shane's almost-headache began to grow. "Excuse me?"

"If you tell us we have to wear lip gloss, we will." She bounced in the saddle. "Because my mom says I'm too young."

"Mine, too."

"But we want to."

"I'm not going to say you have to wear lip gloss."

Four ten-year-olds immediately began to pout.

"Why not?" Mandy asked.

"Because . . ." He sucked in a breath. "Because I'm not going to get your moms mad at me, okay? If your moms get mad, they might say you can't ride anymore. Do you want that?"

They exchanged glances, then shook their heads. Then Mandy smiled at him.

"You like us."

Shane held in a groan. "Can we get started now?"

345

"Okay, but just so you know, my mom says I can't start dating until I'm fifteen."

"The most important thing is keeping everything clean and sanitized," Heidi said, leading the way into the goat house. "And we're talking about a goat here, so it's not like you can count on her to cooperate."

Annabelle held a pad of paper in her hands, prepared to take notes. The offer to milk Heidi's goats while she was on her honeymoon had been impulsive. It wasn't that she was regretting it, exactly, but she was a little nervous about all the responsibility.

"Do we really have to sell the milk while you're gone?" she asked.

Heidi laughed. "You'll do fine. It's not that hard. Trust me."

"It's not so much an issue of trust," Annabelle told her. "I don't want to get it wrong."

"We'll practice until you're comfortable. Besides, Shane knows what to do."

"Are you sure? He's more a horse guy than a goat guy."

"He knows and don't let him tell you otherwise."

Heidi showed her where everything was kept. In a couple of days, Annabelle would arrive bright and early to practice on an

346

actual goat. Charlie would do the same. At least they would take turns milking.

"You're not going to have to worry about the cheese," Heidi told her as they headed back for the main house. "There are a couple of batches that need work, but May is taking care of that for me."

"Good. Because goats are about my limit."

They paused on the porch. Annabelle turned to look at the ranch. Up on the slight rise was Priscilla's home. The elephant, Reno and Wilbur shared a big fenced-in area. Since May had put a notice in the Fool's Gold *Daily Republic*, locals had been dropping off freshly pruned leafy branches for Priscilla. She enjoyed poplar, willow, maple and ash, along with several varieties of fruit trees. An elephant could go through a lot of branches in a day.

Khatar was in his usual corral. He had shade, sun and plenty of water, along with a view of what was going on. She'd greeted him when she'd first arrived and, for once, he'd stayed in place.

The riding horses clustered together in another corral, while Shane's pricey pregnant mares were in a third. Heidi's goats were out on loan, taking care of lawns and brush for anyone who signed up.

Annabelle liked everything about the

347

ranch. There was a sense of connection with the land, a feeling of belonging. She was happiest when she was here, although a part of that was probably because she was usually with Shane. She could spend her days scrubbing grout with him and still have a good time.

"I picked up my dress," Heidi said, her face bright with excitement. "Want to see?"

"I'd love to."

They went upstairs to one of the spare rooms. Off the bedroom was a small alcove that had obviously once been used for a nursery. A beautiful white wedding gown hung from a big, brass coatrack. The dress faced the rack, with the train spread out on the sheets spread over the floor.

"I'm so paranoid about it," Heidi said. "I couldn't even steam it after I picked it up. I was shaking too much. May did it for me. Now I come in here every day and look at it. I know. I'm such an idiot."

"You're not. You're excited about getting married. Isn't that how it's supposed to be? Honestly, I'd be worried if you weren't looking at your dress every day."

Heidi hugged her. "Thank you."

Annabelle hugged her back, then tugged on one of Heidi's blond braids. "You're welcome. Now show me this fancy wedding gown."

Heidi slipped off her boots and walked to the dress. She carefully lifted the hanger, then expertly turned the dress so the train was still protected by the sheets.

A heart-shaped neckline had been done in pure white silk. The bodice was pleated and fitted. At the waist was delicate beading. The skirt was full with only a few scattered beads. Simple. Cap sleeves added to the air of innocence, while the fabric and pleating were more elegant. The train was long and had the most beading.

"It's perfect," Annabelle breathed. The gown was all things Heidi. Sweet and pretty, with unexpected touches. "How are you wearing your hair?"

"Up, I think. Of all things, May has a diamond tiara that belonged to her grandmother. It's silly, but I actually love it."

"Why not? Every bride should be a princess on her wedding day. Rafe isn't going to know what hit him."

Heidi put the dress back on the coatrack, then carefully smoothed the train into place.

"I hope so," she said as she faced Annabelle again, then led the way out of the room. "I want him to be happy."

Annabelle waited until they were in the

hall to touch her friend's arm. "The man is crazy about you. Seriously. If you're in the room, he can't stop looking at you. When he talks about you, he grins like a teenager on his first date. Do you really have any doubts?"

"No." Heidi drew in a breath. "But sometimes I can't believe I got so lucky. Six months ago I would have told you I didn't believe in love and if someone convinced me it was real, I would never trust it. But then he was here and I couldn't help myself."

"The irresistible man?"

Heidi laughed. "Something like that. I never thought I could be this happy. First buying the ranch, then almost losing it, then having Rafe fall in love with me."

Annabelle enjoyed her friend's happiness, even as she felt a little knot of worry in her tummy. She wanted what Heidi had. Wanted to feel those feelings, wanted to be secure in knowing she was loved. She'd never had that with Lewis. Deep inside she'd always sensed she wasn't a partner in their relationship.

For a while she'd assumed she was simply one of those women who wasn't destined to find love. That she would make her life fulfilling in other ways. But now, with

Shane, she found herself wanting her happy ending. Wanting him to be the one.

She just wasn't sure it was possible.

"It's a faucet," Shane said. "For a kitchen. Don't I only need one?"

"Yes," Annabelle said patiently. "One is great. So which do you like?"

He stared around in obvious bewilderment. Normally she would have taken advantage of the situation and mocked him, but right now she sort of understood his confusion.

On the advice of his contractor, they were in Sacramento at a bathroom and kitchen fixture specialty store. They were going to be able to make all the decisions regarding plumbing at once. There was only one problem. The store was the size of a grandstand and there were hundreds of choices for each option.

Shiny, brushed, stainless, copper-colored, brass, black, white. There were tall faucets and stubby faucets. Faucets that bent or sprayed or filtered water. She was half expecting to see one that talked.

There were even more choices for the bathrooms, along with sinks and tubs and shower fixtures. Oh, and there were rows and rows of toilets.

They were being assisted by a well-dressed thirty-something man named Marcus who had received the contractor's email with the list of what Shane should be buying.

"We'll start easy and work up to what's difficult," Marcus said, attaching their list to a clipboard and then handing it to Annabelle. He pulled out a touchpad device and started entering information.

"What's easy?" Shane asked warily.

"The kitchen. A faucet and a sink."

Annabelle knew that wasn't exactly true. There would be appliances and lighting, not to mention countertops, backsplashes and flooring. But none of that was Marcus's problem.

"Farm sinks are very popular," Marcus told them, leading them over to the kitchen area. Several displays showed the sinks and faucets in an actual kitchen-like setting.

"They're large, which gives you a nice working space. Deep enough for pasta pots. Some people don't want their sink split into two parts."

Shane stared. "It's a sink."

Marcus gave a little sigh and pushed up his rimless glasses. "Yes. I hear that a lot."

"This is important," Annabelle told him.

"Why?" Shane looked genuinely confused.

"Are you going to be washing any small

livestock in the sink?" she asked.

"No."

"Then let's get a traditional two sink configuration. With the one side deeper."

Marcus nodded and led them to that part of the display. They debated stainless versus the other materials. Marcus asked about a faucet over the stove. As Shane laughed, Annabelle told him, no, that hadn't been ordered.

She quickly narrowed the faucet selection down to three and he picked the one he liked best.

"Why that one?" she asked as Marcus led them to the bathroom fixtures.

"It was the biggest."

"I figured," she said, linking arms with him. "You're such a guy."

"It's one of my best qualities."

They reached the showers. Before Marcus could explain much, his cell phone buzzed.

"It's one of my suppliers. Would you excuse me please while I take this call?"

"Go ahead," Shane said.

"Thank you. There's coffee over there, if you'd like."

He quickly walked away.

Shane stared at the displays of showers.

"Don't," Annabelle told him, looking down at the inventory list. She couldn't remember if the house had two or three full bathrooms.

"Don't what?"

"Say 'it's just a shower.' You were going to."

"I wasn't," he said, but he sounded a little defensive.

She glanced at him and grinned. "You so were."

"Maybe on the inside."

She found the right part of the list. "There are three full baths, including the master, a half bath and a sink in the mudroom."

"I need coffee."

She followed him over to a coffee station complete with a sofa, a small table and chairs and several plates of cookies. Shane poured her a cup, then a second for himself.

"It's too much," he said. "We should have gone somewhere with a smaller selection."

"Most people appreciate all the choices."

"Most people are idiots."

"You'd rather be back doing horse stuff," she said.

He raised his eyebrows. "You did not just say horse stuff."

She held in a smile. "I did."

"You're in big trouble now."

"Are you going to punish me?"

Instantly his features sharpened as his gaze

centered on her mouth. "Have you been bad?"

"Very."

"I like your honesty."

He continued to look at her. She felt the temperature in the room rise about ten degrees and her skin got the pre-kiss, tingly tightness. It sure didn't take much for Shane to get her distracted.

She cleared her throat and searched for a safer topic. "So, um, how's Wilbur settling in?"

"You really want to talk about the pig?"

"It seems safer."

He glanced around, then returned his attention to her. "Good point. They probably don't want us taking one of the tubs for a test drive."

"It could be awkward. I'm not sure Marcus would approve."

"Wilbur's fine. Reno likes him more than Priscilla does, I think. It's not like they share their innermost feelings with me. But he's settled in and now the odd duet has become an even stranger trio."

"I'm glad Priscilla isn't alone. She must have been lonely by herself. Elephants are social animals."

"Someone's been doing research on the internet."

"A little," she admitted.

"Study any horse stuff?"

She laughed. "Some. Khatar is my one true love. I need to understand him."

"He's a pretty simple guy."

"As are you." She linked her arm with his and enjoyed the socially polite feel of his body next to hers. "Come on. Be a brave little toaster. We're going to look at showers. This is going to be fun because some of them come with gadgets."

"What do you mean?"

"You can get a steam shower if you want. Or one that you can program the temperature. You punch in what you want it to be and it tells you when it's there."

"I like technology."

"I thought you might. There are also showers with heads coming out the side, so every part of you gets clean."

He glanced at her. "I don't need that. I have a woman come in every morning to wash me."

"Really? I haven't met this woman. What's she like?"

"Beautiful. Naked. It's how I start my day."

She drew back. "Interesting. I think I liked you better when you were frightened of the sink choices."

He wrapped his arm around her and pulled her close. "Don't be jealous. She's a professional. It's a business arrangement."

"The strange woman who bathes you every morning?"

"Uh-huh. But you could try out for the job. I'm a very easy grader."

They'd arrived back at the bathrooms. She pointed to the electronic display. "See if they have a setting for icy cold. Because that's all you're getting from me."

"I'm wounded." He faced her and put his free hand on her waist. "If it really bothers you, I'll get rid of her."

"I think I'd like to meet this mystery woman of the professional washing."

"You'd have to come over very early."

"I guess I'd better get used to waking up early if I'm going to milk Heidi's goats."

"You should probably spend the night, just to make it easy on yourself."

She found herself getting lost in his dark eyes. This was the Shane she liked most, she thought, wanting to lean in and feel his mouth on hers. The teasing, fun guy who made her heart beat faster.

Nearby, someone cleared his throat. Annabelle saw that Marcus had returned. She took a quick step back and sipped her coffee.

Shane didn't look the least bit chagrined. "We were discussing the digital temperatures in the shower."

"Ah, I see. You should look at this one. It changes color as the temperature changes."

Shane grabbed her hand and drew her along after Marcus. "It changes color. I like that. Maybe we can find one that makes the water different colors, too."

"You did really well," Annabelle said four hours later as they drove back to Fool's Gold. "We got everything you needed from the store. It will be shipped to the job site and make your contractor very happy."

"Good. Because she has serious attitude if she's not happy."

Annabelle didn't want to think about how much money Shane had spent in a single afternoon. All those fixtures added up, especially since he tended to choose high-end materials. She supposed she was going to have to integrate the fact that he wasn't just a guy who worked with horses. He was a successful breeder and racehorse owner. She had a feeling he paid more in taxes than she made.

"With the measurements for what you bought, construction can continue," she said.

"Yeah. I'll get a two-day break and then she'll be on me about lighting fixtures."

"The electrician is going to need to know what goes where."

He turned off the main highway for the road to the ranch. "Want to pick them for me?"

"No, but I'll go with you."

"Thanks."

Their eyes met for a second and she felt the familiar flutter in her chest. He was good, she thought. Better than good.

As he made another turn, they passed a flatbed truck with the name of a delivery service going the other way. Shane groaned.

"What did she buy now?"

"At least it's not an animal," Annabelle said, looking at the flatbed, hoping to see a clue. "They always come in enclosed trailers."

"Unless it was in a cage or something. Like a lion."

"Your mother wouldn't buy a lion."

"You sure about that?"

Annabelle thought about May's eclectic menagerie. "Um, no. Not really."

They drove onto the ranch only to see a shiny new red truck parked by the house. It was big, with massive tires and an extended bed.

Shane slowed his truck and stared. "Because the Cadillac wasn't enough?" he muttered.

"Cadillac?" She stared at the truck. "You think Clay bought it?"

"No one else would want anything that flashy. That has my little brother written all over it."

"When does he arrive?"

Shane came to a stop and turned off the engine. "Earlier this afternoon."

She glanced toward the truck and saw a man standing on the porch. He was obviously a Stryker brother — with dark hair and eyes. The same broad shoulders and long legs. But he was also different.

He wasn't just good-looking. He was handsome in a whole other league, his features just a little more perfect than everyone else's. And his appeal didn't stop there. The man had an amazing body, expertly shown off in tight jeans and a form-fitting T-shirt.

"You can close your mouth now," Shane grumbled.

Annabelle tore her gaze away from Clay. "My mouth wasn't open."

"It kind of was. Don't worry. We're used to it. Clay has always been the pretty one in the family. Try not to drool. It makes things awkward."

He was joking. Sort of. She looked at Shane and thought of how much she enjoyed everything about him. Then she undid her seat belt and leaned toward him.

"You're very concerned about my reaction to your brother. I think the person you really have to worry about is your bathing lady."

As she spoke, she put her hand on the back of his head and drew him to her. When he was close enough, she leaned in and kissed him. She thought about how he made her laugh and how she looked forward to spending time with him. Then she thought about all the ways he amazed her in bed and let her kiss do the talking, so to speak.

When she finally drew back he smiled. "Nice."

She raised her eyebrows.

"I got the message," he added.

"Good. Remember that."

As she got out, she wondered if Shane's reaction to her looking at Clay had been about her or if this was another example of his dealing with his ex. Had she been a little too interested in Shane's brother? Because if she had been, this was more proof of Annabelle's uphill journey to prove she was someone Shane could trust. That she would never betray him or trick him or hurt him.

Easy enough to say, she thought. But much, much harder to prove.

CHAPTER SEVENTEEN

"I'm so happy," May said, checking the roast she'd put in the oven, then closing the door and straightening. "All my boys are home with me."

Shane collected plates and flatware to set the table, as instructed. "Were you this excited when I moved back?" he asked, his voice teasing.

"Of course," his mother assured him.

"Only Clay's a little more special," Rafe called from the sideboard by the table. He pulled the cork from the bottle of wine May had insisted they would have with dinner.

"He's rarely here," May told them both. "That makes it special."

"Face it," Rafe said, returning to the kitchen to get the wineglasses. "He's her favorite."

May put her hands on her hips. "I love all my boys the same. You two know it, too."

Rafe paused to kiss her cheek. "We do,

Mom. But sometimes it's fun to mess with you."

It was just the four of them for dinner that night. Heidi and her grandfather had gone into town to leave the Strykers to enjoy their reunion in private.

Clay strolled into the kitchen and walked up to his mother. "You're even more beautiful than the last time I saw you," he said, pulling her close and hugging her. When he released her, he turned to Rafe. "Hey, there's some white dress upstairs. You know anything about that?"

Rafe narrowed his gaze. "You didn't touch it, did you?"

"No." Clay held up both his hands. "I just looked." He winked. "Marriage, huh? What does she see in you?"

"More than she'd see in you."

Clay slapped him on the back then turned to Shane. "See my truck?"

"It's hard to miss."

"If you ask real nice, I'll let you drive it."

Shane grinned. "No, thanks. By the way, I took the Cadillac to San Diego. Got it all broken in for you."

Clay's dark eyes widened. "No," he said slowly. "You didn't."

"That baby can corner and she's got some speed in her."

Clay lunged forward, Shane ducked out of the way, then caught his brother as he turned. The mock wrestling had May shrieking at them to stop. She grabbed a dish-towel and attacked them both with it.

"Not before dinner," she yelled, slapping them in rhythm with her words. "Stop it, both of you. This is the first time our whole family has been together in three years and you're not going to ruin it."

Shane released Clay and straightened. He glanced at Rafe, who stared at May. Clay looked just as uncomfortable as he straightened his shirt.

"Not our whole family, Mom," Clay said.

May's happy expression shifted to wary. "No," she said quickly. "I mean the four of us. Of course Evangeline isn't here. Which is too bad."

Shane felt the familiar boil of anger. "I'm going to check on the horses," he said, heading for the door. "I'll be back in time for dinner."

"I'm just putting on the potatoes," his mother called after him. "Twenty minutes. No longer."

Shane went outside and drew in a deep breath. He told himself getting pissed off wouldn't help anyone. That a case could be made he was as much to blame.

Behind him, the back door opened. He turned. Rafe stepped out beside him. The brothers stared at each other.

"It's not your fault," Rafe said quietly. "None of it. You were a kid."

Shane shrugged. "If I hadn't brought him home," he began.

Rafe grimaced. "Don't make me beat the shit out of you."

"You really think you can?"

"I could make a dent." Rafe moved next to him and leaned against the back porch railing. "You were eight, Shane. Eight years old. You'd lost your dad and heard your mom crying herself to sleep every night. You were trying to help."

"It didn't help. It made things worse. I'm glad we have Evie, but that guy . . ."

Some twenty-six years ago, after the death of their father, Shane had met a cowboy in town. At eight, he'd been unable to understand everything happening around him. All he knew was that his mom missed his dad and Randy, the cowboy he'd met, was nice and had agreed to come over for dinner.

Apparently Randy had stayed for more than dessert. Nine months later, Evangeline had been born.

"She should have given Evie up for adoption," Shane said flatly.

Rafe stared at him. "How can you say that? She's our sister."

"I know who she is and I know what she's been through. The youngest by enough years that we were all too busy for her. Mom never bonded or connected with her, or whatever you call it. Evie spent her whole life knowing she wasn't welcome, wasn't wanted. You think that was easy for her? Better for her to go to a family who wanted her."

"She's our sister," Rafe insisted. "We love her."

"Sure. From a distance and when it's easy. I talk to her maybe once a month. Clay does the same. You haven't spoken to her in what? Eight or nine years? And Mom does her best to pretend she doesn't exist."

"I saw her a couple of months ago," Rafe said.

Shane turned and stared at him. "What?"

"Drove down to L.A. and found her. We had coffee." One corner of his mouth turned up. "She wasn't exactly happy to see me, but we've stayed in touch since."

Shane had a little trouble believing the words. "You're stubborn and pigheaded. She didn't do what you wanted. Are you saying you've forgiven her?"

Rafe looked at him. "I'm the one who

needed forgiveness. She was a kid who lost her way. I should have been there for her and I wasn't. I feel bad about that."

"None of us were really there for her," Shane said.

His sister had always been the guilty secret of the family. May had always acted as if Evie didn't exist and he and his brothers hadn't done a whole lot better.

"Maybe you're right," Rafe said slowly. "Maybe adoption would have been a more rational choice. She would have felt that she belonged. I asked her to come to the wedding. She said no."

Shane was impressed that Rafe had even bothered with an invitation. "You can't blame her for not wanting to be here. I'm sure she doesn't remember much about Fool's Gold, so the town's not a draw. As for a family event, that has to be her idea of hell."

"I know, but it would have been nice to have her around."

The back door opened again and Clay walked out. "Mom wanted me to check on you two." He lowered his voice. "Talking about Evie?"

"Yes," Rafe said. "I was telling Shane I invited her to the wedding but she refused."

"Would you want to come if you were

her?" Clay asked, then seemed to brace himself. "Hell, I wasn't sure I would be welcome here."

Shane knew the comment wasn't directed at him. He waited while his younger and older brother faced each other.

"I'm glad you're back," Rafe said quietly.

Clay waited.

"I mean it," Rafe added. "It's good to have you home."

Clay relaxed. "Okay. Thanks."

"You're welcome."

Clay turned to Shane. "I can't believe you drove my car to San Diego."

Shane grinned. "You said for me to take care of it and I did. You never said not to drive it."

"Didn't think I had to."

"Then that's your problem."

Clay started to say something else, then turned slowly and stared past the barn. "Is that an elephant?"

Rafe laughed and slapped him on the back. "Welcome home, kid. You've got a lot of catching up to do."

Charlie picked up her latte and took a sip. "You're the one who called this meeting," she said, as she set it down.

Dakota nodded in agreement. "I did and I

have a reason."

"I figured."

Her friend's hesitation was an indication that Charlie probably wasn't going to enjoy the topic. Still, she liked Dakota and respected her. So she would listen. *Then* she would get upset.

"You talked to Pia about IVF," she began.

"I did. She made it sound both great and awful."

Dakota wrinkled her nose. "Aren't there hormone shots involved? I would hate that. I'm a true baby when it comes to needles."

"I don't love them, either, but if it's for a good cause, I could deal."

Dakota drew in a breath. "I don't want you to take this wrong. I'm saying it with love."

"You're avoiding saying it with love."

"You're right. It's just . . ." She reached a hand across the small table and touched Charlie's arm. "I think you're doing this in the wrong order. You want to have a family and I completely respect that. And you. The decision to be a single parent isn't an easy one. Many single parents have the situation thrust upon them. They don't get to choose and you do."

Which all sounded great, Charlie thought. "But?"

"But in my opinion, you're making that choice for the wrong reason." She met Charlie's gaze. "What happened to you is awful. And that you were unable to get any kind of justice only makes it worse. No one should go through that. There's no excuse for what that man did to you. You've suffered for a long time. Now you're coming out of your pain and thinking about having a family. Which is great, but what you're not dealing with are the rest of the consequences."

Charlie didn't want to hear any of this. She wanted to get up, toss her coffee cup into the trash and stalk out. Which would make excellent TV, but this was her life. Dakota was a friend. She was also a trained psychologist. Charlie should probably listen to her. Even if every word made her uncomfortable, like being trapped in a small, dark box.

"Go on," she said softly.

"If you didn't want to be with a man because you'd given relationships several tries and they weren't for you, then fine. But you're avoiding men because you're afraid. Afraid of trust, afraid of intimacy, both physical and emotional. You keep people you fear at bay by intimidating them. You're one of the strongest women I know,

Charlie, and one of the weakest. To simply cut off a piece of yourself out of fear isn't who you are."

Charlie curled her hands into fists. She told herself to keep breathing, that she would get through this conversation and then she could smash something.

"You need to get this fixed before you bring a child into your life," Dakota told her. "That doesn't mean you have to have a man around. I think you'd be a great single mom. But you do have to heal the wound. Otherwise, you won't be able to teach a baby all the lessons you need to. Being a parent is hard enough. We're all flawed. But you want to start from the best position you can and right now you're not there."

Dakota's gaze never left hers. "I want the best for you. I want you to beat this."

"I don't like it," Charlie told her, fighting faint nausea and more than a little shame. "I don't like it a lot."

Dakota waited.

Charlie rubbed her face then nodded once. "Okay. Maybe you're right. Maybe this is a problem. The guy thing."

Dakota's mouth curved into a smile. "Just maybe? Do you know how many degrees I have?"

Charlie grinned. "Yeah, yeah, book smart.

I know." Her humor faded and she leaned forward. "I don't know how to fix it. I'm not a therapy kind of person. I'm too impatient. I don't want to talk about my feelings."

"There are different kinds of therapy. Not all of them require you to talk about your childhood. I could help you find a trauma specialist who would only focus on the rape itself. When it happened, no one believed you. So you not only have to process the damage done by the physical act, but also the betrayal of those you should have been able to trust."

Charlie wasn't in the mood to process anything. "Can I just have sex with a guy and call it a day?"

"Would that make you feel healed?"

"Since I haven't wanted to since, then yeah. That wouldn't hurt." Honestly, she couldn't imagine trusting anyone enough to do that. Nor could she picture herself wanting to.

"Then sex is a great place to start. Any candidates?"

"No. Men aren't my thing."

"It doesn't have to be a man."

Charlie stared at her. "Ah, no. I didn't mean it that way. Given the choice, I'll go with a man."

Dakota looked amused. "Just checking. Because whatever works."

"You're incredibly weird. You know that, right."

"I can live with my idiosyncrasies."

"And I should learn to live with mine," Charlie said. "I'll admit I don't like what you're saying, but in my gut, it feels right. So I'll listen."

"Let me know if you want my help in finding a therapist. I know a few who specialize in trauma. You'd have to go to Sacramento for sessions, but it shouldn't take very many."

"I'm not sure which would be worse. Therapy or sex."

Dakota grinned. "Which is part of the problem. For most people, sex with a great guy would be the preference."

"I guess." She looked at her friend. "Thanks for being brave enough to take me on."

"I'm here for you. I can also help you find a guy, if you'd like."

"Ah, no, thanks. Great offer, but I think I should humiliate myself in private."

Dakota tilted her head. "Why would there be humiliation?"

Charlie shook her head. "Now you're going all therapist on me. Change of topic.

How are the kids?"

"You're trying to distract me."

"Yes, and you're going to let it work, because you love me."

Dakota laughed. "You're going to be the best mom. Seriously. Get this fixed, Charlie, because you have babies just waiting to come into your life."

Charlie hoped she was right. The road to healing wasn't going to be much fun, though. Therapy or a man? Honest to God, she couldn't figure which road offered the least pain. With a man, she wouldn't have to haul her ass to another town. With therapy she wouldn't have to have sex. Of course it was possible her therapist would tell her to start dating, which meant the worst of both worlds.

She would get it figured out, she promised herself. Because she was ready to be part of a family.

Annabelle leaned against Khatar. "For us to take our relationship to the next level, you're going to have to be supportive of reality TV. There's no other way around it."

The horse rubbed the side of his face against her arm, as if nodding.

"Really?" she asked. "You wouldn't mind a *Project Runway* marathon? Or a night of

America's Next Top Model?"

"Does he ever answer?"

Annabelle looked up and saw Clay standing by the fence. He was still the most incredibly good-looking man she'd ever seen, but she was getting used to having him around. Not that she had any interest in the man. For her the world had been reduced to a single man she couldn't get off her mind.

"Sometimes," she said with a grin. "I speak fluent horse."

"There's a talent." Clay eyed the stallion. "I heard he was mean."

"I did, too, but it's silliness. Khatar is a sweetie."

"He tried to kill a guy."

Annabelle rubbed behind his ears. "I refuse to believe that."

"Maybe Shane started the rumor to get the horse's price down."

She laughed. "I doubt he would do that."

Clay studied her. "So you're one of those, are you?"

"One of what?"

"A woman who thinks my brother has principles."

"Are you saying he doesn't?"

"No. I'm messing with you. Shane's a good guy."

Which was an opening to a conversation she'd wanted to have with someone. Maybe Clay would help her out.

She walked toward him. Khatar followed.

"Can I ask you something?"

Clay put one foot on a railing and studied her. "Am I going to like the question?"

"I don't know."

He shrugged. "Go ahead."

"Am I like the infamous Rachel?"

Clay's perfect mouth twisted. "If you are, you need to get the hell out of my brother's life." He swore under his breath. "Has she been around?"

"Not that I know of. I'm sorry to bring her up. It's just she seems like a constant presence in Shane's life. He's judging me by her." She leaned against Khatar. "The first time Shane saw me, I was dancing on a bar. I wasn't drunk." She explained about the dance of the happy virgin. "I guess because of his ex, it made him wary. I want to know what she and I have in common."

"From what I've heard, almost nothing. Rachel . . ." He rested his forearms against the top railing. "Rachel lived big. She was always going and doing. Pretty enough, I suppose. But she knew how to attract men. All men." He looked at her. "Rachel wasn't happy unless every guy in the room wanted her."

Annabelle swallowed, wondering if maybe she'd started down a path she didn't want to follow. "I'd heard she cheated on Shane."

"She didn't just cheat. If a guy wasn't paying enough attention to her, she came on to him. She needed to be the center of attention in every situation. She claimed to love Shane, but I don't think she has a clue what love is."

Annabelle bit her lower lip. "Did she ever come on to you?"

Clay's look was hard. "More than once. Rafe, too. We didn't know what to do. Did we tell him? Did we ignore it? We had no idea if he wanted to know or not. He tried to make the marriage work, but finally figured out it was a lost cause. So he left. She came after him. They got back together. It was a cycle that continued for a few months until he was finally done."

She thought about her first marriage, about what had gone wrong. Lewis had a lot of culpability, but she'd been looking for more than any husband should have to provide. They were both at fault. It sounded like Shane had been trapped in a situation he would never win.

"Shane's biggest problem is that he's a

man of his word," Clay told her. "He wasn't willing to think the worst of his wife. I would have dumped her the first time she cheated. But he's loyal and didn't want to give up on the marriage."

"He's a good guy."

"He is. Which leaves me in the uncomfortable position of wondering if I should ask your intentions." He grinned. "There's something I never thought I would say. But he's family, you know?"

She didn't know. She'd heard. She'd seen other families. On a personal level, she'd always wanted to belong. She'd wanted it so much, she'd pretended to see characteristics in Lewis that weren't there.

She looked at Clay. "You sure you want to know?" she asked.

"I can take it."

She waited for a second, letting the truth wash through her. She'd been avoiding it for a while now, but there was no escaping reality.

"I love him."

Clay grinned. "That's putting it on the line. Does he know?"

"I haven't told him."

Clay held up both hands. "Don't think I'm gonna do it."

"I didn't. That would be very strange

coming from his brother."

Clay put his hands back on the railing. "He might be a bit of a jackass about the whole thing. Because of Rachel."

"I've already seen hints."

"Don't give up on him."

"I won't."

Because she'd finally found where she belonged. Now all she had to do was convince Shane that she was worth a second chance.

Shane headed toward the house to wash for dinner. He was sorry he hadn't said he was heading into town. He hadn't seen Annabelle in a couple of days and found himself wanting to see her and talk to her. He should have asked her out to dinner.

Which he could right now for tomorrow, he thought as he grabbed his cell phone. Just then the alert signal chirped, telling him he had a text message. He pushed the button and read, then grinned.

Miss you. Want to come over tonight?

He quickly texted back, Absolutely. Say when and I'll be there.

7:30 okay?

Perfect. See you then.

He walked into the house grinning.

Two hours later he parked in front of her

house. He'd showered and changed. On a whim, he'd stopped by a florist shop on the main street and picked up a bouquet of roses. Hokey, maybe, but still a classic choice. He'd gone with pink rather than red, to keep things light.

She opened the door before he had a chance to knock. She was wearing one of her strappy summer dresses and no shoes. Which meant she barely came to his shoulders. Her hair was long and loose, all curls. Her toes were a bright pink. She was walking, breathing sex and the second he saw her, he wanted her with the desperation of a man who'd spent the past twenty years alone on a desert island.

"For me?" she asked, smiling up at him. "Thank you. Wow. That's unexpected. But lovely."

Barely able to control his need, he handed her the flowers. She took them, breathed in the scent, then drew him inside and shut the door.

She put the flowers on a small table by the door. After turning back to face him, she put her hands on his shoulders and drew him close.

"Hey, handsome cowboy. I haven't seen you in a while," she murmured.

He went willingly, pulling her against him

and kissing her deeply. Even as he ran his hands up and down her back, he thrust his tongue into her mouth. She met him stroke for stroke, arching against him, rubbing herself against his rapidly growing erection.

He moved his hands from her hips to her rear. He squeezed the curves. When that wasn't enough, he found the zipper and jerked it down. After grabbing her dress by the shoulders, he gave it a tug.

Several things happened at once. Annabelle moved back slightly, so her dress could fall off her arms and drift down to the floor. He opened his eyes to watch the show. A heartbeat later, he saw she wasn't wearing anything under the dress.

Nothing. As in naked.

She smiled up at him. "I missed you."

He had to swallow before speaking. "You, ah, mentioned that in your text."

"I wasn't lying."

"I get that."

"Good." She took his hand, then turned and led the way to her bedroom. "I thought we could play doctor. I have a few places that need attention. Want me to show you?"

He wasn't sure how he'd gotten so lucky. Annabelle was funny, smart and caring. She was also something of a wildcat in bed. No one looking at her reading a story to kids at the library would guess that. Unless the person knew about the dance of the happy virgin and had had the pleasure of kissing her into moaning surrender.

Need pulsed through him in time with his heartbeat. He was hard enough to ache, and more than ready to play any game she wanted.

They reached her bedroom. She turned to face him again. "Oh, Dr. Shane, can you help me?"

As his hands settled on her breasts, he leaned in to press his mouth to hers. "Yes, ma'am, I can. Let me see if I can figure out where it hurts and then I'll kiss it and make it all better."

Chapter Eighteen

Annabelle waited around the side of the barn. The day was warm and clear, with a light breeze. Two afternoons ago a storm had blown through, dropping enough rain to wash everything clean. Now the ground was dry, the flowers bright, the moment perfect. Wedding perfect.

"I feel ridiculous," Charlie muttered, tugging on the waistband of her dress.

"You look great."

She did, Annabelle thought. The pinkish-melon fabric complemented her coloring, while the sweetheart neckline and fitted bodice showed off unexpected curves. One of the Gionni sisters — both helping the bridal party and on a truce for the wedding — had curled her short hair then used product to add an edge to the curls. Makeup, applied by a very brave Nevada, accentuated her blue eyes and long, dark lashes.

"You can dress up a pig, but it's still a pig," Charlie muttered.

"Wilbur would look very handsome in a tuxedo, and you're not a pig. You've spent your whole life trying to be the opposite of your mother. May I point out she's not here, you're a woman and every now and then it's fun to dress like you remember that. You look beautiful. Yes, it's a compliment. Suck it up and go with it."

Charlie blinked at her. "For a short person, you have a lot of attitude."

Annabelle laughed. "I'm also wearing four-inch heels which I could use as a weapon. Don't piss me off."

"I guess I won't."

Heidi came around the side of the barn. Glen and May were with her, both helping hold up the gown.

Heidi looked at them and sighed. "What was I thinking, wearing a train on grass? Once we get through the ceremony, I won't care about stains but until Rafe sees me, I want to be perfect."

"You've succeeded," Annabelle told her, taking in the upswept hair, the sparkling tiara and the graceful dress. "You're stunning."

"She's right," Charlie told her, voice thick. "Damn, I'm getting all misty."

"Thank you," Heidi told them. "For everything. For being my friends and helping me and —"

"Stop it right now," May said sternly. "I mean it, girls. Stop it or you'll all start crying. There's still the ceremony and then pictures. You can mess up your makeup all you want then. Do you hear me?"

"I'd listen if I were you," Glen told them, his mouth twitching as he tried not to smile. "She can be mean."

May gave a laugh, then started to straighten Heidi's gown. When it was in place, Annabelle handed the bride her bouquet. May left to be seated up in front.

Glen moved next to Heidi and offered his arm. "You ready for this?"

Heidi nodded. "Thanks, Grandpa. You know I love you, right?"

"Nearly as much as I love you. Rafe's a lucky man."

"I'm lucky, too."

Annabelle felt her eyes start to get a little misty. She blinked several times to avoid tears. The music changed to the last song before the bridal march. She looked at Charlie, who squared her shoulders, like a soldier heading to battle.

"I'm ready," Charlie muttered. "Let's get this over with."

"Ever the romantic."

Charlie gave a strangled laugh, then started around the barn. Annabelle waited about fifteen seconds, then followed. She turned left and was able to see the seated guests and the archway where the couple would be married.

Rafe stood up front, with Shane and Clay at his side. Annabelle did her best not to stare longingly at the middle Stryker brother, aware that in this crowd anything could be fodder for town gossip. But it was hard not to be impressed by the well-cut dark suit and the handsome man wearing it.

She walked slowly up the petal-covered center walkway and took her place by Charlie. Off to the side a string quartet, compliments of the California University Fool's Gold music department, seamlessly transitioned into the wedding march. The guests rose and the bride appeared.

The ceremony was quick but meaningful, with Rafe and Heidi reciting vows they'd written, followed by the traditional love, honor and cherish. The kiss was just passionate enough to assure everyone this couple was going to make it, then they straightened and were introduced as husband and wife.

An hour later the pictures had been taken. Heidi's dress had one more surprise — the overskirt came off, leaving the bride in a reception-friendly long dress, absent extra layers and the heavy train.

The quartet was replaced by Fool's Gold's favorite party DJ and guests began to dance. Annabelle was just going to find Charlie when Shane came up and captured her hand.

"You've been avoiding me," he said, pulling her close as the music shifted to something slow and romantic and they began to move together.

"No, I was giving you space."

"Why?"

"You might have brought a date to the wedding."

He looked genuinely confused. "Another woman?"

"Or a man. I'm not going to judge."

Shane pulled her to the side of the dance floor. "Annabelle, what are you talking about? Why wouldn't I be with you?"

She stared up at him. The four-inch heels helped, but honestly nothing could change the fact that she was just plain short.

"We're spending time together," she told him. "But we haven't talked about anything. I didn't want to presume."

"That we're together?"

She nodded.

He sighed. "I've been out of the game a long time if I'm doing it this badly." He put his hands on her shoulders and stared into her eyes. "I'm with you. What did you think the other night was about?"

"Enjoying each other."

He frowned. "Are you enjoying yourself with anyone else?"

She smiled. "No. You have me firmly captivated." A safer truth than the fact that she loved him. She would get into that later, assuming this conversation went well.

"Good. I want to captivate you. Because you've got me under your spell. There's no one else. I'm only seeing you."

Her heart gave a little flutter and she did her best to look interested but not giddy. "So if we were in high school . . ."

"I'd give you my letterman's jacket, carry your books and beat the shit out of any guy who asked you out."

She raised herself on tiptoes and kissed his mouth. "And I'd let you go all the way after prom."

He touched her face. "I could never resist you."

"I like that in a man."

"Any man?"

"No. Just you."

For a second, they stared at each other. She willed him to say more. To tell her he loved her. That he'd let go of the past and no matter what, he was going to trust her. But before he could say anything, May announced the buffet was open and that everyone should enjoy the food.

Shane put his arm around her. "Buy you dinner?"

Aware the moment had been lost, she smiled up at him. "I'd like that very much."

Four hours later, Annabelle was feeling the champagne. It was a sneaky liquid, all bubbly and friendly. Going down so easily. Then it snuck up and bit you in the butt. Or in her case, the head. Because everything was just a little spinny.

It was her own fault. Because of all the work there'd been getting everything ready for the wedding, she hadn't eaten and her trip to the buffet had come after the champagne. So the single glass she'd consumed had hit her hard. Good thing arrangements had already been made for rides back to town for the partygoers. May and Glen had rented the school buses. So driving wasn't an issue, but she had a feeling she might be in for a rocky morning.

"A problem for another time," she murmured, making her way back from the restroom. She walked, or maybe swayed, her way around the dance floor, searching for Shane. Clay stopped her instead.

"You're drunk," he said with a grin.

"Not drunk. You can't say drunk," she informed him. "*Buzzed* is a much better word. Seriously, I've had one glass, so how bad could it be?"

"You're a pretty cheap date."

She stared at him, trying to figure out what made him so attractive. A quirk of genetics. Appearance was all about math. She knew that. Symmetry and spacing. And . . . something else she couldn't remember right now.

"You're very handsome," she told Clay. "I mean that in an objective way. I'm not the least bit interested in sleeping with you. Because the sex with Shane is amazing. Seriously." She hiccupped slightly, then covered her mouth and leaned against him. "Sorry."

Clay's mouth twitched as he put his arms around her and held her upright. "You have it bad."

She wasn't sure if he meant the liquor or the man and decided it didn't matter. "I'll be fine."

"I'm not so sure. Are you going to remember this conversation?"

"Of course. Probably. I'm not sure. Is it important?"

He laughed, moving his arm to her waist to keep her from swaying. "If you forget, I'll tell you again. I talked to Mayor Marsha earlier. She mentioned the festival and dance you're doing to raise money for the bookmobile. She said you're still looking for a male sacrifice. I'll do it if you want."

It took Annabelle a second to process his words, then her eyes widened. "Really? You have to wear a loincloth and get your heart cut out. Not really. The heart bit. It's pretend."

"Sure. I've worn less than a loincloth."

"You've been naked," Annabelle said in a whisper. "I've seen your butt in the movies. It's nice."

"Thank you."

She held up her hands, wanting to be clear. "I'm still not interested. You know, in you."

"I got that. Because you're into Shane."

She nodded and motioned for him to come closer. "I'm still in love with him. I don't think that's ever going to change. He doesn't know yet."

Clay surprised her by hugging her. "I'm

glad," he said in a low voice, when he released her. "He deserves someone like you."

"I think so, too."

He put his hands on her shoulders and turned her. "Shane is watching us. He's that way."

"Okay. Thanks."

She started walking. The music seemed really loud and suddenly her stomach wasn't as happy as it had been. Her champagne buzz became a little more of a headache.

This couldn't be good, she thought, wondering if her happy time was about to catch up with her. She turned, thinking maybe she should head to the house and lie down for a few minutes, then spun back, deciding she would find Shane first. As she moved, she ran into Nevada.

"Sorry," she said quickly. "I wasn't looking."

Nevada laughed. "No, it's me. I'm not paying attention." Nevada squeezed her hand, practically beaming. "Wasn't the wedding wonderful? Isn't everything perfect?"

Annabelle studied her friend. "Are you okay? You seem, um, different tonight." Because saying "too happy" was a little too blunt. While Nevada was a lot of fun, she was rarely giddy. "Or are you enjoying the champagne as much as I am?"

Nevada drew in a breath, then sighed. "It's not champagne," she admitted. "I haven't had any." She glanced around, then lowered her voice. "Tucker and I just found out I'm pregnant. It's totally unexpected. We've been using protection. But we're newlyweds and we've been busy, so I guess we beat the odds. The plan was to wait for a couple of years, but here we are."

She smiled widely. "I'm so happy."

"Congratulations," Annabelle told her. "That's great news. Is it still a secret?"

"Yes. We're not telling everyone until next week. We just found out yesterday and we didn't want to take away from Heidi and Rafe's wedding." Nevada hugged her. "I'm so lucky. First Tucker and now a baby." She laughed and then released Annabelle. "I need to get back to my sisters. Let's have lunch next week."

"I'd like that."

Annabelle watched her walk away. She started to walk toward Shane, then stopped as her champagne-induced buzz disappeared as if it had never been. Cold sobriety hit her along with an impossible possibility. Nevada's words rang in her head, as loud as bells, as frightening as the thunderous roar of an approaching train.

An unexpected pregnancy. They'd used protection. An unexpected pregnancy.

"No," Annabelle whispered. "No. I'm not. I couldn't be."

They'd been careful. All those long nights of making love over and over again. They'd been careful.

If she was pregnant, Shane would . . .

She couldn't begin to imagine, but it would be bad.

She told herself to stop it. Not to worry. That there was no way she was going to have a baby. But the knot of worry that had quickly formed wouldn't go away. Which meant she was going to have to find out for sure. As soon as she could.

Shane stabbed the straw viciously, wishing it would fight back. He was pissed and had nowhere to put his anger. He'd been awake since dawn, taking care of Heidi's goats then cleaning out the stable. The hard work had done nothing to dull his sense of betrayal.

To think he'd been the chump who'd offered to relieve Annabelle of her offer to milk Heidi's goats while the happy couple was spending the weekend in San Francisco. Had she secretly been laughing at him the whole time? Why not? Here he was, being played again.

"You're up early."

He glanced over his shoulder and saw Clay had walked into the barn. His younger brother had a mug in his hand. He held it out.

"I brought you coffee. Mom said you were gone before she could make any."

Shane put down the pitchfork and walked to his brother. He took the mug of coffee, set it on a nearby bench, then drew back his fist and hit Clay squarely in the jaw.

His brother went down like a sack of potatoes, landing on his butt. He stared up at Shane with an expression of disbelief.

"What the hell is wrong with you?"

Shane rubbed his stinging knuckles. Despite the pain, he actually felt a little better. "Stay away from my girl."

"What are you talking about?"

"Annabelle."

"I know who, asshole. What is this about?"

Shane picked up the coffee and took a drink. When he'd swallowed, he stared at Clay, still on the ground. "Yesterday. At the wedding. You were all over her."

Clay moved his jaw back and forth. "Good thing I'm out of the business. You can't hide a bruise in a picture that's going to be on a billboard." He sat up straighter and rested his arms on his knees. "Listen. I heard from Mayor Marsha that Annabelle still needed someone to help her with her festival. Something about a male sacrifice. I told her I'd do it. That's it."

Shane's relatively good mood faded as the fury returned. "You are not going anywhere near her."

"I'm helping your girlfriend. That's what brothers do."

"Sure. Pretend you're helping. What else are you doing? Are you seeing her? Were you with her last night?" Because he'd planned to spend the evening with Annabelle, but she'd pleaded a headache and had gone home early.

"I was here," Clay told him. "With you. What is going on? Why are you —" Clay's expression of outrage shifted to something more like compassion. "I get it."

"What?" Shane demanded.

Clay climbed to his feet. "She's not Rachel," he said quietly. "She's nothing like her. For what it's worth, I think you're damn lucky to have found someone like Annabelle. You're my brother, Shane. When Rafe was being a jerk, you were always there for me. We've been close our entire lives. You know I'd never do anything to hurt you. I never touched Rachel and I would never get between you and Annabelle. But you already know that. What I can't figure out is why you're looking for trouble. Are you worried that she's like Rachel, or terrified that she isn't? Because if she isn't, if she's just what she seems, then you're going to have to step it up and be worthy."

"You're talking like a girl."

"You're avoiding the question and the truth. You're not mad at me. I don't think you're even mad at Annabelle. You've got a burr up your butt about something and you need to figure out what."

With that he left the barn.

Shane stared after him, then turned back to his work. But he'd lost the energy for it. His brother's words mocked him as he wondered if they could possibly be true. Was he looking for trouble where none existed or was he seeing things clearly? And if this was just leftover trash from his first marriage, how did he get rid of it and believe in someone else?

Annabelle paced the length of her living room. "I'm going to throw up."

Charlie eyed her cautiously. "Is this drama, or are you serious?"

"I don't know." She pressed a hand to her roiling stomach. She hadn't felt right since the wedding, two days ago. She wanted to blame the champagne, but couldn't. Maybe it was hormones.

She turned to the sofa, thinking she should sit, then realized she was too upset and that the walking back and forth helped.

She looked at her friend. "This is so bad. Really, really bad. He's just starting to trust me."

"Shane," Charlie said, in a tone that indicated she was still playing catch-up.

Annabelle reminded herself she'd called the other woman and begged her to come over without telling her why. Explanations were required.

She dropped to the ottoman in front of Charlie's chair. "Shane was married before."

"I know that part."

"From what I've been hearing, she was pretty awful. Wild and unfaithful. Shane isn't the kind of guy who gives up easily. His word matters. So he tried to make the marriage work and she kept cheating and then it was over."

"Nearly everyone deserves a second chance," Charlie said cautiously. "Now he's done with her. What's the problem?"

"Sometimes he thinks I'm like her. That I'm wild and flighty."

"You're not."

"I know, but the first time he saw me was after he'd moved back. The night I did the dance of the happy virgin at Jo's bar. It painted a different picture."

"I can see that. But now he knows you. He trusts you."

"He was starting to. I think. I hope. But then Lewis showed up and we weren't really divorced."

"Not your fault."

"Agreed, but it was awkward. It seems like every time he starts to get close, something happens."

Charlie stared at her. "And something has happened again?"

"I'm pregnant."

Charlie's mouth dropped open. She closed it and swore. "Seriously?"

Annabelle fought tears. "Yes. I found out this morning. I suspected at the wedding." She hesitated. Nevada hadn't announced her good news, and she didn't want to steal her thunder. "I was thinking about how great things were with Shane and suddenly I wondered. I went to the drugstore as soon as it opened and got a test."

She pressed her lips together. "I'm happy about the baby, of course. It's shocking, but good. Honestly, I can't wrap my mind around that part of it. I'm so caught up in

400

wondering how bad this is going to be with Shane. Just when he's starting to trust me, you know? He's not going to believe this is an accident. He's going to think the worst of me. He's going to assume I did it on purpose."

Which wasn't true, she thought sadly. She hadn't had a clue. Which had meant an emergency visit to her gynecologist, stick in hand, to find out if she'd done anything bad by drinking a glass of champagne at the wedding. Thankfully Dr. Galloway was used to hysterical pregnant women and had taken a few minutes to reassure her before sending her off to schedule a regular visit.

"He's as much responsible as you are," Charlie told her. "This isn't your fault any more than it's his. You used protection."

"Faithfully."

"Then you tell him he has good swimmers and he should be proud."

"I doubt he's going to see it that way," Annabelle murmured. "This is so much worse than Lewis. That was just a paperwork error that didn't affect him directly. This is a baby!"

Charlie leaned forward and grabbed her shoulders. "You didn't do anything wrong. Give Shane a chance to screw up before you assume the worst. He might surprise you."

"Good advice," Annabelle whispered. Too bad she knew Shane well enough to believe he wasn't going to surprise her this time. At least not in a good way.

CHAPTER NINETEEN

"Shouldn't your business partner be doing this with you?" Shane asked as he followed his brother into yet another building in the center of Fool's Gold. So far they'd looked at three potential office locations. To Shane they were all the same — open spaces with windows and doors. Weren't all offices the same?

"Dante's hiding out in San Francisco," Rafe told him, using a laser tape measure to take quick calculations. "Resisting the inevitable."

The inevitable being the company's move. "Dante's not a small-town kind of guy," Shane pointed out. "I'm not sure how he'll fit in here."

"He'll do fine." Rafe nodded appreciatively. "I like this one. I wonder what's upstairs?"

Temporary space was needed for Rafe's company. He and Dante had bought a building on the edge of town, but it needed major remodeling and wouldn't be ready for at least eight months. Which meant either commuting to San Francisco, something Rafe didn't want to do, or getting a temporary location.

Shane wasn't sure why he'd bothered tagging along. Getting away from the ranch had seemed like a good idea, but now that he was standing alone in the big open office space, he realized he could still hear himself thinking. He needed more of a distraction.

"Would you take it as is?" Shane asked, checking out a small alcove that was obviously a break room. There was a refrigerator, microwave, table and chairs, cupboards and plenty of counter space. Nothing fancy, but workable.

"Yes. I don't want to put any money into remodeling. It's only for a few months. We can make do."

Shane walked back into the main room. "There aren't any private offices."

Rafe grinned. "Dante is going to love this place."

"Why do you want to torture your business partner?"

"For sport," Rafe admitted. "Yup, this is it. We can get all the desks in here. Half the staff will be staying in San Francisco until the new building is ready, so there's plenty of room."

He made a few notes on a tablet, then clipped the laser tape measure onto his belt. "Let's go talk to the owner about a short-term lease. I want everything signed before Heidi and I leave for Paris in a few weeks."

Shane followed him out. When they reached the sidewalk, Rafe paused.

"You don't have to go with me," he said. "If you have somewhere else you'd rather be."

"Like where?"

"The library. Don't you want to see Annabelle?"

They were standing by the stairs that led to the second-floor businesses. A couple of young girls — maybe ten or eleven — walked by and started up the stairs. Shane shifted to the left to give them room.

"You're still pissed," Rafe said when the girls were out of earshot.

"No."

"You are. I can tell. You're being an idiot."

"You didn't see what happened," Shane told him, feeling his temper rise.

"I heard about it. Clay agreed to be Annabelle's sacrifice for her dance and they hugged."

Shane kept telling himself that was all

there was to it. But he couldn't shake the feeling of being played for a fool. Something he'd felt too often with his ex.

"If it was more —" he began.

Rafe cut him off with a shake of his head. "Isn't the bookmobile important to Annabelle?"

"Yes."

"Isn't that why she came to see you in the first place? To learn to ride and do the horse dance?"

Shane shoved his hands in his pockets and nodded.

"Didn't she tell you about the program and ask you to be the sacrifice? Didn't you refuse?"

"Stop being logical. This isn't about that."

"No. It's about you being stupid. You're making this more than it is. The worst part is deep inside, you know that, too. You're so busy worrying about Annabelle being like your ex-wife, that you're pushing her away when she's done nothing wrong. But you'll never be free from your past until you learn to let go."

Rafe stared at him. Shane turned away. "Don't you think I know that?"

"Apparently not, based on how you're acting. Clay offered to help your girl. *Your* girl. You think he doesn't respect your relationship with Annabelle? You think he'd want to get in the way of that?" Rafe paused as two more girls hurried toward the stairs and ran up to the second floor.

Rafe lowered his voice. "You're crazy about her and you're blowing it. Do you think you can do better?"

"I don't want to do better. I want to be sure."

"Sometimes caring about someone requires taking a leap of faith. This is that time. Go talk to her. Let her know you're going to need a little help getting through this. But you can, if you have a little faith in her. And maybe yourself."

Shane thought about punching his brother, but knew Rafe wouldn't take it as well as Clay had. Plus, there was a chance Rafe might be right. About all of it.

"Marriage suits you."

Rafe grinned. "Heidi suits me. You've been given a second chance, bro. Don't blow it."

Annabelle let Khatar pick his way over the open ground. She'd come to the ranch earlier, planning on sitting down with Shane and telling him about her pregnancy. But when she arrived, May told her that Shane had gone into Fool's Gold with Rafe to look at temporary locations for Rafe's business.

Rather than spend her time pacing and getting more upset, she'd decided to go for a ride.

Over the past couple of weeks, she and Shane had been taking long rides together. They worked on the dance steps with Khatar then headed out past the fence lines and toward Shane's property.

Now she urged Khatar in that direction. He went easily, remembering the route.

They walked by a grove of trees, then circled around to the edge of Shane's property. From there it was a ten-minute canter to the construction site.

She stayed back far enough not to spook the horse. The stables were nearly finished and the house had been framed. Shane had taken most of her suggestions and his contractor had called to thank her for keeping him on track, as far as picking out fixtures, surfaces and appliances.

She could already see the finished house in her mind. She knew what the front door would look like, could imagine stepping into the entryway. There would be a light overhead, a switch to the left. From there it was a short walk to the great room. The kitchen was bigger now, with more counter space and more storage. They'd chosen everything together. There was even a jetted tub for two in the master.

"I'm playing a dangerous game," she whispered. "Falling for a man who might never trust me again."

Once he found out about the baby.

She had hopes, of course. The fantasy that he would hear the news, gather her in his arms and tell her he would love her forever. That the baby was the best surprise ever. Unlikely, she thought sadly. While she was at it, she could add movie music that swelled as the credits rolled. Because the odds of that happening seemed so small.

One of the construction guys spotted her and waved. She waved back. She leaned over and patted Khatar. "We should probably head back," she told the horse and began to turn him. He took a couple of steps, then stopped, his ears forward as if listening to something unfamiliar.

Annabelle was quiet, listening. Then she heard it, too. A warning rattle. Her whole body went stiff with fear as she stared down at the ground, searching for the owner of that scary sound.

The snake was coiled by a bush, inches from Khatar's hoof. Annabelle sucked in a breath and carefully drew the horse back. She didn't know what would happen if he was bitten, but knew it wouldn't be good.

"Come on," she said quietly. "Back. Get back. We'll leave him alone."

Khatar did as she requested, taking a step away. Then the snake lunged forward and the horse went on the attack.

There was very little warning. Khatar rose on his back legs, then came crushing down. The snake was pulverized, suffering an instant death. Annabelle did her best to hang on to the saddle while keeping hold of the reins. Then she felt herself starting to slip. She screamed.

Khatar rose up again, as if determined to reduce the snake to little more than a stain on the dirt. Her left foot slipped out of the stirrup, the reins fell from her fingers. She reached for them just as Khatar came down hard on his hooves. He rose again and she went flying.

The sense of soaring through the air shocked her but not as much as the hard ground. She landed on her back, all the air rushing from her lungs. Yet breathing was the least of it, she thought in a panic, her hands covering her belly, as if offering protection.

The baby, she thought as Khatar stepped close and snuffled her cheek. The baby. She inhaled the scent of the horse, saw the sky go black and then there was nothing.

■ ■ ■ ■

"You're very lucky," the doctor said.

Annabelle was sure he'd introduced himself, but right now names were the least of her issues.

"Nothing broken," he continued. "Your bump on the head isn't serious. We're going to keep you overnight, for observation. If all goes as we expect, you'll be released in the morning."

Annabelle put her hand on her stomach. "I'm pregnant," she said quietly, trying not to panic. "Is the baby okay?"

The doctor, an older man with gray hair, glanced down at her stomach. "How far along?"

"I'm not sure. Around six or eight weeks."

"Do you see Dr. Galloway?"

Annabelle nodded.

"I just saw her in the hall. Let me tell her you're here and check if she can see you."

"Thank you."

He left. Annabelle swallowed against the tightness in her throat and told herself that everything would be fine. That even though she felt as if she'd been run over by a truck, the doctor had assured her she wasn't hurt. The baby was small, right? Protected? If she was okay, then her child would be, too. Except she knew that fall could be bad for an unborn child.

She shivered, then pulled up the blanket and tried to get warm. The steady throb of a headache made it hard to do anything but get lost in the fear.

A few minutes later, Dr. Galloway entered the room and walked over to Annabelle.

"What is this I hear?" the doctor asked as she took Annabelle's hand and gave her a warm smile. "You fell off a horse?"

"I didn't mean to. He was protecting me from a rattlesnake."

"Then he sounds like a good kind of horse. How do you feel?"

"Beat up."

"Any cramping?"

Annabelle shook her head.

"Excellent. I've ordered an ultrasound. They should be here for you shortly and then we'll have a look and see what happened. Until then, try not to worry. I know that sounds impossible, but make the attempt. Babies are surprisingly resilient."

"All right," Annabelle whispered.

Three hours later, she was wheeled back into her room. A pretty nurse bustled in to check her vitals and offer her a sandwich to tide her over until dinner.

"We've been flooded with calls," the nurse added with a smile. "Word got out about your accident and the whole town wants to know if you're okay."

Annabelle couldn't imagine ever feeling hungry or tired or sad again. Not when the news had been so good. The baby was fine. She had, in Dr. Galloway's terms, fallen exactly right to protect a growing fetus. Her bones and organs had cushioned the growing life inside of her, which meant she would be sore for a few days but the child would be unaffected.

She let the relief spread over her and knew she would always be grateful. "A sandwich would be great," she said. "As to my friends, you can tell them everything is perfect. I'll be home in the morning. And yes, that's actual permission to give out the information. I know you have strict confidentiality guidelines."

"We do and I appreciate the specific instructions. There are a few people outside in the waiting room. Is it okay to send them in?"

"Sure."

Annabelle realized she probably looked awful, but that didn't matter, either. Her baby had survived. Right now he or she was growing. In a few months she would be holding an infant in her arms. That was going to be her priority.

As the nurse left, Annabelle wondered if Shane had heard about the accident and if he was one of the people waiting. At the thought of him, her heart quickened. As soon as they were alone, she wanted to tell him about the baby.

She loved him and hoped for the best. Hoped he cared about her as well, that he loved her and wanted to be with her. But even if he didn't, she would be fine. That's what she'd decided while waiting for her ultrasound. That she would make it work in every way possible. She'd grown up knowing she wasn't wanted by either parent. She would do everything in her power to make sure that never happened to her child. She was strong and had a good job. She lived in a wonderful place and had supportive friends. She would get through this and she and her child would thrive.

But everything would be so much better if Shane came along for the ride.

Heidi and May burst into her room.

"Are you all right?"

"What happened?"

"Are you broken?"

They were speaking over each other as they rushed toward her. Heidi ran around

414

to the other side, then they hugged her together.

"I'm fine," she said. "I'm going home in the morning. Nothing is broken. Just a few bruises."

She didn't tell them the best part, but as she spoke, she rested a protective hand on her stomach and sent all the love she had to the growing life inside of her.

"You are Shane Stryker?"

Shane nodded at the woman in the white coat. She'd found him pacing in the waiting room.

"I'm Dr. Galloway."

The woman was in her late fifties, with steel-gray hair and glasses. Her eyes were kind and she didn't look like she was delivering bad news.

"Is Annabelle okay? The construction guys saw what happened. Khatar reared. Ah, that's a horse. I thought maybe he was trying to throw her, but there was a snake. He killed it. I think he was protecting her."

"That's what she said, too. Annabelle is well. Nothing broken. She hit her head, but even that seems to be minor. We'll keep her overnight and release her in the morning."

Shane released the breath he'd been holding. Relief rushed through him. "You're sure."

The doctor motioned to a sofa and chair in the corner. "Let's sit," she said.

He followed her and then sat. She angled toward him.

Dr. Galloway smiled at him. "The baby is fine. It's so tiny and there's so much cushioning. We did an ultrasound. All is well. I knew you'd want to know."

She said something else. They both stood and shook hands. Shane might have spoken in return, but he couldn't say for sure. It was as if his mind and his body had separated. He could see himself moving and talking, but it wasn't him doing it. He was on the outside, watching.

Baby? Annabelle was pregnant?

The words echoed and repeated. They turned upside down, then righted themselves. They formed images. A baby. She was having a baby. His baby.

He thought of all the times they'd been together. How they'd used protection. Condoms, which worked most of the time, but not always. He thought of her dancing on the bar at Jo's and how she laughed and the way Khatar would literally break down walls to be with her. He thought of how he felt when he was around her and knew that as much as he wanted not to be played, he didn't have a choice.

Annabelle watched the door anxiously. She'd had a steady stream of visitors, but had yet to see Shane. It was nearly six and she could smell the dinner trays being distributed. She'd barely touched the sandwich that the nurse had brought even though she knew it was important to eat. Yet all she could think of was that she wanted to see Shane.

And then he was there, walking into her room. Tall and handsome, everything she could want in a man. His gaze met hers.

"You scared the hell out of me," he told her.

"Sorry. It wasn't Khatar's fault."

"I know. I saw the snake. Or what's left of it."

"He was very brave and determined. The snake didn't stand a chance. But I lost one of the stirrups and started slipping and then I was flying through the air. I don't remember much after that."

There was something in his eyes, she thought, feeling a little uneasy. Something about the way he was looking at her. She raised the bed a little, so she was sitting up.

"Shane? What is it?" She couldn't tell what

he was thinking, but he didn't look happy. "Is Khatar all right?"

"He's fine. Rafe took him back to the ranch." His gaze intensified. "All right, Annabelle, let's get married."

"What?" Her voice was breathless, as she did her best to grasp the words. "Married? What are you talking about?"

Because he wasn't acting like a man out of his mind with love. He seemed . . . resigned. As if they'd been in a battle and he'd lost. But they hadn't been. They didn't fight. They weren't that —

Oh, God. She'd told Dr. Galloway it was okay to talk to Shane. She'd meant it was okay to tell him she wasn't hurt. But Dr. Galloway was a gynecologist. By definition, she would assume Annabelle meant the baby.

He wasn't proposing, he was giving in. He was assuming she expected that if she was pregnant, she would want him to marry her. He was accepting responsibility. Because that's what Shane did. The right thing.

He was an honorable man. A man who took care of his own. In his world, if a man got a woman pregnant, he married her. He would be her husband and the baby's father and for the rest of his life, he would believe he'd been tricked into all of it.

It was as if everything she'd wanted, everything she'd dreamed of having, had been resting right there on the palm of her hand. All she had to do was close her fingers and she would have it forever.

She couldn't even hate him, she thought, resigned to the inevitable. Because she loved his honor as much as she loved everything else about him. But forever duty wasn't forever love. And she'd promised herself she was never going to settle again.

She was grateful to be in the bed because right now there was no way she could stay standing. Her legs felt weak and she hurt. Not just from the fall, but from the inside. Where her heart had already started to crack.

"While that's a lovely invitation," she told him, "thank you, but no. We won't be getting married."

"You're having my baby."

"That's true. But one has nothing to do with the other."

His mouth twisted. "You're going to make me beg?"

"I'm not going to make you do anything, Shane. Yes, I'm pregnant. Obviously it's yours. But that is the only relevant information on the table. I'm sorry Dr. Galloway was the one to tell you. I came out to the ranch this morning to talk to you myself. You were gone, so I took Khatar out. My plan was to tell you when you came back. This is what happened instead." She kept her gaze steady. "Marriage is not on the table."

His expression tightened. "You're making this a game."

"I'm not. I'm telling you that I didn't deliberately get pregnant to trap you. I'm not that person."

"You're going to have the baby on your own?"

"Yes. I can do that. I can do a lot of things. I'm very capable."

"And I just walk away?"

"You'll do what you want," she told him flatly. "The baby is a long way off. We have time to come up with a plan if you're interested in shared custody or being a part of the child's life. But understand this. I know what it's like to be in a relationship based on assumptions and dreams rather than love and reality and I won't be part of that again. I won't live a lie."

She willed him to see she was telling the truth. "Believe me when I tell you I won't marry you, Shane. I won't marry you because it's the right thing to do or because of your sense of responsibility. That's your problem, not mine. I want someone who loves me and needs to spend the rest of his life with me. I want a man to adore me the way Khatar does. I want messy, passionate love. I don't care if it's inconvenient. I want it all and I deserve it. What I don't deserve is a man who has once again been caught in a situation that leaves him feeling trapped."

Her throat tightened and her eyes began to burn. Tears were not far away and she didn't want Shane to see her break down.

She swallowed. "You should go now."

"We're not done talking about this," he told her.

"You're wrong. About me and this situation. We're completely and totally done."

CHAPTER TWENTY

Charlie held her close. Annabelle let her friend tell her everything was going to be okay, then sniffed and straightened.

"You know I don't believe you," she said, as she grabbed another tissue and wiped her face. "About any of it."

Charlie looked stricken. "I know. I can't help saying everything will be fine. What I'm thinking is Shane is a complete jerk and I should run him over with a fire truck."

"Don't. You'd go to jail and then I'd really be alone." Annabelle gave a strangled sob. "How selfish is that?"

"It's not. I appreciate you missing me."

Annabelle nodded as more tears fell. "I would. You're a good friend. I think you should brace yourself. I'm going to be a little needy for the next few months."

"I'll be here. I don't scare that easily."

"Are you mad about the baby?"

Charlie frowned. "Mad? Why would

I be mad?"

"Because you've been talking to Dakota and Pia about IVF and maybe adopting and here I go and get pregnant."

Charlie hugged her again. Strong arms held her tight, then released her. "That's twisted, even for you. It's not like there's a limited number of babies and you took the last one. I can still have one, too. Or an older child. I haven't decided. If you're happy, I'm happy."

"Thank you." She pressed a hand to her chest. "I can't tell you how much this hurts. All of it. Losing Shane, finding out he doesn't believe in me, that in his mind, I'm still like his ex. How can that be?"

"You know it's not about you, right?"

"What? Of course it's about me."

"No," Charlie told her. "This is about Shane and his inability to trust. The pregnancy is a simple and easy way for him to express his deepest fears. It's kind of good it happened sooner rather than later. Either he'd deal or he wouldn't. And if he doesn't . . ." She pressed her lips together. "Sorry. Sometimes I get too logical."

Annabelle touched her hand. "You're being a good friend and I appreciate that. You're right. I don't want to hear it, but I know you're making sense. If Shane can't get over Rachel, I need to know that."

"Whatever happens, you're going to be a mom."

Annabelle managed a watery smile. "I'm happy about that." She reached for more tissue. "Can you do me a favor?"

"Sure."

"Would you not tell anyone about this for a while? I know I'll be smothered in sympathy and right now I can't deal with that."

"Of course. Whenever you're ready. We'll invite the girls in and —" She scrunched her nose. "I guess we won't be doing the margarita thing, what with you having a baby."

"I picked a bad time to figure out the man I desperately love isn't in love with me, huh?"

"There's never a good time for that."

Shane didn't know what the hell he was supposed to do now.

He still had plenty of work. Talking to the trainers working with his racehorses, keeping tabs on the mares, working with Khatar and planning the next step in his breeding program. Work he liked. Work that satisfied him. There was the construction on his land and the constant stream of questions. His family. He was a busy guy with a lot of responsibility. None of which kept him from thinking about Annabelle.

He hadn't seen her in seventy-two hours. Long hours that were empty and made him ache. He hadn't realized how much he was used to having her around until she was gone. The righteous anger that had taken over at the hospital had faded, leaving only confusion. Because he was a man at war . . . with himself.

His gut and his head said Annabelle was a woman he could believe. That she would never hurt him, never trick him. But his heart — his heart remembered and was slow to trust again.

He wasn't dealing with the idea of a baby at all. He couldn't. Not until he'd figured out what he was going to do about Annabelle. From where he was standing, he either believed her or he didn't. There was trust or not.

Annabelle loved kids. He'd seen her with them, both at the library and here at the ranch. She inspired them such that they offered her all the money they had to help bring a bookmobile to Fool's Gold. Because she'd shown them that reading was a gift. A key to worlds beyond their imagination.

He'd also seen her with Khatar. One rule on any ranch was when a person couldn't get along with horses or dogs, he or she wasn't worth having around. The difficult Arabian had become a gentle, easy mount because of Annabelle. He was still the brave leader of the herd — his desire to protect Annabelle had proven that. But whatever had caused him to be vicious was gone. Just last week, he'd slipped out of his corral to be with the girls during their lesson. He'd walked around with them, the fifth horse in the procession, following the steps perfectly.

Annabelle had given herself in so many ways. Helping Heidi with the wedding, offering to take care of the goats. She'd helped him with his house. She'd been a good friend and a generous lover. She put herself on the line — personally, professionally, sexually. When Lewis had shown up, she'd been completely honest about what had happened.

He missed her. Seeing her, talking to her, touching her. He'd wanted to call, to check on her, but hadn't been able to make himself pick up the phone. Last night at dinner, Heidi had mentioned she was completely recovered and he'd been relieved.

A familiar car drove into the yard and parked by the barn. Shane took a step toward the vehicle, both surprised and gratified she'd shown up. They were supposed to have one more practice before the parade on Saturday. He wasn't sure he would see her, or even if it was okay for her to ride.

He hurried toward her, needing to hear her voice. Even if all she did was to tell him to stay the hell away from her. Then the passenger door opened and Charlie got out. The other woman's expression was hard and determined. Obviously Annabelle had told her friend everything. Charlie wasn't here to watch the practice, she was going to act as a buffer. To make sure Shane didn't hurt Annabelle anymore.

Then it didn't matter because Annabelle was walking toward him and she was all he could see. She wore jeans and boots, and a T-shirt that teased "Research This!" She was all curves and sex appeal. A thinking man's perfect 10.

Except the smile he adored was missing and her eyes were sad. She looked as if she'd lost a part of herself, as if something precious had been stolen. Pain twisted in his belly when he realized he was the thief in question.

"I want to run through the steps one more time," she told him. "Charlie will be with me, so you don't have to stay."

A dismissal, which he deserved, he told himself. "Are you all right?" he asked. "Are you feeling well enough to ride?"

She shrugged. "I'm still sore, but it's not bad. I saw my doctor yesterday and she cleared me to practice and ride in the parade. We do everything at a walk, so that's safe. I'll hang on with both hands for the big finish. It's fine. Khatar would never hurt me."

The last words were spoken with a defiant lift of her chin.

"I know he wouldn't," he told her, then glanced past her to where Charlie stood guard. "Can I talk to you later?"

"Sure. Maybe after the parade."

He wanted to tell her he was sorry he'd hurt her, but knew the words were feeble and insulting. Not meaning to hurt her didn't make the pain any better.

Khatar came trotting around the barn. Shane wasn't even surprised.

"I'll get him saddled," he said.

"That's okay. Charlie can do it. Khatar likes her, too."

Then Annabelle deliberately turned her back on him and walked to the horse. Shane watched her go and knew that he'd just lost something important. Something he could never replace.

Not knowing what else to do, he started for the house. As he walked up the stairs to the back porch, Clay stepped out of the house.

"Is Annabelle here?" his brother asked. "She called and wanted to know if I could practice with her. For the ceremony on Saturday."

Clay kept talking, but Shane was too busy charging him to listen. He bent at the waist and slammed his shoulder hard into his brother's midsection. Momentum drove them back.

Shane straightened, already swinging. Clay dodged both fists, slapping Shane's arm away when he got too close. Shane knew his brother was holding back and it pissed him off.

"Fight back," he demanded.

"Not happening. You do remember I've been studying martial arts for ten years, right? If I hit you, I'm going to break something."

"Cheap talk," Shane growled.

Without warning, Clay's booted left foot shoved against Shane's middle. The power of the push had Shane falling to the porch and sliding a few feet backward. Before he could figure out what was happening, Clay was on top of him, one fist lightly pressing against his chest, the other threatening to cut off air at his throat.

"Want to see the black belt?" Clay asked coolly.

Shane was still busy trying to get air into his lungs from the kick. Clay drew back, grabbed a hand and pulled Shane into a sitting position. Then he dropped down to the porch and stared at his brother.

"You're not mad at me," Clay said. "You're mad at yourself. Because you're a jackass."

Shane concentrated on breathing. It was easier than facing the truth.

"She cares about you," Clay continued. "We can all see it. What's stopping you? Rachel? How long are you going to let her keep winning?"

His brother's words sank in. Shane knew he was right about everything. It was easier to worry that Annabelle was like his ex-wife than to face the truth.

That he'd fallen in love with her and that scared the hell out of him.

"I've screwed up everything." Shane stared at his brother. "What if I've lost her?"

"You haven't lost her."

"You can't know that."

"Yes, I can. She obviously cares about you, although for the life of me, I can't figure out why. That's not going to change overnight. But you're going to have to figure out a way to convince her you're worth a second chance. I haven't got a clue on that one."

Shane thought about Annabelle, how she made him laugh and how he looked forward to being with her. He thought of all he knew about her and what was most important to her. It wasn't a matter of convincing, he realized. Love wasn't about words, it was about actions.

"I know how," he said. "But I'm going to need your help."

The morning of the festival dawned warm and clear. Perfect weather, guaranteeing big crowds. Good news, Annabelle told herself as she secured the circle of flowers in her hair. Plenty of money would be raised today. Hopefully enough to cover the purchase price of the bookmobile along with the cost of all the books and supplies. Anything left over would go toward the little things like gas, insurance and, hey, paying a driver.

Problems for another day, she told herself. She shook her head a couple of times to make sure the flowers would stay in place as Khatar rose on his rear legs, then pulled on the white Máa-zib-inspired dress she would wear.

The full skirt would keep her covered as

she rode astride. She was supposed to be barefoot, which was easy enough. She was also supposed to look fierce, or at the very least happy. Neither of which seemed very likely.

She couldn't stop thinking about Shane, which wasn't a surprise considering everything. He'd said he wanted to talk. Even though she kept telling herself that the only subject of interest was the baby, she wanted him to have meant something else. That maybe he'd finally figured out she wasn't playing games with him, that she didn't want to "win" anything. Her only goal was to be with the man she loved and have him love her back.

She would know more tomorrow, she thought, wishing she had suggested they have their conversation after the ceremony today. At least that would cut down on the wait time.

She slipped her feet into sandals and left her house. The walk to the beginning of the parade route was short. She waved at people she knew as she went and was pleased to find a large crowd already lining the streets.

When she slipped past the barricades into the prep area, she was surprised to see Mandy and her friends there and in costumes that looked a lot like hers.

"Surprise!" the girls shouted, then rushed toward her.

"What are you doing here?" she asked.

"We're in the parade, too!"

"Shane's been teaching us the steps with our horses and everything."

"He said he wanted this to be the best parade ever so we would get a lot of money for the bookmobile."

"He did?"

She told herself not to wish for too much. He would have had to start practicing with them weeks ago. Long before he'd found out she was pregnant and had decided to assume the worst.

"Our horses are here and everything," Mandy said, pointing.

Annabelle saw Rafe leading the last of the riding horses down the ramp of a trailer. The other three were already saddled and tied up to a makeshift railing. Khatar was there as well, with flowers in his mane and his white coat painted to match the trim on her dress.

Khatar and Rafe and the girls and their horses, but no Shane.

The hope she'd been holding on to died. Shane didn't want to talk to her about the two of them. About a future. He was going to have a child and he would want to protect his interests. If he cared about her, if he believed in her, he would have been here.

She walked over to the big Arabian stallion and rubbed his face. "You're very handsome," she whispered, fighting tears. "Thank you for doing this for me."

Rafe came over. "You ready?" he asked.

She nodded.

"There's a big crowd," he told her. "You're going to get your bookmobile out of this."

"Then it's all been worth it."

He smiled at her. "My brothers and I talked last night. We're going to set up a trust fund for the bookmobile. It will cover maintaining the program. It was Shane's idea."

She stared at him. "I don't understand. Why would he do that?"

"I'll let him tell you." He touched her shoulder. "Don't give up on him. He's a good guy."

"I know that. Loving him isn't the problem."

"Then maybe it's time to have a little faith."

He moved next to Khatar and laced his fingers together. Annabelle slipped off her sandals, gathered her skirt in one hand and pushed off the ground. When she'd settled in the saddle, Rafe helped her straighten her skirt, then handed her the reins. He got each of the girls ready and then it was time.

The sun was high in the sky as they started the parade. The Fool's Gold High School Marching Band went first, followed by the cheerleaders. A few local businesses had decorated cars with banners and flowers, then Pia signaled for Annabelle to start.

"This is it," Annabelle told Khatar as she guided him into place then lightly touched his side with her bare heel. "We're the main attraction."

The parade route went through the center of town and ended at the park. Huge crowds lined the sidewalk, cheering and calling out. The smell of popcorn and hot dogs mingled with the scent of suntan lotion and barbecue. Children waved small flags and a couple of balloons drifted toward freedom and deep space.

Khatar took it all in and seemed to enjoy the attention. He zigzagged along the parade route, carefully performing his steps. Annabelle found she didn't have to offer much in the way of encouragement. He tossed his head and pranced, a happy horse adoring the waving audience.

When they reached the edge of the park, Annabelle saw the altar where Clay would be waiting. After Khatar performed his big finish, she would dismount — hopefully without flashing the crowd — and climb the two steps to where Clay was tied up. She would take the fake knife from her belt and pretend to cut out his heart. Easy enough, she thought. Then she could make her escape, go home and have yet another good cry. This one, she promised herself, would be her last. Her heart might still be breaking, but sobbing every day couldn't be good for the baby.

She and Khatar came to a stop near the dais. She gave him the signal and he gracefully rose onto his back legs. His front legs pawed impressively. The crowd gasped, then cheered. When he came down to solid ground, she swung her leg over, gathered her skirt around her and slid to the ground. The second cheer surprised her.

She offered a little wave, then gave Khatar a scratch behind the ears. "You were great," she told him.

The stairs were on her left. She started up, just wanting this all to be over. She had a few words to give, then she would pretend to cut out the heart of her sacrifice and call it a day. Only she realized the loincloth-clad man wasn't Clay at all. It was Shane.

He lay spread-eagle on a bed of hay. His face had been painted like a Máa-zib male prisoner would have been hundreds of years ago, his wrists and ankles wrapped in rope as if he were bound, although she knew he wasn't. He had a chain of flowers around his neck.

She climbed the second step, then stared at him. "What are you doing here?" she asked in a low voice, aware there was a microphone somewhere.

He smiled at her. "If you're going to cut out anyone's heart, it's going to be mine."

She heard someone murmur in the crowd. No doubt everyone was waiting for the big finish.

"I'm not mad at you," she told him in a whisper.

"I know." He sat up. "You're hurt. I hurt you, Annabelle, and I'm sorry."

She glanced around, aware of several hundred people watching them. "It's okay. We can talk about it later."

"I think we should talk about it now." One corner of his mouth twitched. "Then you can cut out my heart."

"Shane," she began, but he shook his head.

"No, me first." He scrambled to his feet. "I know you're nothing like my ex-wife. I know you're good and kind and caring and loyal. I like everything about you, Annabelle

Weiss. More than that, I love you. I'm sorry it took me so long to figure that out, but I did and I'm standing here to say I love you. I want to spend the rest of my life with you and our baby."

She heard the hum of conversation. But all that mattered was staring into Shane's eyes and seeing the truth of his words in his beautiful eyes.

The pain inside of her faded until only happiness was left. Happiness and the promise of all that would be.

"You're telling me this now? Here?"

"Sure. The festival is important to you and you're important to me. I figured you'd appreciate a big finish." He cupped her face in his hands. "Marry me. Not because it's the right thing, or because of the baby, but because you love me."

"I do love you," she whispered.

"Good. Because I want to spend the rest of my life taking care of you, supporting you, being your partner and husband. I have my flaws and I'll work on them, but once I commit, I don't give up easily."

Tears filled her eyes. Tears of joy and promise.

"I'll marry you," she murmured.

A cheer went up from the crowd. Confused, she started to turn, but before she could, Khatar leaned in and nudged her from behind. She fell into Shane's arms. He caught her and kissed her.

There was another cheer and yells that they should all be invited to the wedding.

Annabelle got lost in Shane's kiss for a second, then drew back and looked around. "I forgot about the microphone."

"I didn't." He kissed her again, then grinned. "I wanted to prove to you I meant what I said. Now we have witnesses and if I don't treat you right, the whole town will get on my butt. That should make you happy."

"You make me happy," she said, leaning in and kissing him again.

He pulled her close, then murmured, "I think they're going to want us to reenact this every year. Game?"

"With you? Always."

ABOUT THE AUTHOR

Susan Mallery is the *New York Times* bestselling author of over one hundred romances and women's fiction novels. Her funny and sexy family stories consistently appear on the *USA Today* and the *New York Times* bestsellers lists. She has won many awards, including the prestigious National Reader's Choice Award. Because her degree in Accounting wasn't very helpful in the writing department, Susan earned a Masters in Writing Popular Fiction. Susan makes her home in the Pacific Northwest, where she lives with her husband and toy poodle.